In all things of nature there is something of the marvelous.

—Aristotle

THE
RIVER KING
A Fly-fishing Novel

ROBERT J. ROMANO, JR.

*I hope you
enjoy your time with
the River King!
Best Regards
Bob Romano*

Cover Art by Emily Rose Romano
Original Map by Trish Romano

Printed and Published in the United States of America

First Edition

10 9 8 7 6 5 4 3 2 1

ISBN: 978-0-9996155-0-8
Library of Congress Control Number: 2017956042

To view a complete list of other books by Robert J. Romano, Jr., you are invited to visit the author's website: www.forgottentrout.com

ACKNOWLEDGEMENTS

I would like to thank the folks of western Maine, so many of whom
have graciously shared their lakes, rivers and streams with those of
us from away. This one's for all of you and for Emily Rose—thanks
for accompanying your parents on their magical mystery tour.
Thanks also, dear daughter, for your invaluable assistance with the
long and sometimes frustrating process of editing. A special thanks to
Tom Tolnay, with whom my words would never have made it to the
page. And to Trish—Lord knows why she puts up with this old fool.
And to you, dear reader, for allowing me to share with you my love
for the Rangeley Lakes Region and its people.

About the Author

Bob Romano lives in the northwest corner of New Jersey with his wife, Trish and their two Labrador Retrievers, Winslow Homer and Finnegan. Trish Romano has contributed artwork and a map to *The River King* as she has done with each of Bob's books. Their daughter, Emily Rose Romano, has contributed the cover art for *The River King*.

For more than thirty years, Bob and Trish have maintained a camp in the Rangeley Lakes Region of western Maine, which is where they spend much of their free time.

You can obtain more information about Bob's books by visiting his website: forgottentrout.com or his author's page on Amazon.com.

Also by Robert J. Romano, Jr.

Fishing with Faeries

Shadows in the Stream

North of Easie

West of Rangeley

Brook Trout Blues

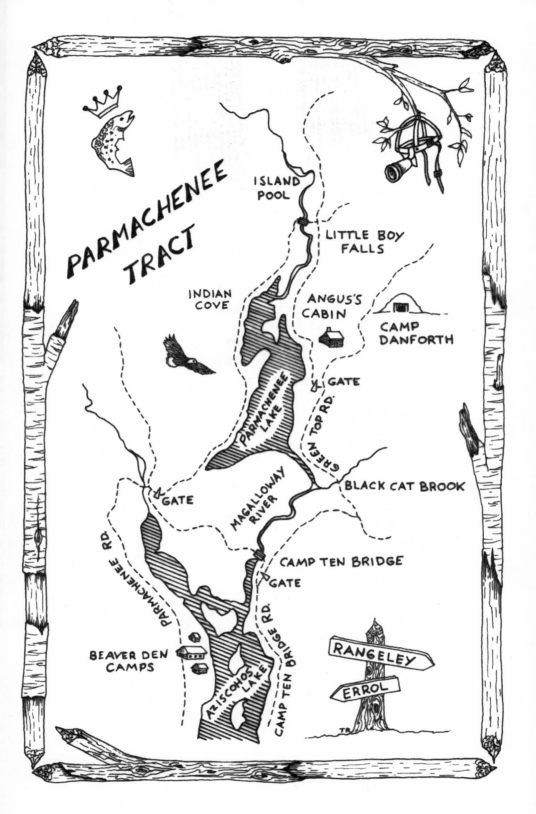

Rangeley, Maine is a real place as are many of the lakes, rivers, streams, logging roads, sporting lodges and businesses, which I have attempted to faithfully describe in the book you are about to read. However, this is a work of fiction and some of the locations will not be found on any map or chart of the region. Although sports staying at Bosebuck Mountain Camps may find similarities with Beaver Den Camps and residents of Oquossoc, with the fictional town of Easie, any such resemblance to these places is purely coincidental. All names (unless used with permission), characters and incidents are either a product of the author's imagination or used fictitiously.

—*Robert J. Romano, Jr.*

· Chapter One ·

It was Gilroy's idea. We were sitting at our usual table, the one in the far corner of Sparky's. The wheels had been turning all night. Hell, fumes were coming off the guy's head, although it was hard to say for sure with the room shrouded in a cloud of cigarette smoke.

Like a trout rising through the fog-drenched surface of a lake, Thelma Louise appeared through the haze and placed two longnecks on the table.

"I'll be back to collect the empties." It was after ten and the place was filling up. A combination of voices, clinking glasses, and music from the jukebox required her to shout.

Looking away from the television that was bolted to the wall in the opposite corner of the tavern, Donnie Gilroy stole a glance down Thelma's blouse. When she spun around we could see the upper portion of her tramp stamp visible above those low-rider jeans she liked to wear.

I could recall the night the three of us hitchhiked down to Farmington to celebrate Thelma's sixteenth birthday. High on beer and weed, Gilroy dared me to walk into Mr. Adams, a tattoo parlor located on Farmington Falls Road. An hour later Donnie stumbled out with a brook trout inked across his forearm and T. L. with her devil girl winking back at anyone who might be sneaking a peak whenever she bent down. Me? I sobered up real quick when that needle came out.

Gilroy looked back at the screen. Lifting one of the bottles to his lips, he muttered, "Damn Yankees."

Boston was playing at New York. We had spent the night watching the bombers beat up on the Red Sox in a stadium where we couldn't afford a decent seat.

I grabbed the other bottle. Gilroy groaned when Jeter slammed a two-run double down the right-field line. He raised a middle finger toward the television as the New York fans rose to their feet.

"I'm tellin' ya Harry, this time of year the hogs only come out at night."

I frowned. Unlike Gilroy, I'm a worrier. Have been, my whole life.

As a kid, I worried about my mother's health and how I might grow up to be like my father. As a man, I worried about making a living in Rangeley, the town where I was born—a town where smelt, a fish no bigger than Gilroy's middle finger, leave the lakes every spring and swim up the brooks and creeks to spawn. A town where each year, everyone I know puts away their snow machines the week after ice-out. They wait for dark and sneak out to their favorite spot, hunkering down until the early morning hours while drinking beer and scooping up buckets of the abundant baitfish. You see, smelt is a delicacy the people of western Maine have enjoyed since we took the land from the Abenakis. They are also the reason why the region's brook trout and landlocked salmon grow so large and why every so often the wardens find some drunken fool face down in a foot of freezing cold water—collateral damage of the early-spring slaughter.

Although many of the jobs in our town are dependent upon tourists and vacationers, mostly anglers who travel to the region for the opportunity to hook a trophy fish, few locals give much thought to how all those buckets of dead smelt affect the size and numbers of the trout and salmon that depend upon the baitfish as their principal source of food.

While Willie Nelson sang, "My Heroes Have Always Been Cowboys," I caught every other word Gilroy was saying as he moved his arms around wildly. With his hands gesticulating, he explained how by the end of June the largest brook trout only come out after the sun goes down.

"That's when they whack anything that moves!" Gilroy leaned closer as if to share a secret. "Smelt, crayfish, younger trout. Hell, they'll even go for the occasional small duck if it's stupid enough to waddle out after dark. Has something to do with the Wolf Moon." He tended toward the dramatic when it came to fishing.

"You mean the Strawberry Moon," I corrected him.

He looked momentarily confused.

"Wolf Moon's in January," I explained. "In June, the full moon is called the Strawberry Moon." Gilroy took another swig of beer. "Bro, you've been watching too much Weather Channel."

"Anyways, how we suppose to see at night?" I asked.

"Leave that to me." Tipping back his bottle, Gilroy took a long pull.

Donnie Gilroy rarely worried, living in the moment, out there on the edge. Where I might slip a toe into the water to judge its temperature, Gilroy would jump in with both feet.

The crowd in the bar moaned in unison when A-Rod slammed a ball against the left center wall. Gilroy mumbled something I didn't catch. He slammed the bottom of his empty longneck on the wooden table.

"But what about the high water?" I wasn't entirely sold on his plan.

The tail end of a tropical storm had powered up the coast and then swung inland. After stalling for three days, it left six inches of rain in its wake.

Gilroy shifted in his chair. He looked from side to side as if we might be spied upon. After a moment, he reached into his shirt pocket.

Ignoring my question, he whispered, "Check this out." A maniacal smile spread across the guy's lips as he handed me a six-inch-long mouse. Holding the creature between my thumb and second finger, I studied its beaded eyes and little leather tail while admiring the body of neatly sculptured deer hair.

"Kinda big, don't ya think?"

Gilroy swiped the deer-hair pattern from my hand and dropped it back into his pocket. "With all that high water those hogs will be lookin' toward the surface to pick off whatever comes downriver. And this baby'll float over any rapid no matter how rough." Gilroy waited a moment for his revelation to sink in and then added, "I can see those bruisers now, cozying up to poor little mousy. Badges? We don't need no stinkin' badges!"

The two of us liked to stay up late watching black-and-white movies like *The Treasure of Sierra Madre*. We'd get stoned and binge on snacks, Gilroy preferring Doritos; me, Cheetos.

Too busy scribbling lines and arrows on a crumpled napkin, Gilroy didn't notice Thelma Louise graze my arm when she gathered our empties, not even when she smiled that smile that can drive a guy nuts.

Without looking up, he asked, "Got a smoke?"

Reaching into my breast pocket, I pulled out a pack of Marlboros.

After taking a long drag, Gilroy spread out the napkin.

I followed my friend's finger as it traced a wiggly line that looked a lot like an X-ray I once saw when they removed a part of my grand's lower intestine. *Either that or the trail leading down to Widow Maker*, I thought.

The part of the Magalloway River from the dam down to the small bridge on Route 16 is only a mile or so long, mostly fast water that holds decent-size brook trout and landlocked salmon. The river's calf-deep riffles are able to sweep a portly sport off his feet. The faster rapids can rise above your waist and easily take out an experienced angler. In between, enormous fish hold court in a number of deep runs. These leviathans rarely leave their lairs, preferring to remain in the shadows cast by boulders the size of small dinosaurs.

Since graduating high school, I've made my living guiding anglers like those who've been traveling to our little town since the 1800s. When not guiding, Gilroy and I fish the water for fun. I carry this long two-handed net my great-uncle built and gave to me for my tenth birthday. Although both deep and wide, it barely manages to hold some of the brook trout Gilroy has taken from the Magalloway, fish measured in pounds rather than inches.

It's a wild river, dangerous to the uninitiated, and Widow Maker is its most dangerous run, especially after a heavy rain. It is even more treacherous at night. Gilroy was convinced it contained his Moby Dick. I figured it would drown us both.

Before the rain, there had been three weeks of drought that caused my regulars to cancel their previously scheduled appointments. Luckily for me, one of Teddy Alick's crew had shown up for work with a hangover, causing the guy to break his leg in two places after tripping over a stack of shingles and falling ten feet off the side of a cabin. Left with empty pockets and time on my hands, I had jumped at Teddy's offer to complete the roofing job on some rich dude's camp that was located on one of the islands in the big lake. For three days, I boated across the water in my Rangeley Boat, completing the job the afternoon before the rain began.

Earlier in the evening, Ted had settled up with me, and when Gilroy trudged toward the men's room, I walked over to Thelma Louise and paid our tab, adding a five-dollar bill to what we owed for the beers. Thelma, who was standing behind the bar cleaning a glass with a dirty rag, winked at me before turning toward the cash register.

Outside, the stars stared down at us in cold silence. The bar noise evaporated when the tavern's massive oak door swung closed. We took no notice of the large sign hanging on the outside wall that declared in faded block letters:

SPARKY'S — WHERE OLD FRIENDS MEET

Although regular customers, we'd never stopped to wonder why "old friends" managed to end most evenings in a brawl requiring the intervention of the police.

I swatted a mosquito that drew blood on the back of my neck. After we piled into my pickup, Gilroy bummed another cigarette. Gravel splashed out behind us when the old Ford's back wheels spun out.

"Stop at my place first?" he asked as smoke swirled out of the open window.

After his brother left town, Gilroy moved into the basement of his mother's home. The Cape Cod style house where he was born was built on a lot that was only a block off the main street of town and just a few blocks away from our local watering hole. With its swayback roof and rickety porch, the building had seen better days. Although Gilroy promised his mother to fix it up, he never seemed to find the time to do so.

I kept the truck running as he trotted toward the back door. It was a warm night. With the air conditioning on the fritz since last summer, I had the windows of the pickup rolled down. When Muddy Waters' growl broke through the static, I stopped fiddling with the radio.

For a while after Gilroy had gone away, I'd given up my dream of guiding. Thelma Louise had convinced me that a degree from Franklin County's Community College might be our ticket out of town. I spent a while commuting to the school, located forty-five minutes away in the bigger city of Farmington, but dropped out when Gilroy returned home. Thelma Louise wouldn't talk to me for three weeks after that. About the only thing I got out of those months was an appreciation for the music played on the college's radio station.

After a few minutes, Gilroy appeared, carrying a nicked-up cane rod and tattered vest. He'd changed from jeans to cut-offs and knotted a green paisley bandana over his shaved head.

"Where're your waders?" I asked.

"Goin' wet." Gilroy had replaced his work boots with a pair of black high-top sneakers. He placed his rod and vest behind the seat, which is where I kept my gear from May through September.

"I'm a hoochy-coochy man," Muddy moaned from the dash.

"What's that shit?"

I ignored the comment, knowing Gilroy hated any music not accompanied by a steel guitar.

Driving back through the center of town, we passed the Building and Supply and a moment later, the fancy bowling alley that had opened during the short-lived boom years after 9/11 when anglers decided it was better to motor to Maine than to fly to some exotic destination. That was before the banking bust resulted in FOR SALE signs posted on every other vacation cottage. Weekdays, the bowling alley rarely has more than a few vehicles parked outside its double oak doors, but the owner is cute for her age, the food surprisingly good, and it still hops most Saturday nights.

"You have a couple of those mice for me?" I asked.

"Sure." Gilroy reached back and pulled out a large box from the pocket of his fly vest. He flipped it onto my lap. With one hand on the wheel, I looked down. Six deer-haired mice stared back at me through the clear plastic.

"I'm a mean mannish boy," Waters grumbled as we drove past Dodge Pond and out of town.

"You know Billy Kozlowski?" Gilroy took back the mice.

I nodded.

Koz had been a year ahead of us in high school. He'd played fullback, first string and dated Suzy Warner. Billy proposed to Suzy soon after they graduated. Little Suzy was the bomb, but a year and a half after they married, she ran off with the bass player from some country western band that had passed through town. After that, Koz humped over to Berlin each morning, a forty-five-minute drive across the New Hampshire border, where he worked at his uncle's used car lot until enlisting a few months after 9/11.

"He's in Iraq, Special Forces or some crap," I mumbled, still thinking about Suzy.

The truck rolled up a steep hill and then back down the other side. The moon glowed through a film of cloud.

"He's on leave. Staying at his uncle's house." Gilroy flipped his cigarette out the open window. Plucking the remains of a joint from his shirt pocket, he pushed in on the truck's lighter.

"You know the place?" he asked as we passed the fields around a farm. Under the glow of the full moon, Gilroy glanced at a barn. Its sides were slumped inward, the washed-out paint, a mere memory of its once bright red color.

I looked over at him, but he had leaned forward to pull the lighter from the truck's dash. It wasn't like Donnie to invite someone to fish with us.

After taking a few quick tokes, Gilroy passed the joint to me. I turned off of Route 16 and rumbled over the stone bridge that led into the smaller village of Easie. A moment later we passed between the town's general store and its sporting goods store. With the exception of a lamp over the deck outside the general store, the street was dark. The joint made a sizzling sound as I inhaled, the tip glowing in the darkness of the cab. I passed it back to Gilroy. The truck bounced haphazardly over a pothole as we turned onto a dirt road. A few moments later, I pulled into a short gravel drive. The number six was painted on the mailbox nailed to a post that leaned to one side. I stopped behind a tan minivan.

"Stay here." Gilroy crushed the roach in the ashtray. "We don't want to spook him," he cautioned.

The humidity, unusual for western Maine, even in high summer, slipped in behind the storm that had dumped more rain in a few days than we had seen in all of the previous month. I pulled out the pack of Marlboros. Lighting one, I looked across a lawn of dandelions and crabgrass. A Chevy Blazer sat on blocks beside the minivan. The sullen headlights of the aging SUV stared back at me. Queen Anne's lace bordered a slate walkway that led to the front door. Beside the door, a few black-eyed Susans were interspersed between clumps of daisies.

The thin layer of clouds had broken apart. I looked past the small house at the moon's reflection on the pond that was named after the town's founder. I took a drag on the cigarette. The humid air smelled like a basket of damp socks.

Ten minutes later, Gilroy bounded out of the house. Beads of perspiration had formed across his brow. A narrow ribbon of sweat slipped from under his bandana and down his left cheek.

"How much money you got left from that roofin' job?" He slipped off the cotton cloth and ran it over his face and across his damp scalp.

"I thought we were goin' fishing."

"Trust me, dude."

Flipping the cigarette out the window, I dug down into the pocket of my jeans and came up with seventy-three dollars. Donnie grabbed the bills and ran across the unkempt lawn. I lost sight of him in the shadow cast by the cottage.

When he returned, he had a canvas rucksack slung over his right shoulder. Billy's last name was stenciled across it. I was pretty sure we were in for a long night. I might take the occasional toke, but it was Donnie who had gotten into some deep shit after high school. Even so, I kept my mouth shut as we drove down the dirt road that swung around the western shoreline of Hawley Pond.

Gilroy turned in my direction, saw the concerned look on my face and said, "Chill."

· *Chapter Two* ·

I HAVEN'T THOUGHT ABOUT IT UNTIL NOW, BUT LIFE REALLY CAN BE like a river, with its ebbs and flows, the current oftentimes even, running at a modest rate, the days slipping by one after the other. On occasion, our banks become awash with happiness, more often with grief. And like a river, a life can take a turn when we least expect it, sometimes opening upon a vista, other times sliding through shadows. Sudden spates cause us to crash violently against some unmoving obstacle while bending around others. We either return to the contours with which we have become familiar, or follow a new and unfamiliar course. I suppose, to understand any of what happened, you have to go back to the beginning, to the headwaters so to speak. Take Thelma Louise for instance.

Like most everyone else I know, Patti Ellis (that was Thelma's mother) grew up in our little town. She lived with her two sisters and their parents, Herman and Sheila Ellis, until an accident at the mill where Herman worked resulted in his death. Sheila Ellis never remarried, working weekdays as a waitress in one of the fancier restaurants in town and weekends at Fletcher's Fly Shop, the predecessor to the Rangeley Region Sports Shop that remains located on the main street of town and around the corner from the little cottage where Sheila raised her three daughters.

Sheila Ellis was known for the streamers she created. These colorful imitations of smelt fashioned from feathers and fur and arranged on long hooks became sought after by anglers throughout western Maine. While her mother worked at the shop, Patti sat beside her on a stool behind the counter. Or at least that's how Thelma tells the story.

According to Thelma, as her mother grew older, Patti Ellis watched with envy as each year tourists and vacationers came and went.

In the spring, while rain and sometimes snow whipped down off the dark hills surrounding the town, Thelma's mother would stare out of the window as men looked up at the sign above the door that told them they had arrived at the Land of Fishing Legends. Much like the Knights Templar arriving in the Holy Land at the end of their long and perilous journey, these true believers, mostly middle-aged brothers of the angle, wandered into the shop. They wore chest waders rather than chainmail and baseball caps instead of helmets, their fly-fishing vests pulled over protruding stomachs, eyes wide on unshaven faces. They came to purchase Sheila Ellis's streamers, laying out their dollars on the counter in the hope that they might catch the fish of their dreams.

Although she found these strange men amusing, it was the summer people who Patti Ellis truly envied.

In August, after the heat drove the anglers back to their homes and thinned out successive clouds of black flies, mosquitoes and no-see-ums, families walked through the town in shorts and sandals. Spending time lakeside at a rented cottage or cabin, the vacationers frequented the stores along either side of the town's main street.

Patti wished she could afford the jewelry, silk blouses, and fleece pullovers displayed in the shop windows just outside of her reach. She longed to have a meal at the upscale restaurant where her mother worked nights.

Seated on her stool in the little fly shop, she watched those "from away", as they're called by us locals, come and go.

In September, fishermen returned, once more chasing the trout and landlocked salmon that begin their spawning runs in the fall, followed by "leaf peepers" who arrived to take in the color of the maples, oaks, and aspens along Route 16. In winter, snowmobilers rode their machines through the groomed trails that extend throughout the forests of western Maine into northern New Hampshire. Skiers rented condominiums along the nearby slopes of Saddleback Mountain. Many of them drove into town at night to spend their money at Sparky's, the Red Onion, or one of the upscale restaurants in town.

Someday, Patti Ellis told herself, *one of those handsome vacationers will fall in love with me.*

The young girl never understood why anyone would settle in western Maine. Those that did came from southern New England, a few from New York, and a surprising number from New Jersey. They were drawn, she supposed, by the beauty of the surrounding forest and sparkling waters, while unaware of how difficult it was to earn a living in a region of the country that lacked well-paying jobs.

Patti was in high school about the time Mexicans joined the crews who cut lawns and patch roofs on vacation cottages and cabins. To this day, these men with dark skin and strange accents provide cheap labor for those owning vacation homes. We never did learn how people from south of the border found their way so far north, but they work hard and mind their own business. Unable to afford the prices charged in the shops lining Main Street, most of the transplants, like those of us born in western Maine, work two or more jobs while barely able to make ends meet. Patti knew from talking with the children from away that they had no idea how difficult the locals had it, and although most people from our town wouldn't dream of trading their lives for those from the outside, Patti Ellis would.

Thelma's mother yearned for the day when she might meet a boy from Boston or Hartford, maybe Nashua or Danbury; a boy who would take her away from the spruce-and-balsam forest. For a young girl who had no interest in her mother's fancy streamers or the fish they promised to catch, the clear, cold streams and sparking blue lakes held little promise. Instead, the way Thelma tells the story, her mother married Johnny Shannon.

Johnny was a real charmer. The seventeen-year-old with wavy blonde hair and sky blue eyes fell for the guy with the quick smile and a shock of raven-black hair that he liked to comb back on his head. The plan had been to move to Boston as soon as they graduated, but six months pregnant, Patti had been forced to leave school early, marrying Johnny

Shannon the month before she was due. The newlyweds rented a house located a few blocks away from where they had gone to school.

Even without degrees, they did pretty well. Johnny, who was a middling mechanic, found work at Daniel Fogerty's garage, while Patti, when not working at the IGA, took care of Dylan and later, Jake. But it wasn't long before Johnny was spending most of his days palling around with his buds, rather than working at the station and his nights screwing around with whomever he could manage to pick up. At least he had the decency to stay away from Sparky's, where Patti's friends hung out. Instead, he drove over to Errol or Rumford. But Johnny always had money, more than Patti thought he could earn working at Fogerty's, and the guy paid their bills. Patti had to give him that.

It all went to shit when Johnny was sent away for a year, having pled guilty to receipt of stolen property, a reduced sentence from the crime of breaking and entering that the cops couldn't pin on him. As a condition of his release, her husband had to drive down to Farmington once a month, where wouldn't you know, the bastard ended up shacking up with his parole officer. Without Johnny's money, Patti did her best to take care of the two boys between shifts behind the meat counter. Falling two months behind in the rent, she feared they might be evicted. Although more than a year had passed since Johnny took up with the parole officer, neither had yet filed for divorce. One night, Patti left the boys with a friend and walked down to Sparky's for her first girl's-night-out since the split up. It was the same night that Gil Kelly's eighteen-wheeler chugged up Route 4 on his way to Gorham, where he was supposed to drop off a truckload of pulp. Deciding to stop for a quick one, he strode over to where Patti was seated with two of her friends and asked if he could buy her a beer.

A few weeks later, "uncle" Gil walked out of Patti Shannon's one-bedroom ranch and drove the cab of his logging truck back down to Sparky's Tavern. It was an especially cold evening during an especially cold September, and after four shots and as many beers, he stumbled outside where the sky was spitting down pellets of freezing rain. Gil Kelly pulled out of the lot in front of the tavern and never looked back. After crossing the New Hampshire border, he stopped in the town of Errol and jumped into bed with a waitress, who worked at the Bull Moose Restaurant and Lounge.

Four months later, Patti accepted Susan Gilroy's offer to drive her down to Portland to take advantage of the state's free legal clinic. Donnie's mother had held Patti Shannon's hand as they walked up Federal Street. Susan told Patti everything would be all right as they approached the gray stucco building where Pine Tree Legal Assistance has it offices.

After she swallowed a fistful of Tums, Patti collapsed onto a metal chair that hurt her butt. She chewed the multi-colored pills like candy to help keep down the acid that had built up since the second month of her pregnancy. Patti tried to ignore the discomfort while answering the young lawyer's questions, excusing herself twice during the interview to pee.

An hour and a half later, she was back on Federal Street, walking arm in arm with Susan. The two women stopped to stare at the graffiti scrawled across the gray stucco that reminded them of the slogans and symbols spray-painted by the local kids across the ramps and pipes of a skateboard park built beside the regional high school, that was located a block behind the town's main street. After squeezing back into Susan's subcompact, Patti agreed when the other woman suggested they stop at a McDonald's, where she washed down two big Macs and a large bag of fries with a super-sized Coke.

Johnny hadn't bothered to answer the court papers when they were served upon him, and the divorce was finalized three months after Patti had returned from Portland. Par for the course, he also failed to pay a nickel in support for his two boys, let alone alimony. While Johnny ignored the judge's order, Patti worked behind the meat counter until a few days before her due date. Meanwhile, twice during those last few months a member of DSER, Maine's Division of Support Enforcement and Recovery, had attempted to serve her ex with papers, but both times he was nowhere to be found. The few times they spoke by phone, Johnny had said "he wasn't going to pay no whore who was having some other man's baby." Johnny was a charmer all right.

All of this led up to the day Thelma Louise received her name. The way Thelma tells it, her mother stood at the front door of her rented house on a chilly morning in the month of May. She wore a pair of Kelly green socks under her unlaced Sorels and a flannel nightgown that pressed against her extended belly.

Patti Shannon watched her two boys, Dylan, who was seven, followed by Jake, now six, plod toward the yellow bus idling outside the one-story ranch. When the bus' doors folded open, Greta Hanson, the same woman who had driven the vehicle when Patti went to school, waved her big paw of a hand. Patti waved back as the doors of the bus, like Jonah's whale, appeared to swallow her sons.

With the boys off at school, their mother had the little house to herself. Patti shuffled to a kitchen cabinet and dragged out a box of Cheerios. She found a spoon leaning in the plastic dish drainer. After washing out a bowl from a sink full of dirty dishes, Patti grabbed a carton of milk from the refrigerator. The effort was too much for the woman who had approached the end of her term, and she sat in a chair to catch her breath. After a few moments, Patti filled the bowl with the cereal.

Tears filled her eyes as the last of the milk barely covered the circles of grain. Raising the spoon to her lips, Patti once again worried how she could remain in the house on the meager wages she received from her job at the IGA.

Fuckers, she thought to herself.

Patti was forced to set aside her concerns when a series of gurgles beginning in her stomach spread down through her intestine. Raising one of her buttocks, she released the pressure. While giggling at the flatulence, another sound, this one emanating from her mouth made her laugh even harder. Not some petite bird-like little burp, it was a loud and long belch that started in the depths of her swollen belly, worked its way past the acid-scorched lining of her throat and erupted like that volcano from all those years back, the one that blew the top off of some mountain out west. *This kid better be coming soon,* she thought.

Pushing aside her empty bowl, Patti waddled toward the broom closet. A white-footed mouse sat on its haunches in the corner. The tiny rodent grasped a sunflower seed in its paws. With her own eviction looming, Patti wished the mouse good day while filling a plastic bottle with seed from a bag on the floor. Opening the kitchen door, she stepped outside and poured the seed into a feeder that hung above the kitchen window.

Back inside, she watched a chickadee flutter down. The black-capped bird stripped off a shell and then flew away with the inner seed in its beak. A few moments later, a titmouse did the same. Patti waited, staring out through the glass onto an unkempt yard surrounded by a forest of spruce, pine, and balsam. She pressed her hands against the small of her back, which made her belly protrude farther against the red-and-white checks of the flannel nightgown. A chill had followed her inside the house. She closed the door after a nuthatch followed the titmouse's example. *Maybe I'll call her Birdie,* she thought to herself.

Shuffling into the living room, Patti fell back into the cushion of a couch that sank under her weight. She lifted her bloated legs onto a green hassock while ignoring the batting that stuck out of a long tear across its top.

What she really wanted was a cigarette. The doctor at the clinic had told her it could hurt the baby, but she had smoked through her first two pregnancies and the boys were none the worse for it. Even so, the pack of Kools sat on top of the television and she was too damn tired to raise herself up again. Leaning on her side, she stretched out an arm as far as it would go. Grabbing the remote from the arm of the couch, Patti clicked through the channels before settling on a movie.

Thelma's mother dozed off halfway through a commercial about some pill that promised to cure her depression if it didn't make her commit suicide. Patti Shannon awoke in time to watch the last thirty minutes of a movie she had seen once before. She smiled as Susan Sarandon and Gina Davis led the cops on a cross-country chase. The sudden ring of the phone caught her by surprise. Grabbing the remote that had fallen under her butt, she lowered the sound of the television while letting the machine pick up. After listening to a message telling her that she had been selected as a finalist to win a two-week vacation cruise to the Bahamas, Patti turned the sound back up just as Gina Davis entered a diner, a few moments later telling Susan Sarandon how she had left a much-too-young-and-awfully-handsome Brad Pitt alone in a hotel room with the women's money.

"Fuckers." This time Patti Shannon said the word out loud.

· *Chapter Three* ·

IT WAS NEARLY MIDNIGHT BY THE TIME I DROVE OUT OF TOWN. A single vehicle was parked outside the general store. A younger guy Gilroy and I knew was seated on the steps beside a girl with curly blonde hair. The guy raised his beer as we passed by.

"Looks like Mikey might get lucky tonight," Gilroy quipped.

After driving back over the stone bridge, I turned left onto Route 16 and headed west. Ten minutes later, with Donnie hanging out of the window, we drove under the shadow of the concrete dam located at the bottom of Aziscohos Lake. Staring up at the full moon, the young Ahab howled like a coydog. I turned up the radio, straining to hear Gillian Welsh lament the fate of some beauty queen from Ohio that made me think of Thelma Louise Shannon.

A quarter mile down the two-lane blacktop, I pulled up next to a sign maintained by Florida Power and Light, the utility company that regulated the flow of water coming out of the dam at the bottom of Aziscohos Lake. As I'd feared, the figures scrawled across the chalkboard confirmed that 1,800 cubic feet of water was ripping downstream every second. After parking the Ford in the gravel lot adjacent to the river, we sat inside the cab listening to the sound of the powerful current. I looked over at the satchel that lay between us on the front seat. I was no longer thinking about fish, certain that a car would be waiting, maybe an Escalade full of Colombians, or worse, a Lexus with Russians carrying Uzis, waiting to complete a drug deal. But there was nothing. The only sound—that of the river—roared over the rapid beat of my heart. After Gilroy climbed out of the cab, I reluctantly opened my door.

Clouds had rolled in, thicker and lower than before. Without the moon, the two of us rigged our rods by the light of the pickup's open doors.

Donnie asked, "You got that long-handled net of yours?"

I reached inside the truck and pulled the net from behind the seat while Gilroy swung Kozlowski's rucksack over his shoulder.

"You go on. I'll follow." Stooping down to lace my wading boot, I stared out into the darkness. My worry mounted, convinced that my friend was in over his head. That thought, combined with the lingering effect of the marijuana and beer, made my head ache.

The fish below the dam remained active throughout the season, even in the warmest weather thanks to the cold water periodically released from the bottom of the lake. A hydroelectric tube constructed below the dam to generate power provides additional cold-water discharges into the long dark pool alongside the parking lot where I often met my sports.

Gilroy grabbed a penlight from one of the pockets of his fly vest. He strode over to the wire fence that enclosed the small concrete building containing the controls to regulate the hydroelectric tube.

A moment later, I fell in behind him. The two of us walked single-file along a footpath between the fence and a steep slope covered with dandelions, daisies, and black-eyed Susans. Gilroy's light momentarily flashed across the words: DANGER HIGH VOLTAGE–F.P.L. printed on a metal sign that hung from the fence.

Like two river spiders, we scrambled over a series of large boulders at the end of the narrow trail and climbed down to the bank where the edge of the current lapped over waist-high Joe Pye weed. Before entering the river, I took the penlight from Donnie's hand and directed its narrow beam into the shadows cast by the forest until I found two wooden staffs. I reached down, handing one to Gilroy while retaining the other.

The rain had filled the lake to its capacity. The release from the dam was many times its normal rate while the tube's discharge added to the river's ferocity. Even so, we knew that the better fishing lay along the far side of the river and that the only place to ford was above the opening of the hydroelectric tube.

Below us, the current widened into a deep run, but above the hydro it compressed into a series of rapids that rushed over a line of large boulders. We entered the water while gripping the poles that I kept stashed beside the river. With the current pounding at our thighs, we waded out to the nearest boulder. After resting for a few moments, we struggled farther into the river, stopping behind another boulder. In this manner, we took nearly ten minutes to cross the narrow gorge. Extending a hand toward Gilroy, I helped him scramble up the far bank. We dumped the poles where they could be found on our way back and followed the penlight's beam down the trail along the east side of the river.

Staring at the rucksack hanging over Gilroy's shoulder, I wondered what was inside. I was expecting a blade-wielding Jason to appear at any moment, but passing by Warden's Pool we encountered neither machine-gun drug dealers nor hockey-masked psycho-killers. Tree branches grazed our shoulders. Once, we heard the sound of a small animal rustling in the brush, possibly a porcupine or raccoon, or maybe a skunk. Then, a few moments later, the sound of something larger crashed through some branches.

"Moose, maybe moose." Gilroy liked to quote expressions from an old *Bert and I* album he liberated from his mother's scratchy LP collection.

We had spent the previous night hanging out in his basement apartment, watching another black-and-white movie, this one starring Alan Ladd as a private eye. Donnie had nodded out sometime after two in the morning, while I channel surfed until coming upon a film about a bunch of British POW's forced to build a bridge for the Japanese during World War II. The tune from the movie had stuck in my head and I whistled it while we hiked through the darkness.

"Almost there," Gilroy muttered as we approached another deep pool. Although I couldn't make it out in the dark, I knew a trail cut through the forest on the other side of the river that began across the road from the fire warden's house and terminated at the bank of the somber run. Gilroy lowered the rucksack to the ground. We listened to the current crashing into the pool that is well known by locals, who like to park their cars alongside the macadam and walk down the path for a few casts before heading off to do whatever it is they are supposed to be doing.

Removing the neckerchief from his head, Donnie bent down to wet the cloth in the river. After wringing it over the back of his neck, he once again slung the rucksack over his shoulder and headed down the path. I took a knee to splash water on my face, then rose, following a few steps behind. For a brief time the narrow footpath rose along a steep slope. Gilroy was wheezing as we stopped a second time to catch our breath. Below, we could hear the swollen current. Tramping down the other side of the hill, we once again found ourselves alongside the river.

Running ahead in anticipation, Gilroy called, "Over here!"

I found him kneeling beside the rucksack in a field of summer grass that had grown tall. Donnie lit another joint. The tip glowed hot when he drew in breath. The sound of the angry river grew louder as I walked closer to the bank. I'd sweated out the beer and pot and declined when Gilroy raised the joint in my direction. While lighting a cigarette, I stared out into the darkness.

The longest run below the dam, Widow Maker was deceptive. Because it was wider than the other pools, the river's velocity was more evenly distributed, allowing anyone unfamiliar with the river to wade without fear of being swept away, until possibly stepping into a hole, of which there were many. Unable to gain purchase on the slippery rocks below, the swift current could easily sweep an unsuspecting angler off his feet.

I'd heard of at least three anglers losing their lives in this way. A few years back, a friend of my grand's was found jammed against a sweeper. The following year, hikers discovered the bloated body of a young man draped around a boulder a few hundred yards downriver. Just last season, a sport was lost while wading with one of his buddies. He had fished the pool under the watchful eyes of Rusty Miller, an older guide working out of the sporting goods store in the town where Koz lives.

The story Rusty told the wardens began with a hog of a salmon that tail-danced halfway across the river before breaking off from his sport. Later, while settling up, the guy had expressed his intention to return the following day. The guide was careful to describe the danger and suggested that the sport try one of the less difficult runs.

Rusty explained how he'd tried to convince the guy not to return to Widow Maker on his own, but the sport's friend told the wardens that they didn't take the guide's advice, figuring Rusty wanted to keep the honey hole to himself.

According to the friend, everything had gone well until the sport hooked a big fish. One moment he was calling out, the next he'd disappeared under the current. Both the guide and the friend had joined the wardens in their search. They found the sport lodged against the center beam of the little bridge that crosses the river a quarter mile or so downstream.

"Damn, but that looks tough," I called over my shoulder. Having fished the pool many times over the years, I felt safe wading it in daylight, but it was another story at night and in such high water.

"No problemo." Gilroy loosened the cord around the canvas sack.

I crushed out my cigarette. Walking over, I picked up the penlight from the damp grass and directed its slim beam over Donnie's shoulder. Instead of drugs, Gilroy pulled out a metal gizmo. Painted flat green, it had a single scope extending outward from what looked like an expensive pair of binoculars.

"Dark ops. Real high tech. Koz says they call 'em green death over there."

"Sweet." I smiled for the first time since we left Sparky's.

"They're ours for the night," Donnie said as he handed me one of the devices. "Gotta return 'em tomorrow."

I adjusted the harness holding the goggle over my eye. With my hands free, I grabbed my bamboo rod and walked toward the sound of the current.

Five minutes later we were waist-deep in the Magalloway, the river sweeping over our legs, the surface shimmering through a haze of green light. I watched Gilroy, a Joker-like grin plastered across his lips, as he cast the deer-hair mouse. He looked like a green Cyclops, with his paisley neckerchief tied over his head and the single scope protruding out from the military glasses. The mouse wiggled each time he twitched the tip of his rod. On his second cast, the maw of a heavy fish broke through the surface. Gilroy hauled back, putting a deep bend in the 8-weight cane rod, shouting "Huah!" when his reel began to sing. We cast those deer-haired mice into the early hours of the morning, two fly-fishing commandos fighting impossibly large brook trout, most fish breaking off, but a few coming to the net while the tip of the joint Gilroy kept in his mouth glowed red whenever he inhaled.

I met Donnie at the diner behind the town's Historical Society building sometime after five on the following afternoon. Between two mugs of black coffee, I devoured a plate of eggs, sausages, and hash browns while Gilroy worked on a big stack of pancakes with a side of Canadian bacon. I removed my phone from the front pocket of my jeans when it began to vibrate.

"It's Petey Boy," I told Gilroy, as he smothered his pancakes with raspberry syrup.

"Put him on," I said to Petey. When an unfamiliar voice asked if I was available the next morning, I answered, "No problem. One sec."

"Bernice," I called to the aging waitress, who worked at the diner for as long as any of us could remember. Borrowing her pen, I scribbled a guy's name and a time on a napkin and then said, "Tomorrow morning. Right. Six thirty. I'll meet you at the station."

Half an hour later, Gilroy and I hobbled down the town's main street, walking across the sand-and-gravel lot outside Sparky's.

Inside, a number of old men sat at the bar. They hunched over their shots and beers like vultures hovering over roadkill. I nodded at Thelma Louise, who nodded back. We walked down to our usual table in the back of the tavern and waited for her to bring us a pair of longnecks.

"I'm telling ya Harry, they've been taking stripers all week. Just look at this webcam." Donnie Gilroy swung his phone in my face.

"I checked the charts and the tide'll be turning not long after midnight. If we leave by nine, we can be on the coast just as the action is heating up."

I could see that my friend was working himself into another fishing frenzy.

· *Chapter Four* ·

D ONNIE GILROY'S LIFE WAS SHAPED BY TWO EVENTS THAT OCCURRED within only a few months of each other. The first began innocently enough on a pleasant Saturday afternoon. Like a hundred-year flood pouring down through the headwaters of a river, blowing out logjams and sweeping away cobble, this single event, more than any other up until then, resulted in the erosion of those fragile underpinnings that held his current in check while gouging out a new course from which he'd never return.

Even at the age of nine, Gilroy was obsessed with catching the biggest fish in the river, although back then we caught more perch than we did trout. It was the week after school let out for the summer. Donnie was hanging out at the dock behind The Town and Lake Motel, where his mother worked cleaning rooms. His attention turned to a Ford Bronco that pulled into the lot in front of the public beach adjacent to the motel's dock. A bunch of older kids spilled out of the two doors of the blue-and-white SUV. Gilroy recognized the three older boys, who were clad in cut-offs and T-shirts, but not the girl, who had long legs. A black bikini accentuated her pale skin. He assumed she was from out of town, about to begin her summer vacation.

Two of the boys strode down to the water. They began splashing around, doing their best to draw the girl's attention away from the third guy. Ignoring their laughter, she spread out a towel and lay down on her stomach. Eventually, the two teenagers walked over to the dock and took turns diving off the end. Donnie pretended to stare out onto the wavelets caused by an easterly breeze while watching the third boy kneel beside the girl with the long legs and pale skin. When the girl undid the pencil thin strap of the black bikini-top, Donnie Gilroy felt a stirring that he didn't quite understand. After the two teens came up for air, they swam back to the dock, where they stood waist-deep in the water. Seeing their friend reach down to rub lotion across the girl's back, they decided she wasn't worth their time and made plans to fish the upper stretch of the Magalloway River.

Back then, my grandfather, Harold, would drive Gilroy and I to the river below the Aziscohos Lake dam. He wouldn't allow us to wade through any of the more treacherous rapids, but looked on as we fished close to shore. We once watched the old man play a large salmon through Warden's Pool. I remember how the mist fell off the water above the deep run creating a tiny rainbow that only added to the magic of the moment. I never forgot the image of that fish tail-dancing across the surface, not once, but three times.

Gilroy figured that anyone approaching his parents' age was old and anyone as old as either my grand or his brother, my great-uncle Angus Ferguson, was ancient; which meant that their friend, Daniel Fogerty, had to be as old as dirt. Old man Fogerty had been born in a house a block behind the service station once owned by his father. By the time Harold and Angus arrived in town, Fogerty had inherited the business that was located between the post office and what is now the Rangeley Region Sports Shop.

A number of times during the previous summer my grand's long-time fishing buddy had dropped us off at some small brook or streamlet, leaving Gilroy and I free to explore on our own. Fogerty would return before dark to buy us hamburgers and fries at the Pine Tree Frosty or a small pizza from the Red Onion. But it was the river above Aziscohos Lake that we longed to explore.

The upper part of the Magalloway River flows through wild country known as the Parmachenee Tract. Like a jewel in an ancient crown, the bright waters of Parmachenee Lake sparkle clear and cold from an otherwise sullen conifer forest. Beginning as a tannin-stained whisper, the headwaters of the Magalloway slip over the Canadian border following a serpentine path through bogs that ooze mud and are pocked with prints of beaver, otter, black bear, and deer. Gathering volume over the next few miles, the river widens while twisting and turning until reaching Parmachenee Lake at a point not far above Indian Cove, a dark backwater where moose like to gather.

Below the lake, the Magalloway reappears, sliding past Black Cat Cove and over the remains of a wooden dam that was once used by loggers to raise the water level, allowing timber to slide above the river's boulder-strewn bottom. From here, the stream descends at a rapid pace until entering Aziscohos Lake.

This tract of semi-wilderness is locked behind gates, the keys to which are held only by a lucky few, including the owner of Beaver Den Camps, a sporting lodge at the head of Aziscohos Lake. A half-dozen or so owners of camps scattered along the banks of Parmachenee Lake also possess keys as do loggers who harvest timber for the paper companies that own most of the great expanse of forest known as the Great North Woods.

Fogerty had told us that the little lake held in the palm of the dark forest was named after a Native American princess. My great-uncle liked to say that the stream connecting the lake above the gates with the man-made impoundment below reminded him of the Highland rivers of his youth.

Few locals have ever fished inside the Parmachenee Tract and fewer have explored the forest surrounding its shores. Gilroy assumed that the teens either had a key or were lucky enough to own mountain bikes that could traverse the logging roads, which extend beyond the gates. Always keeping his ear out for piscatorial news, my friend had heard whispers among the fishing guides describing shadowy pools containing enormous brook trout. He once overheard Fogerty describe to one of his customers a fish that measured from the tip of his middle finger to above the crook of his elbow.

Families from away who were able to afford half-a-million-dollar cabins claimed ownership of the handful of camps built along the shores of the wilderness lake. Although these wealthy few might only spend the occasional weekend at their vacation homes, they guarded their keys as jealously as their portfolios. We knew of only one local man who owned a camp behind the gates—my great-uncle, Angus.

Shorter than most men and blessed with no fear of heights, Angus Ferguson could climb the side of a ninety-foot spruce quicker than a red squirrel. While a young man, Angus had earned his living as a tree topper, one of the most dangerous jobs in an extremely dangerous occupation. He was responsible for limbing the tops of tall trees before they were felled, that is, until a chainsaw ended his career. Although the doctors saved his leg, the little man would walk with a limp for the remainder of his life. As part of a settlement reached with Boise Cascade, he was given a lifetime lease for an acre of land overlooking Parmachenee Lake. It was land he could never afford to purchase outright from the large corporation, which along with a few other paper companies owned most of the region's forest.

The small cabin and a few out buildings cost little to construct. Angus used lumber his logger friends had left for him to build the modest structure. He performed the work with the help of his brother Harold, old man Fogerty, and a few of the other men in town. Located more than thirty miles outside of Rangeley, the drive to Angus's camp could take as long as an hour, sometimes longer, depending on the condition of the logging roads that wound up through the forest from Route 16, the macadam road that connected our town with New Hampshire and the rest of the world. Back then, my great-uncle had yet to invite us to his cabin, and so Gilroy and I could only imagine what wonders lay behind the gates.

"Mr. Fogerty says he'll take us next Sunday." Gilroy nearly spit the words out. The froth around his lips made me worry that perhaps a rabid dog had taken a bite out of him.

After hearing the two older boys discuss their plans, Gilroy had begged the service station owner to drive us to the gates. My friend spent the following week tying Black Ghosts, the only streamer he could manage to construct at that age. To play it safe, Gilroy plunked down a dollar fifty to purchase a Hornberg from the fly shop.

The Hornberg, a traditional pattern that can be fished as a streamer or dry fly, was created by a Wisconsin game warden to imitate an adult caddis, stonefly, grasshopper, moth, or any other big bushy bug when skittered across the surface of the water. Although too difficult for Donnie to tie, the pattern was known back then, as it still is today, to possess magical powers. It's a mouthful-of-a-streamer able to entice the biggest fish from the stream. Or at least that's what Gilroy had explained to me on the following Sunday as we pedaled our bicycles toward old man Fogerty's gas station.

The sun had barely crested the hills to the east of town. Shadows slipped over one side of Saddleback Mountain. They fell across the snowless ski trails that cut through the pine-studded slope like stitches over a wound.

Gilroy and I appeared at the station shortly after six that morning. When, two hours later Fogerty pulled in beside the gas pumps, he found us asleep on the curb in front of the door to his little office. After loading our bicycles in the back of his Suburban, the station's owner drove out of town. Heading west, he stopped at the general store beside the southern end of Aziscohos Lake to buy grinders and a couple of bottles of orange pop.

A little more than forty-five minutes later, he pulled up to a gate, where a hand-written sign warned: PROPERTY OWNERS ONLY–VEHICULAR TRAFFIC FORBIDDEN! The old man reached into the back of his vehicle and pulled out a small cooler that held the sandwiches and bottles of soda he had purchased for us. While helping Gilroy tie the red-and-white ice chest to the handlebars of his bicycle, Fogerty said he'd be back at four to pick us up.

"Be sure to duck into the woods if youse hear a car coming, and for Christie's sake, pull those bikes well off the road when you find the trail."

Fogerty thought for a moment, then added, "And don't forget ya not to mention my name if youse get caught!"

On the drive in, he had explained that although it was only unauthorized vehicular traffic that was forbidden behind the gates, the camp owners, having paid a tidy sum for their cabins, didn't cotton to those who biked or hiked in, and if caught we should expect swift retribution. Since Gilroy and I had never been behind the gates, Fogerty drew us a map on a napkin that he stuffed into my shirt pocket.

It was a long bike ride to the river and I remember sweating profusely by the time we crossed the wooden bridge that spanned the dark current. After walking our bikes a few feet into the wood, we hiked single file down the trail outlined on the napkin. The conifers were closely packed on either side of the narrow path, and I could smell the balsam in the heavy June air. As the sound of the current filled our ears, Gilroy was unable to contain his excitement. Pushing past me, he scrambled down to the side of a waterfall that stretched across the river. A few seconds later, I swung Fogerty's cooler onto a picnic table that was set in a small clearing beside the stream.

Donnie hurriedly rigged the old cane rod he had purchased at a yard sale the previous summer.

"It's just like Fogerty said!" he yelled back at me.

The spray from the falls felt good after the long bike ride. I walked over to a large boulder. A bronze plaque bolted to its side commemorated a visit to the river by President Eisenhower.

"Fogerty says they stocked this pool with so many trout Ike could've walked across their backs to get to the other side." Gilroy was talking while knotting a Black Ghost to his line. I drew closer to the long run that spread out below an outcropping of boulders polished smooth by what the napkin confirmed was Little Boy Falls.

Donnie cast the Black Ghost into the white foam at the bottom of the falls while I strung line through the eyes of an eight-foot Leonard fly rod that was a hand-me-down from my great-uncle. As the current took hold of the streamer, he stripped back line, imitating the action of an injured baitfish. On his third cast, a salmon, as big as the one hooked by my grand in Warden's Pool, rocketed through the surface.

Yet to make a cast, I dropped my rod and grabbed the net that hung from a clip on the back of Gilroy's fishing vest. Wading behind him, I watched the fish jump a second and then a third time.

It seemed like an eternity before I was able to slip the net under the salmon's side. I remembered to hold the fish under the water the way my grand had taught me while allowing it to regain its strength. We marveled at the salmon's beauty. Its silver-and-black scales reminded me of the type of armor I'd seen in a book my mother liked to read to me about King Arthur and his Knights of the Round Table. Careful not to injure it, Gilroy gently removed the hook before we slid the big fish back into the cool water below the falls.

During the next few hours Donnie released two more salmon, each smaller than the first, while I wandered farther down the trail, taking a few small brook trout from a wide run known as Landing Pool. After lunch, we switched positions.

I was checking Fogerty's watch, about to call out to Gilroy, to tell him it was time to head back, when he began to frantically holler my name. While I scrambled over the boulders beside the shoreline, my leaky hippers made squishing sounds each time my feet hit the ground.

"Jesus, Harry!" Gilroy yelled when I came into sight of the pool. "He's gotta be the king of the river!"

Gilroy's rod was bent forward, vibrating with the life force on the other end of the line.

"Have ya seen 'em yet?" I cried while wading toward him.

"Only his maw. After that he went deep and stayed there." Donnie took back line, but after three turns of the reel, the fish powered across the deep pool, on a long run that caused the reel to sing out in frustration.

"Gotta be a brook trout."

"Seems more pissed than scared." Sweat saturated the back of

Gilroy's shirt.

"Bigger than the salmon, for sure," I muttered, my voice lowered to a reverential whisper.

"Was ready to call it quits, playing around with that Hornberg I bought, letting the breeze take it into the air, slapping it back down on the surface, when the bastard raises its head and grabs the thing out of the air." Wild-eyed, Gilroy stared at me, his voice raised, although I was standing a foot or so beside him. "That was the last I saw of him."

I watched the fish take more line. It was nearly into the backing.

Donnie worked the trout, gradually reclaiming much of the line previously lost while I strained to catch a glimpse of the Leviathan.

"Sonavabitch," cried Gilroy, when the brook trout suddenly broke through the surface. I was sure it was the biggest fish we'd ever see however long we might live. It made the salmon look like a smelt. No way it'd fit in the net, I thought, afraid to voice my concern.

"You two belong to those bikes up the trail?" An angry voice suddenly called out. Startled, the two of us turned at the same time to find two men breaking out of the forest beside the stream.

Donnie turned back to the fish while I continued to stare over my shoulder. Shiny gadgets dangled from the fly vests of the two men. The shorter one wore a wide-brimmed hat. His belly pressed against his chest waders. The shadow cast by the brim of a dark blue baseball cap hid the taller one's face. Both men held expensive graphite rods in their hands.

"Time to go boys," the man under the cap called out.

"Don't make us call the warden." The fat man dropped his rod in the grass and waddled onto a cobble bar that spread out into the river.

Gilroy was trying desperately to bring the fish to his side while leaving me to decide whether to bend forward with the net or engage the two men.

"Didn't you see the signs above the gate? You're trespassing!" The taller man waded past his companion. He too had abandoned his rod on the bank.

"We didn't use no vehicles," Donnie called back weakly.

"Unless you're a guest of a camp owner, you have to go."

I could now see the face of the man with the baseball cap. Deep creases cut through his brow. Combined with skin that was tight against his high cheekbones, the guy reminded me of one of the dead brought back to life in a movie Gilroy and I had seen. The zombie was almost upon us. His sweating companion huffing and puffing a step behind.

"C'mon mister," was all I could think to say.

"NOW!" spit out the fat man.

As the zombie with the cap reached for my arm, Donnie momentarily looked away from the fish. That's when the trout turned, falling upon the horsehair-thin monofilament connecting Gilroy's line to the Hornberg. Hardened by age, the fish's jaw was impervious to pain, but the unrelenting force that had pulled it ever closer to shore had suddenly ceased. The river king slowly finned back into the depths from where it had risen to strike at the annoying bug with the surprisingly nasty sting.

That was the day that forever changed Donnie Gilroy's life; the storm that caused his river to flow over its banks, creating a flood that turned the river from its original direction down a course from which it would never return.

· *Chapter Five* ·

IWOKE TO THE SOUND OF THE SHOWER IN THE NEXT ROOM. Sun streamed in from the edge of the curtain that was drawn across the window. Rolling on my side, I focused on the clock radio. It was six fifteen. I scratched my head, trying to remember the events of the previous evening. Scanning the room, I noticed a red bra and matching thong lying beside the bed. Women's clothes were strewn about, some hanging off the back of a chair, others out of a dresser drawer that hung open. Another pile flowed out of the open door of a closet.

I remembered wishing Gilroy well, watching his faded pea-green Subaru spin out of Sparky's parking lot and onto the main street of town. I also recalled walking back inside the tavern, finding a seat between two of the vultures and nursing a longneck until Thelma Louise closed up the place sometime after one in the morning. Jack Daniels—Thelma's go-to drink when she decides to let loose—blurred the rest of my memory.

Although the drought had discouraged my sports from booking time with me, news of the recent rainstorm had spread quickly, with two of my regulars, a father and son from Boston, calling to reschedule their previously canceled date. A third, an older guy from a small town outside of Waterbury, Connecticut, did the same.

It was going to be a busy few days, which was fine with me, but if I didn't hurry, I was going to be late for another sport, the one waiting for me at old man Fogerty's gas station.

I stared at the alarm clock that had ticked away four more minutes that I'd never recover. Grabbing the remote from the bed stand, I clicked through the higher numbers. The Weather Station was predicting overcast skies with a chance of showers. *Not a bad day to be on the river*, I thought.

After checking out the scores on ESPN, I clicked off the TV and stared up at a crack in the ceiling that reminded me of a sweet little trout stream running into the south end of Rangeley Lake.

"Hey babe." Thelma Louise padded across the room in her bare feet. She had a pink towel wrapped around her body and a baby blue one around her hair. Judging from her smile you'd never guess that only a few hours before she had drained a half bottle of Jack while drinking me under the table.

I could smell the shampoo as she unwrapped the towel around her head. After shaking her hair like a dog after a swim, Thelma kissed me on the cheek. I looked over her shoulder at the clock on the bed stand: Six-thirty. It would take me at least fifteen minutes to shower and dress and a few more minutes to drive the short distance from Thelma's apartment to the gas station. I ran my fingers through the mélange of brown roots that rose into a shaggy mop of dirty blonde, with a few purple streaks thrown in for shits and giggles. The color of Thelma's hair changed as frequently as the weather in western Maine.

I began to worry, but then said the hell with it, telling myself that once the sport hooked his first fish he'd forgive me for being late. That was about the time I found the spot below T.L.'s ear that drives her crazy. When she tumbled onto the bed, the pink towel fell to the floor, landing between the red bra and thong.

Ernest Doyle was pissed. The big Irishman was looking down at his phone as I pulled into the station. It was seven twenty-eight. Fogerty later explained that my sport had walked over to Petey Boy at least three times to ask if he knew when I'd be arriving. Petey had just smiled that handsome smile of his while shrugging his shoulders.

Later, while on the river, Doyle would explain how he had sold software to protect the computers of municipal transportation systems from cyberattack. He had done well on a contract with the New York subway system and even better with another from New Jersey Transit, but it was the stimulus money handed out like candy by the Feds after Wall Street melted down that enabled him to retire at age fifty-two. It was a good thing for the retired entrepreneur that I didn't learn until the following afternoon what he had said about having a plan to spend the rest of his life sampling trout streams around the world and not standing around waiting for a fishing guide recommended by a retard with a Marlon Brando smile.

Doyle now leaned against a four-door Range Rover parked off to the side of the gas station. He was texting on his phone and did not look up when I pulled behind a late-model Suburban that was parked beside the pumps. Petey Boy had his arm inside the back window. He looked up as I climbed out of my truck.

"Hey Harry." There was that smile.

Daniel Fogerty stood in the entrance of the small office attached to a concrete building that contained a single large bay.

"How they hangin', Har," he called as the Suburban's driver walked toward the office where an ancient cash register collected dust beside a credit card machine.

The head of an enormous German Shepherd followed Petey's arm as he slipped it back out of the vehicle's window.

"Hey bud." I clapped my hand on Peter Jordan's shoulder while nodding toward Fogerty, who then turned to follow his customer inside the office.

Petey tilted his head toward the balding man standing beside the shiny Range Rover. Doyle continued stabbing his meaty fingers at the screen of his phone.

"He's sure mad at you, Harry." Petey frowned.

Ernest Doyle was a big man, a bit over six-two, weighing somewhere north of two-fifty. He had small eyes sunk into a round face and a tiny nose. He reminded me of a big sow I once saw at the Fryburg Fair. I remember Gilroy making oinking noises at the poor thing while Petey called out Piggly Wiggly.

My sport scowled as I walked toward him. "You're late," the big man grunted, without looking away from the phone's small screen. Slipping the device into his pants pocket, he clasped the hand I extended in his direction.

"No worries," I mumbled, unaware of the insult Doyle had directed at my friend.

After introducing myself, I explained that we would be taking my truck to the river.

"He says you're the best guide hereabouts." Doyle pointed toward Petey Boy.

"He can get carried away," I replied. While helping the sport carry his gear toward the truck, I quickly added, "Overcast skies, the water up with the rain, you're in for a good day."

With the help of one of the staffs I'd stashed at the edge of the forest the night before last, Ernest Doyle was able to wade across the river above the hydro-tube. The big man handled himself well enough. Casting with a high degree of proficiently, he was soon into fish, a small brook trout and then a larger one.

As I had predicted, my sport's initial petulance faded after a salmon zinged off thirty feet of line in a single run.

"Call me Ernie," he said after I took a photograph of him releasing the fish.

By lunchtime, Ernie had released another large salmon and two brook trout, one much shorter than the salmon. The other, a fat fish, measured nearly fifteen inches. The first trout had been cruising through a set of rapids below Warden's Pool, the other taken a quarter mile downstream from a deep gorge formed between the bank and a boulder. The rock's shoulder leaned into the current the way Billy Kozlowski once bullied his way over goal lines.

"What's with your friend?" the retired software salesman asked as we looked over a set of rapids that contained the promise of fish.

"Petey?" I asked.

"Seems a bit off, you know?"

I needed a good tip to help pay my rent and keep me in beer and cigarettes for another month. Fighting a sudden surge of anger, I replied, "Pete's okay. A little enthusiastic is all."

Eager to change the subject, I pointed toward a pool that held a number of decent-size trout. Following my instructions, Doyle cast a nymph, one of many I'd tied over the winter. He allowed it to dead-drift along the far bank. In this manner, the sport worked the pool hard for over an hour. During that time, he took three more trout and two salmon, all of average or larger size. I had remained seated with my back against an enormous spruce. My long-handled net lay beside me should Doyle get really lucky. Raising my face skyward when sunlight slipped through the parting clouds, I thought of Thelma Louise. Like her mother, she too dreamed of making enough money to get a new start in a big city like Hartford or even Manhattan, which got me thinking about what I wanted from life. That's when I rose to my feet, deciding it would be a good time to break for lunch.

The retired entrepreneur sat on a smooth boulder unwrapping one of the turkey sandwiches I'd nearly forgotten to purchase from the diner while on my way to the gas station. The two of us talked fishing, Doyle describing locations I couldn't pronounce and would never have the opportunity to visit and me describing some of what I knew about the local fishery.

While at the diner, Bernice had suggested I add two slices of freshly baked apple pie to my order, saying that it would cost next to nothing and turn a decent tip into a really good one. As Piggly Wiggly ate the second slice, I bent down to pluck another longneck from the edge of the run where it remained cold. At the sound of a cracked branch, we both turned toward the path beside the river.

A moment later, a familiar figure limped down the forest trail. As the small man walked out of the shadows, a shaft of sunlight illuminated his face. Bright blue eyes stared out above a hawk-like nose. Angus Ferguson's leathery brow had wrinkled with age. My great-uncle stood for a moment at the bottom of the path. The old man wore hippers and a faded green cap with a ripped brim. He didn't wear a vest. I was surprised to see him on this stretch of water, knowing he preferred the river above the lake.

The wading staff he carried in his left hand had been cut from a maple tree. The tree's bark remained in a few places, glistening under successive coats of varnish. Unlike the unadorned staffs I kept hidden along the river, my great-uncle had braided a length of rawhide and strung it through a hole drilled through the top that he had slipped around his wrist. His hand gripped a six-inch strip of leather glued below the hole at the top of the shaft. Had he bothered to notice, Doyle would have seen the letters A S F, one below the other, burned into the wood a few inches above the leather grip.

My sport did take note of the nine-foot fly rod Angus gripped in his other hand. Although he fished with graphite, the entrepreneur knew something about cane, identifying the old man's bamboo rod as a three-piece Winston.

Doyle had at least eight inches and a hundred pounds on my great-uncle, while Angus had more than thirty years on the sport. Ernest Doyle quipped that the old guy reminded him of one of the little people his mother had warned him about when he was a kid. "A leprechaun," he chuckled. But as my uncle limped toward us, Doyle changed his mind. "More like an elf," he said, his voice low as the other man drew closer.

"You know, like in that movie. What's it called? The one after the book I never read."

"The Hobbit?" I tried.

"That's the one."

When Angus nodded in my direction, Doyle asked, "Another friend of yours?"

Rather than reply, I busied myself with clearing away the remains of our lunch.

My great-uncle limped past us. "Mind if ah give it ah go?"

Rather than respond, I picked up Doyle's rod while suggesting we head down river, but the software salesman waved me off. Convinced that the little man with the limp could not raise a fish from water he had so thoroughly covered, my sport watched with amusement as my great-uncle removed a rectangular pillbox from his shirt pocket.

After opening the tin container, he slipped a pair of wire-rimmed glasses over the ridge of his sharp nose. Although Ernest Doyle did not recognize any of the peculiar patterns hooked into a foam ridge glued against the tin's interior, I could identify each one. The sport waited as Angus knotted a tiny wisp of feathers to his line. My great-uncle then knotted a second pattern to a short piece of tippet material that he tied around the bend of the first fly's hook.

In his hippers, Angus Ferguson could not wade nearly as deep as Doyle, who made full use of his chest waders while high-sticking his nymph down the run. Nevertheless, with a single backcast, my great-uncle laid out enough line to cover the same water. The sport watched as the tandem rig sunk from sight. The wet flies slipped down the same seam Doyle's nymph had traveled. Employing a technique called the Leisenring Lift that he had taught me sometime before my tenth birthday, Angus raised his rod, then twitched the tip a few times. Doyle looked back at me with a crooked smile when the little man pulled up the line without a strike. But unlike the Irishman, I knew better.

"We should be going," I called. "There are a few other pools I'd like to show you before we hike back up to the dam." Worrying about losing my tip, I did my best to coax my sport away from the run.

Once again, the little man with the tattered cap laid out nearly sixty feet of line with only a single backcast. Once again, the flies landed like faerie dust upon the water, following the same seam Doyle fished less than thirty minutes before. I was relieved when my sport finally tired of the game and turned to follow me down the trail, but it was too late. My great-uncle had once again twitched the tip of his rod. Instantaneously, the Winston arched forward under the weight of a good fish. Although Doyle had missed the take, he could not mistake the sound of the reel and turned to see the cane vibrating with life.

The little elf did not have a net, but a few moments later, he bent forward to release a brook trout without removing the fish from the water.

"How big?" My sport hadn't moved from where he stood on the bank overlooking the run.

Just about every angler I've ever guided has said it wasn't the fish, but the fishing that was important. Some repeat the old adage that a bad day of fishing is better than a good day at work. One of my more literate clients likes to quote Thoreau's famous words, something about men fishing all their lives without realizing that it isn't the fish they are after. Most guys give a passing nod to an especially pretty sunset or whenever the Lady of the Lake flies overhead, but I know better. I understand that the majority of my customers measure their time on the water not so much by their surroundings or even their results, but by how those results stack up against those of others.

"Hard to judge from here," I lied.

No longer smiling, Doyle groused, "Sure as hell bigger than anything I've seen today."

During my brief career as a fishing guide, I've learned that a sport will be content catching a single fish; provided of course, that his friends have gone fishless. Another, catching his limit of small trout will remain inconsolable should his pal catch a lunker. And so I was not surprised when Ernie quickly reverted back to Mr. Doyle. Notwithstanding the dozen or so nine-to-fourteen-inch trout and the three or more larger salmon he released during his half-day on the water, Ernest Doyle's frown was fixed on his boar-like features for the remainder of the afternoon. Thinking about the brookie that swam away with my tip, I decided I'd make a better mind reader than a river pimp.

· Chapter Six ·

I'D MET THE LOCAL GAME WARDEN ONLY ONCE BEFORE. IT WAS WHILE
I was casting one of my great-uncle's flies in the pond beside my home.
When the little pattern sunk to the bottom, I'd strip it back the way he
showed me. The fly's life-like grouse wing drove the bluegills crazy, with
a fat fish striking each time I twitched the line. The warden, a lanky man,
wore a stern countenance that was in stark contrast to his shiny gold
badge. He had stepped out from behind a large spruce tree to make sure
I wasn't dunking worms in violation of the fly-fishing-only sign posted
on a birch tree a few feet from where we stood.

The same warden maintained a severe expression upon accepting
Gilroy and I into his custody. The two sweating camp owners had insisted we be prosecuted to the fullest extent of the law for "fishing with
worms." Although we vehemently denied the charge, Gilroy's trout had
stripped the Hornberg from his line, leaving only our word to rebut that
of the irate camp owners. With our bicycles loaded into his vehicle, we
sat in the back seat of the four-door Jeep. The warden remained silent as
he drove over the bridge above the falls and down the logging road we
had previously traveled. The man's unforgiving eyes stared at us from
the rearview mirror. Instead of stopping at the locked gate, he turned
onto another logging road. This one flanked the east side of the lake. My
anxiety mounted as I worried about my mother's reaction. She had had a
good couple of months. The previous week she'd taken me to Portland to
watch the Sea Dogs play. While there, she bought me a baseball cap with
the team's logo above the bill. I now lowered the brim of the cap over my
furrowed brow. Staring through the window at the sunlit surface of the

lake, Gilroy appeared unconcerned. I was surprised when the warden turned off the logging road and bumped down a two-track for half a mile before parking his vehicle in a dirt turnout. Walking around the back of the Jeep, he pulled out our bikes and herded us up a winding path that led to a cabin on the eastern shore of Parmachenee Lake. My great-uncle was seated on the steps of a porch extending outward across the front of the one-story building.

"Gilbert," Angus Ferguson said as he rose to shake the warden's hand.

The warden appeared at least a foot taller than Angus, although my great-uncle was standing on the first step of the porch. Angus Ferguson nodded once or twice as the younger man in the olive uniform relayed what had been conveyed to him by the two sports. He stared at Gilroy, when the warden came to the part of the story about the enormous brook trout. The old man's countenance matched that of the warden's, an expression that conveyed his intent to deal with us in a severe manner. Gripping the handlebars of my bicycle, I held my head low under the red brim of the navy-blue baseball cap, while waiting with quiet resignation for my sentence to be passed down. Gilroy was scanning the lake that spread out below the cabin, but a kick to his shin brought his attention back to the matter at hand.

The old man's expression did not change as we watched the warden stride back down the path. We stood for a few moments, at first listening to the Jeep's motor over the logging road and then watching the dust rise up as the warden's vehicle sped around the lake and out the south gate that marked the boundary of the Parmachenee Tract.

After we told him our version of the story, my great-uncle's face appeared less severe. To our surprise, he offered to take us back to the pool as his guests if we agreed to clean a number of fish. Their lifeless bodies lay inside a wicker creel that hung from a spruce notch on the wall of the porch. In addition, we were to mow the grass around the cabin for the next four weekends and stack any firewood the old man cut over the same period of time.

"Bin efter that fish fer mony a seasin." Angus looked across at Gilroy who was only an inch shorter than the full-grown man. "Whit did ye say ye wur casting?" he asked.

"Hornberg," Gilroy replied.

My great-uncle thought this over for a moment.

"An honest pattern. Well done, laddie."

Handing the creel to Gilroy, he limped inside the cabin. After gutting and cleaning the brook trout, we followed my great-uncle's instructions, collecting the entrails and depositing them on a stump below an enormous spruce tree.

Upon our return, we watched the old man prepare the fish two at a time in a shallow dish, sprinkling salt and pepper over a combination of flour and cornmeal. After dredging the trout in the mixture, my great-uncle laid them side by side in an oversized cast-iron pan, frying them in hot oil that crackled as he slowly raised the heat on his propane stove.

Angus put out plates on a small table he'd set up on the porch that overlooked the lake. Cutting up a lemon, he placed a slice on each of our plates alongside two of the longer trout. As we took our seats, the old man walked back inside the cabin, pulled a bowl of homemade potato salad from an ancient refrigerator and called out to us, "Whit wull it be then, will ye hae a beer or pop?"

We looked at each other, Gilroy calling back, "Beer!"

Twisting the caps off two bottles of pop, the old man set one in front of each of us and placed a Sam Adams beside his own plate. While we used our forks to flake away the breaded flesh from the bones, Angus grabbed one of the four smaller trout from his plate and holding it by the tail, slipped all six-inches into his mouth.

With the fish still between his lips, my great-uncle pointed a boney finger toward the sky. I put my hand up to the brim of my cap, but it was hard to make out any detail of the large bird gliding down over the western shoreline, until it swung over the lake's sparkling surface. The sun glinted over the white of its head and tail making it clear that an eagle had set down on the top of the tall spruce above the stump where my great-uncle had directed us to place the fish guts. A moment later, the large raptor fell straight toward the ground, her sharp talons clutching at the edge of the stump. A cold yellow eye stared down at the entrails.

"Lady o' th' Lake," Angus mumbled as he drew the trout's spine back through his teeth.

"A few weeks oot o' th' egg, her big brother knocked th' wee lassie oot th' nest. Yer grand 'n' I happened tae be passing in a canoe and teuk it upon ourselves tae see whit all th' sooch was aboot." Angus slipped a second fish into his mouth.

We watched the Lady rip away at a fish intestine with her fierce beak. Pulling the spine of the second fish back out of his mouth, my great-uncle continued his story. "She hud a goosed wing 'n' was squawking like a wee bairn. So, we brought her back 'ere 'n' nursed th' poor thing back tae health. That young vet ower in Easie set th' wing 'n' showed us howfur tae feed the lass. Let her go efter we wur sure she'd healed up."

After we gobbled down cups of butterscotch pudding with whip cream that appeared like magic from the old man's refrigerator, Angus walked over to a rocker and sat back down.

"Ye ever hear th' story o' White Nose Pete?" he asked. "Some fowk call him Pincushion Pete."

When we answered no, he packed his pipe, lit a match and while drawing down on the tobacco began another story.

"Th' wey 'twas telt tae me, Pete lived under Upper Dam ower to Mooselook. Year efter year, that fish pult aff streamers 'n' flies from anglers wha wur unable tae bring th' auld dobber tae net. This wis back afore yer grand 'n' I moved 'ere." He looked down at me, the smoke from his pipe spiraling toward the sky.

I was seated on the porch floor with my legs crossed in front of me while Gilroy, his arms leaning on a cedar rail, stared wistfully out over the lake. As Angus exhaled, the fragrant scent of his tobacco filled the air.

"Weel noo, I believe 'twas sometime doorin th' nineteen twenties that a well-known angler, a fella by th' name o' Shang Wheeler, wrote an Ode tae Pete. Some say Pete haes lived fur ower one hundred years, while ithers insist tis his descendants that continue the legend. Whitevur might be th' truth, tae mah knowledge, althoogh many an expert angler haes tried, auld Pete haes ne'er bin caught."

Angus stared across at Gilroy, who had turned to face him.

"If ye ask me, 'twas Pete's kin ye hooked doon at th' Landing Pool. Mibbie a cousin or nephew."

"Ya think?" It was like pouring gasoline on a fire.

"Aye laddie, ah do."

Angus told us a few more tales about the legendary fish before banging his pipe on the arm of the chair. After sliding it into the breast pocket of his shirt, he leaned back in the rocker and closed his eyes. We took the opportunity to amble around the inside of the cabin that was constructed from hand-hewn beams.

Walking through an open area adjacent to the well-stocked kitchen, we found a short corridor that led to a small room where we sank into the cushions of two easy chairs positioned on either side of a long window. The window overlooked a grassy knoll that sloped gently down to the lake. A statuette of a moose carved out of a chunk of maple stood on the windowsill beside another of a loon. Between the two was a long piece of driftwood that looked like a duck with its head folded back into its wings.

Inside a miniature log cabin Gilroy found a package of thin cylinders made from compressed balsam. Inserting one into the top of the tiny cabin's roof, he tore a match from a pack I found beside the little cabin. Gilroy allowed the match to linger until the top of the cylinder glowed orange from the flame. The smoke swirling upward from the tiny chimney filled the room with a fragrant pine scent.

An old, but comfortable couch leaned against an inside wall between doors that opened into two bedrooms, one a bit larger than the other. A hollowed out wooden cone was nailed to the doorframe of each bedroom.

The cones contained a variety of feathers, a few of which appeared to have been donated by the Lady of the Lake, although we couldn't be sure. Others were from ravens and crows, arranged between those of herons, owls, and hawks, behind those of different smaller species of waterfowl and songbirds. Gilroy identified a primary feather from a cardinal and a tail feather from a chickadee. I guessed that a third might have come from a cedar waxwing.

I rose from the easy chair to inspect two paintings that were hanging over the couch. Drawn on birch bark, each contained an outline, one of a huge brook trout, the other of a salmon. The fish had been captured in watercolors. Inscribed below the brook trout was the date: "September 9th, 1974," with the words: "Island Pool" written above it. Below the salmon was written "May 21st, 1983, Camp Ten Bridge." I made out my mother's initials in the lower right corner of both paintings.

A black cast-iron stove squatted in one corner of the room while a large oak desk dominated another. It was Gilroy who noticed that the desk was shorter than most. Looking closer we could see that an inch or more had been cut from the bottom of each leg. A painting of a great blue heron, also done in watercolors, hung above the desk. It too had my mother's initials scrawled in the corner. After a while we could hear the old man's snores drift through the open windows. I walked over to a shelf built into the wall beside the oak desk and pulled down a coffee table book containing the artwork of Winslow Homer. While I sat down at the desk, Gilroy stared up at the broad array of titles that Angus had collected. Although many were about fishing, interspersed among them we discovered others concerning the local flora and fauna, as well as historical novels, books of poetry, and still others concerning philosophy. Gilroy eventually removed a thick volume titled *Streamers & Bucktails: The Big Fish Flies* that was written by Colonel Joseph D. Bates, Jr.

Gilroy pointed at the author's name. "Didn't Angus say something about Shang Wheeler and a Captain Bates fishing for Pete from a boat below Upper Dam?"

I looked up from a print of an angler straddling a log below a fall of water. "White Nose broke off Shang's streamer just before Bates was about to net 'im. At least I think that's what he said."

"Wonder if it's the same guy?" Gilroy said as he flipped through the pages.

For the remainder of that afternoon, I went through the treasure trove of literature while Gilroy searched through Bates' book for clues that might help him on his quest to capture a fish as great as the regal brook trout that had eluded such accomplished anglers as Shang Wheeler and his young friend, a captain at the time, who later rose to the rank of Colonel.

· *Chapter Seven* ·

PETEY SQUEEZED, BUT THE KETCHUP INSIDE THE PLASTIC BOTTLE missed the fries that were piled on a plate beside his cheeseburger. The top of the table looked like a crime scene. We were seated at our usual spot beside the window and next to the door of the diner located behind the Rangeley Historical Society building. Grabbing a few napkins from a metal container between the salt and pepper shakers, I wiped the table clean while Petey took a swig of vanilla coke. Reaching into my jeans, I pulled out two twenty-dollar bills and handed them to him.

"Put these in your pocket and don't lose them," I said.

"Thank you, Harry." Petey shoved the bills into the breast pocket of his overalls.

He picked up a fry and ran it through the puddle of ketchup I squirted onto his plate.

"Harry?" Petey asked slowly.

I looked across the table. A puzzled expression had formed across his handsome features.

"What's it for?"

"What's what for?"

"The money, Harry."

"It's called a commission. Your cut for turning that sport onto me."

Petey had been chewing on a French fry, but now stopped while he contemplated what I'd said to him. After another moment of reflection, he said, "I don't think he was a very nice man."

Leaning backward, I stared at the ceiling as the front legs of my chair tilted upward.

I looked back at Petey when he asked, "Do you think it's enough to buy a fishing rod?"

On more than one occasion, I'd come upon him standing outside of the sports shop, staring up at an eight-foot fly rod that hung in the window. The Sage's crimson wraps contrasted nicely against the three pieces of forest-green graphite.

Although he'd never acquire sufficient skill to cast a fly, Petey often accompanied us on the water. I knew all this, but answered, "Might be a down payment. Better to give the money to your mom, who can hold it for you."

This seemed to satisfy him. The towhead returned to his cheeseburger while I counted ceiling squares, an exercise I performed whenever perplexed by the vagaries of life. This was not the first time the old man had taken a fish when others could not, but it was the first time my great-uncle had done so below the lakes. I could only wonder why Angus had chosen that afternoon to fish the lower river and why that pool? What I did know was that Ernest Doyle's scowl had remained fixed across his pig-like features when he climbed into his shiny Range Rover, and although the wealthy sport had taken more fish than most, he'd left me with only the most modest of tips.

I've seen my share of sports and like so many of them, Ernest Doyle, for all his proficiency with a fly rod, had little understanding of what fishing with a fly was all about. Although I'm still working that out for myself, I know it has to do with more than catching a larger fish than the next guy. Still, I wished the old man hadn't showed up my sport. I could have used that bigger tip "Ernie" would have provided, had he not turned back into Mr. Doyle.

Petey scrunched up his face when he took a bite of the pickle that came with his burger. A tiny trail of juice slipped out from the corner of his mouth. After a second bite the rivulet extended down his chin.

The legs of the chair tapped the floor as I leaned forward to grab another napkin. Pete's hair was parted on the left, and although his mother combed it neatly to the side, a few blonde strands always managed to fall down across his brow. He looked younger than his actual age. The guy's smile was infectious and his blue eyes turned the heads of younger girls vacationing with their families along the shores of the lake that bears the same name as the town—a fact that should have troubled me, had I given it much thought.

After cleaning Petey's chin, I took a bite of my own hamburger.

"Thank you, Harry," he mumbled through a mouthful of fries.

I smiled before resuming my mission to count the tiles on the diner's ceiling. While tracing a crack that ended in a wide water stain, I thought of my great-uncle alone in his camp at the edge of those sparkling waters with the Lady of the Lake as his only company.

I hadn't been up to the old man's camp for quite some time and rarely fished the Parmachenee Tract while guiding sports. I decided men like Ernest Doyle hadn't earned the right to fish the little stream that trickled over the Canadian border and wound through shadows cast by tall spruce and fragrant balsam, a stream, where trout as large as those caught before the turn of the century continued to lurk.

Munching on a fry, I visualized the river below Aziscohos Lake. A torrent of water released from the dam below the lake joins with that pouring forth from the hydroelectric tube, creating a tailwater fishery within walking distance of the paved road. It was this stretch of stream that I depended upon to make my living as a fishing guide.

As Petey took another bite of hamburger, I wondered how the river compared with the wild water of my Scottish ancestors. I tried to remember the name of the highland river my mother had described to me as a child. Was it the Dentworth, or maybe the Derworth? No, I was pretty sure it was the River Derwent.

"You guys should've been there!" Gilroy had come rushing through the diner's door, taking the seat next to Petey Boy.

We hadn't seen him for three days, which was not unusual. Every few weeks he'd head out of town, usually chasing one run of fish or another.

His forays to the coast could take a day or two, sometimes more. Once he was gone for more than a week.

Donnie's hand shook as he raised a glass of water. His eyes were dilated. His shirt was stained with salt, fish scales and blood. He smelled of sweat and brine.

I looked down at my watch. I was already ten minutes late to meet Thelma Louise. We'd planned to spend the afternoon cruising around the secluded coves on Mooselookmeguntic Lake in my Rangeley Boat.

"Stopped at Fogerty's to gas up and heard about your run in with the old man." Gilroy reached his arm across the table, swiping a fry from my plate.

"The old coot just saunters down to the river like he did that day on the Upper Mag. What was it, eight, maybe nine years back? You remember?"

"You kiddin'? That trout still haunts me." Gilroy's eyes glazed over as they tended to do whenever his mind turned to fish.

"This time I was guiding some rich fucker. The guy wasn't pleased when the old fart took a hog from the same pool he had fished hard." I felt my anger suddenly rise. Had I thought about it, I might have realized that my ire was directed as much at myself for referring to Angus in that manner as it was at Angus for showing up my sport.

Gilroy chuckled as he grabbed a few more fries from my plate.

"Cost me a nice tip."

"Sorry bro, but lucky for you, I brought back a cooler full of fillets. Keep us fed for a month."

"All three stooges together at the same time." Bernice McCue had shuffled over to our table, a pot of coffee in one of her boney hands. The waitress was about Fogerty's age, working at the diner since we were kids. She should have retired to Florida on her husband's pension, if she had a husband and if he had a pension. Instead, she worked six days a week just to make her rent payments.

"Hey Bernie." Gilroy slid a mug across the table.

"Hey Bernie," repeated Petey as the aging waitress refilled Donnie's mug.

"I'll have a turkey club on white toast." Gilroy didn't bother to pick up the coffee-stained menu that hadn't changed since we first started coming there.

"Of course, you will," Bernice replied without bothering to remove the pencil from behind her ear. Looking at Petey, she asked, "One scoop or two, darlin'?"

When Bernice returned with Gilroy's order, she filled a mug with coffee. Grabbing Petey's empty plate, she replaced it with a dish containing two scoops of strawberry ice cream.

"Thank you, Bernie." Petey smiled up at the waitress.

"You're welcome, sweetie," she replied.

With his mouth full, Donnie described wading into the moonlit surf and casting plugs and spoons to stripers that tore through schools of mackerel within twenty feet of shore.

I pulled the wrapper off a new pack of cigarettes. After offering one to Gilroy, I slid my lighter across the table. Petey spooned a dollop of ice cream into his mouth while hanging on Gilroy's every word. He scrunched up his face when Donnie explained how he had cut slices of mackerel to use as bait once the stripers began to ignore his artificial lures.

It took another thirty minutes for him to run out of steam.

Paraphrasing Wimpy from the Popeye cartoons Gilroy still watched, he turned to Petey and said, "I'd gladly pay you Tuesday for a club sandwich today." He winked across the table at me.

Petey reached into the pocket of his overalls.

I knew better than to ask how Donnie earned a living. Like Blanche DeBois, he appeared to depend on the kindness of strangers. Even so, I didn't like anyone teasing Petey Boy, even if it was good-natured teasing. Looking sharply at Gilroy, I said to Petey, "It's okay bud. It's my turn to pay."

I stared over their shoulders when the little bell above the diner door jingled. Thelma Louise Shannon stood inside the door with her hands on her hips and a frown contorting her pretty face. As she strode toward our table, her red high-top sneakers squeaked against the diner's pine-board floor.

· *Chapter Eight* ·

A S A KID, I LOOKED FORWARD TO THE RAIN. I STILL DO. BACK THEN, it meant I might spend the day indoors with my mother if she was feeling up to it. Now, it means the river will be up and the fish frisky. I remember one morning before Gilroy and I had ventured above the Parmachenee gates. The rain had begun early, the first drops falling while I was still asleep. My bedroom was located across the hall from my parents' room, up the stairs of the house where I was raised. I awoke to the sound of the rain falling gently against the roof. I lay under the sheets in my favorite pajamas, the yellow ones that had pictures of batman stenciled on them; the ones I would wear every night until my mother pulled them out from under my pillow to wash them.

On that particular morning, I rose later than usual and padded across the hall to look into my parents' room. My mother lay on her bed. She was fully dressed, with a dampened face cloth across her brow. The shades were drawn and the room was dark. When I walked quietly to her side, she whispered to me that my father had driven to the office to catch up on paperwork. By no means an unusual Saturday in the Duncan household, I received permission to visit my great-aunt and uncle. With a father who spent much of his time at the bank and a mother, who at times, spiraled down a rabbit hole for days on end, I found the company of the older couple comforting.

Pulling a box of corn flakes from a shelf in the pantry beside the kitchen door, I filled my bowl and walked outside in my bare feet. The roof over the pine deck sheltered me from the rain. While eating my cereal, I stared out across the lawn. A pair of black ducks floated among the reeds along the edge of the pond that bordered the backyard of our home. Off in one corner of the yard lay the red canoe that I was forbidden to take out unless accompanied by my mother. When feeling better, she would paddle me around the pond's perimeter as I searched for turtles, sometimes fishing for perch and sunfish. A red squirrel that had been scolding me scurried up the trunk of a nearby spruce when I turned in its direction. I found myself concerned for my mother. Even at that age, I was prone to worry, especially about my mother.

There were times when my mother would take me on a picnic, others when we'd sit by the pond while she read to me about King Arthur and his Knights of the Round Table from a large book with wonderfully painted pictures of the knights in their suits of gleaming armor. Some were on horseback, jousting with long lances, others standing toe to toe as they swung sun-glinted swords. There were also paintings of magnificent castles with brightly colored banners waving from turrets that rose high into picture-perfect skies and others of Queen Guinevere and her handmaidens. Although impressed with the young Lancelot, his hair the same color as Petey Boy's, I remained leery of Merlin, resplendent in a pointed hat that towered above his head and a powder-blue robe with stars and crescent moons embroidered across the fabric. My favorite character was the good King, who always looked a bit sad, with his long flowing beard and creased brow.

But that was when my mother was feeling well. It seemed to me that the migraines were becoming more frequent, and even when not suffering from one of her day-long headaches, she often appeared to be in a fog, unable to leave her darkened room, as if under one of the wizard's spells.

After walking back inside, I cleaned my bowl and set it in the plastic rack beside the sink. Back in my room, I changed into a T-shirt and shorts and slipped on a pair of sneakers. After taking a moment to run a brush across my teeth, I tiptoed back into my parents' room and kissed my mother goodbye.

The warm rain was not unpleasant on that first Saturday in July.

Running up the street, I imagined myself astride a midnight-black mare. The horse's nostrils flared. Golden mail protected its flanks. With spear in hand, I charged through raindrops and around puddles, dodging a giant dragon's fireball at the last instant.

Angus and Matilda Ferguson lived in a small house a few doors down from my grandparents and only a short walk up the block and around the corner from our house.

My mother had told me how her family had come to the Rangeley Lakes Region. Her father, Harold Ferguson, married shortly after he returned from the war, with his younger brother, Angus, following his example two years later. Not long afterward, the two of them decided to move from Boston to Maine, where they found work as loggers. The house Angus and Matilda had purchased was little more than a cottage, but for a little boy it was a magical place. It had only one bedroom and a single bath. The living room looked out onto the street while the kitchen faced a well-tended flower garden. Like the yard behind my home, the surrounding forest framed a lawn, with grass sloping gently toward the same pond that the Pine Tree Frosty backed up against.

Faded photographs hung on the living room wall. In one, my great-uncle and his brother stood among other members of their family outside the Manor House that their grandparents maintained for a Scottish Lord. They weren't much older than I was at the time. In another, their older sister sat astride a pony. A third photograph captured the Highland stream where Angus and Harold learned to fish. Like my mother's shifting moods, I always thought that river looked quite foreboding as it wound through dark moorland.

Three small portraits hung in the hallway of the small house: one of a stern-looking older woman, who Matilda had explained was the Queen Mum; another was of a stiff looking man in a white uniform with medals pinned to his chest. My great-aunt said he had been the King of England during the war. In a third, a young lady, wore a white gown with a light-blue sash draped across the front. On her head sat a diamond-studded crown while a ruby necklace adorned her neck. According to Matilda, the woman was the Queen of England. I thought her young for the job. The queen, in my opinion, appeared a bit uncomfortable. Although her features were plain, I was drawn to her shy smile.

Each December, my great-uncle would pull down a set of wooden steps from the ceiling and climb into the attic. Angus would return with a large display he'd carved from an oak stump and on which he had fastened an oval mirror. His wife had draped a white cloth around the edge of the mirror, adding puffs of cotton to simulate the snowy landscape around a pond. Behind the mirror rose a mountain of paper mâché that was also painted white. As the days drew closer to Christmas, Matilda would add a tin figure here and another there. Some skated on the pond while others tobogganed down the mountain, and still others stood around a wood fire. In one corner, a group of five or six tin carolers stood together. In another, a tiny tin boy was about to throw a tin snowball at a passing automobile also made of tin. By the time Christmas Eve rolled around, I would have spent hours gazing at the idyllic scene.

Matilda was bending over the stove when I opened the front door on that soft July morning. The smell of sugar cookies baking in the oven permeated the little house.

"He's in his room." She turned to hug me, accepting my kiss on her cheek before I darted across the hall.

"Harry." Looking up from a desk cluttered with batches of fur and bags of feathers, the short man with the aquiline nose used my name, as he so often did, as a one-word greeting. Angus Ferguson's blue eyes looked out over the top of his gold-rimmed spectacles as he pushed his chair back. Among the thread and tinsel, bobbins, scissors, and other delicate tools scattered about the top of a maple desk, a spindle hung suspended by a thread. The thread was wound around the body of a tiny barbless hook, which in turn was grasped in the jaws of an ancient metal vise. Angus's unlit pipe lay in a tray beside the vise.

The room smelled of tobacco and gun oil. Between two large

windows, a sofa dominated one wall. Leaves of hardwood trees were embroidered into its forest-green cushions. Its arms were ornately carved out of maple that matched the tables set under each window. Angus had built shelves that extended from floor to ceiling on an adjoining wall. Every shelf was filled with books.

A large upholstered chair, with a tall back and a cushion of the same design as the sofa, hunkered down in a corner beside a wooden case with a glass door that contained a shotgun and a rifle. The desk where Angus tied his flies stood in the other corner. Drawers in a cabinet above the desk contained all types of fur and feathers from animals and birds that my great-uncle and his brother procured from the waters and forests that surrounded our little town. Above the cabinet hung another of my mother's watercolors, this one of a Scottish Highland stream with an ancient castle in the background. The initials in the corner confirmed that this painting had been completed before she'd married my father.

Well-read and versed in many subjects, my great-uncle was always willing to answer the questions of a young boy. However, Angus Ferguson was not the type to volunteer information. A God-fearing man, he accompanied his wife to Sunday service. Although my great-uncle could quote from what he and his wife called the Good Book, he didn't agree with his religion's attempts to proselytize. Prone to keeping his opinions to himself, when I was older, he once said that many of the world's ills were the result of one man attempting to convert another to his own beliefs. He thought this to be true with respect to politics and religion as much as with fishing with a fly.

He once told me, "Th' Bolsheviks battle wi' th' Capitalists fur th' heart o' th' workin' man, while Christians war against Moslems ower oor soul. Even oor fellow Brothers of th' Angle draw up sides aboot whither tis permissible tae use wet flies 'n' nymphs rather than th' dry fly. Tis a shite o' time, Harry, 'n' th' cause for sae much strife in th' world."

My great-uncle was of the opinion that each man was entitled to his own beliefs, provided those beliefs did not impinge upon another's.

Angus motioned for me to unfold a metal chair he kept behind the door. As I sat beside him, the little man shifted his attention to the fly pattern suspended from the vise.

Even at that age I could tie my own flies. I'd spent hours seated by my great-uncle while he fashioned his sparsely tied patterns.

On that rainy morning, I watched the man, who even back then seemed old, as he dubbed a hint of black mole's fur onto the waxed thread of primrose yellow silk, winding it around the hook to form the body of the fly. With a single turn of a grouse feather that he called a "par-tridge" feather, my great-uncle was able to simulate the legs of the artificial insect.

That was about all there was to the soft-hackled patterns that Angus had taught me to tie before I'd learned my multiplication tables. The recipes for these ancient patterns were set forth in a book. Its cover was fashioned from leather cracked with age, its pages filled with faded pencil and ink illustrations, pages I'd memorized before my first day of school. The book contained patterns my great-uncle had learned to tie from his father and grandfather, both of whom had fished the wild rivers and lochs of Scotland.

Some of the patterns had strange sounding names like "spiders" and "bloas," while others had names as delicate as the material used to create them. Some of my favorites were the Water Cricket, Yellow Sally, and Spanish Needle.

My great-uncle described how, before coming to this country, he had watched his grand meticulously copy patterns from books found in the Lord's extensive library, books his grand could never afford. My great, great, grandfather filled the pages of the leather-backed notebook while adding his own thoughts and observations from his many years as the Lord's river keeper.

The imitation he called a Partridge and Yellow fell to the table when Angus unlocked the jaws of the vise. Raising it to my eye, I marveled at the graceful silk wraps and rufous color of the grouse fibers that appeared alive around the tiny ball of mole fur.

When I handed the weightless bit of fluff to my great-uncle, Angus slipped the point of the hook into a ridge of foam glued to the inside of an empty Sucrets tin. There, the tiny soft-hackled fly patiently waited for more than sixteen years, until called upon to take the large trout from under the nose of Ernest Doyle.

· Chapter Nine ·

"**J**ESUS, HARRY." STARING DOWN AT THE THREE OF US, HER HANDS ON her shapely hips, Thelma Louise's hiss reminded me of an angry water snake that once lunged from the shoreline of a New Hampshire lake where Gilroy and I had been casting big bushy flies to largemouth bass.

"Harry's in trouble," Petey giggled.

Thelma's hair spilled out from under a Red Sox cap that she wore with the brim facing backward. There was a hole in the left thigh of her cut-off jeans. I could see the outline of a black bra under a sleeveless blouse she had tied into a knot around her slim waist. The blouse was the same color as her red sneakers.

"I'm sorry, T." I did my best to look contrite.

"Really? That's all you got?"

"I was having lunch with Petey and then Gilroy showed up."

"Give me a cigarette," Thelma Louise growled. She now sounded more like a pit bull than a snake. "And move over." She pushed her thigh against mine. Staring across at Gilroy, she barked, "You stink."

Gilroy yawned. He stretched his arms over his head. After a moment he said, "Whatdoyasay we drive over to the IGA? We can get us a couple of six-packs and head over to Big Boy Falls where I can wash off these fish guts and you two can make up."

I smiled at Thelma Louise. Like a dog with a bone, she clung to her anger, turning an icy glare at Donnie when he suggested that she should show us some love.

As we rose from the table, Petey Boy asked if he could come with us. When he fixed his boyish gaze on Thelma Louise her ire melted under the warmth of his smile.

Shrugging her shoulders, she mumbled, "Guess I'm outnumbered."

I left a couple-dollar tip for Bernice while checking to be sure there was enough in my pocket to pay for the beer. Gilroy and I decided to leave our vehicles beside the diner. The four of us piled into the Wrangler Thelma leased from the Berlin dealership in New Hampshire. I hopped in next to her, leaving Gilroy to squeeze beside Petey in the back seat. After we stopped at the store, Thelma Louise sped back down through the main street of town, passing Dodge Pond. A few minutes later she turned right at the tall wooden bear outside the village of Easie.

Thelma braked at the bridge that crosses over the Kennebago River to allow me to check the water level and then continued west, until turning onto the logging road known as the Morton Cutoff Road. From there we bumped over potholes and ruts, with Gilroy and Petey hanging on to avoid falling out of the back of the open-top Jeep.

Turning left, Thelma Louise followed Lincoln Pond Road to Green Top Mountain Road. A few minutes later, she turned right off the wider logging roads and onto a narrow two-track that followed the west side of the Cupsuptic River, where we stopped for a cow and her calf to cross in front of the Jeep between Fox Pond and a swamp where moose often graze on its water-logged vegetation.

After driving past a few wilderness campsites, we stopped at the end of the two-track. The sound of the waterfall rose through the forest as we hiked the short distance down to the river. With the recent rain, more water than was usual for that time of year tumbled over a series of boulders, before descending a number of feet through a ravine and into a deep pool. Sunshine filtering through the mist above the falls created a little rainbow.

The four of us were sweating by the time we fanned out below the pool. A slight breeze slipped down the river, keeping the black flies in the forest. While I dug bottles of beer and pop into the grit and stone under the water, Thelma removed her blouse and cut-off shorts. Wearing only the black bra and black panties, she began to ascend the side of the falls, the red high-top sneakers protecting her bare feet. Half way up the slick boulders, she stopped, turned the brim of her Red Sox cap around and screamed "Geronimo!" before leaping sneakers first through the air.

"Geronimo!" yelled Petey Boy, who clapped his hands. He was seated on a smooth boulder near the base of the falls. After removing his leather work boots and socks, Petey pulled up his overalls and kicked his feet, splashing water above his head.

Thelma Louise popped up through the surface of the pool. With a single stroke, she was able to stand. I sat beside Petey while Gilroy laid out a towel on another boulder a few feet away. After retrieving her cap, Thelma Louise waded toward us. Droplets of water shone like diamonds along her arms and legs.

Spreading out a beach towel with a can of Budweiser printed on it, she sat down beside Gilroy, who handed her a bottle of Long Trail. With one hand, Thelma raised the longneck to her lips, while with the other, she wrung out water from her hair that was currently dyed jet black, a thin red streak braided down one side.

"One of these days you're gonna break a leg doing that." I frowned at her.

Still gnawing on that bone, she turned toward me and said, "You can be such an old lady, you know that?"

Thelma Louise reached past Gilroy, who was lighting a joint. As she ruffled Petey Boy's hair, Gilroy took a long drag and then passed the jay to Thelma Louise. When Petey asked if he could take a hit, she looked over at me. Rising from my towel, I bent toward the water's edge and reached down to pull up a can of Vanilla Coke. I handed it to Petey. Carbonated soda streamed into the air, splashing down onto his upturned face when he pulled on the tab.

As Petey Boy slipped into the water to wash off, Donnie stripped down to his boxers. After dipping his shaved head under the surface, he jumped up beside Petey. With his hands high and his fingers clenched like claws, Gilroy roared like some balding sea creature. I yelled at him to stop, telling Petey it was okay.

Once he washed off the brine and fish guts, Gilroy grabbed a beer and climbed back out of the water. Lighting another joint, he took a deep breath and raised his face toward the sun. It wasn't long before Donnie Gilroy was drifting with the clouds on an aimless journey through the sky.

I had scrunched up my T-shirt under my head and was lying on my back in a pair of khaki shorts with my eyes closed. The marijuana had also worked its magic on Thelma Louise, who lay on her stomach beside me, neither hissing nor growling.

With the lakes in western Maine frozen in ice until the beginning of May and spates of snow not uncommon before the leaves are off the trees in the fall, we'd grown to appreciate those few insect-free days when the sun's warmth momentarily relieved our day-to-day concerns. While Petey swigged his favorite soda, we spent the next few hours talking shit and sipping beer to even out our high.

"Look at me."

I had nearly nodded out, but rose on one elbow to watch Petey Boy doggy paddle around the pool.

"Be careful," I called.

Thelma Louise punched my shoulder.

"Let him be," she whispered before her lips found mine.

Gilroy stretched his arms above his head. Having left the pool, Petey wandered along the side of the river, where he engaged in one of his favorite pastimes, searching for rocks, feathers, and other bric-a-brac that struck his fancy. On his feet again, Gilroy gazed at a large bird that spiraled high above us. He wondered out loud whether it was the Lady of the Lake.

Since that afternoon at my great-uncle's cabin, we imagined every eagle we saw to be the Lady. Like my great-uncle, she was nearing the end of her reign, having by that time flown over the skies from the

Parmachenee Tract to the Kennebago Divide for over twenty years, a long life for an eagle. Squinting through the smoke curling upward from another joint, Gilroy watched the majestic bird drift eastward until she disappeared above the conifer-studded hills that surrounded the river.

A few minutes later, with a roach clasped between his teeth, Gilroy hobbled around the rocky shoreline in bare feet. Climbing over boulders, he began to claw his way up the side of the falls. Looking down, Gilroy called out, "Do or do not, there is no try."

Thelma Louise turned in my direction. With a hand raised to shade my eyes from the sun, I explained, "It's his new thing, quoting Yoda."

I sat up as Gilroy climbed above the rocks where Thelma Louise had dived into the pool.

"Don't be an idiot!" I called above the roar of the falls.

Thelma sprang to her feet when she realized what Gilroy was about to do. Cupping her hands around her mouth, she yelled, "C'mon Donnie, you got nothin' to prove!"

The current descended over the top of the falls for more than forty feet before splashing into the pool that at its deepest was only a few feet above our heads.

"Gonna end up like his father," I mumbled to no one in particular.

"Geronimo!" called Petey, who had returned with pockets bulging from all the sticks and stones he had collected.

Gilroy continued his climb toward the top of the falls. Once again quoting Yoda, he shouted down to the three of us, "Named must your fear be before banish it you can."

I knew there was no talking to him.

Thelma Louise and I stood together. We nervously watched Gilroy's progress. Petey, who remained at the back of the pool, clapped his hands.

Donnie Gilroy looked down at us upon reaching the top of the falls. His smile appeared almost angelic. Raising his arms above his head, he rose on his toes and pushed off.

"Geronimo!" Petey screamed once again as Gilroy dove headfirst through the narrow ravine.

"Goddamn it," I yelled, running to the edge of the water. Too frightened to move, Thelma Louise held her breath.

It took a moment or two before Gilroy surfaced. I stared across the pool at his devilish smirk.

"Asshole," was all I could think to say.

· *Chapter Ten* ·

PETEY BOY IS TWO YEARS YOUNGER THAN GILROY AND ME AND ONE year younger than Thelma Louise. On most summer afternoons, Petey stops at the Pine Tree Frosty between twelve and twelve fifteen to purchase a strawberry ice cream cone with sprinkles. You can set your watch by it. He's a familiar figure in our little town, riding his bike the two blocks from his home, turning at Fogerty's service station and continuing down the town's main street to the food stand. Like old man Fogerty, most locals wave as he passes them by.

Petey first saw the bicycle when he accompanied his father to the Walmart located fifty minutes south of our town in the bigger city of Farmington. After that, he always asked his parents to take him with them whenever they made the trip down Route 4. Afterward, the family would stop at Friendly's for lunch and an ice cream sundae.

While his parents pushed a cart through the store, Petey would remain standing in front of the bicycle. He was enthralled by the fire-engine red body and shiny chrome handle bars. Most of all, it was the set of crimson-and-silver streamers hanging from the end of each handle that captured his fancy. Petey could imagine those ribbons bellowing outward as he pedaled through town. Like one of the knights from the book my mother once read to me, he imagined himself riding on an armored horse. Other times, he pictured himself like the Lady of the Lake, who Gilroy had told him was the Queen of Parmachenee, gliding silently up high in a soft-blue sky.

His parents presented the bike to their son on his tenth birthday, but it would be a number of months before I took the time to teach him how to ride the thing and even then, he needed the assistance of training wheels.

The same summer that Petey turned eleven, Thelma found work at the Pine Tree Frosty after lying about her age. Each day, she served ice cream, hot dogs, and lobster rolls to vacationers.

As kids we depended on each other, perhaps even more than we depended on our parents. I suppose it wasn't their fault, but our parents, for one reason or another, seemed to never be around when we needed them. That's just how things were, and we more or less accepted them that way.

Take Thelma and Petey, for instance. Every day, Thelma Louise would look for Petey Boy, who would ride his bike down Main Street, the streamers trailing behind him. He'd pull into the ice cream stand at his usual time each afternoon, flashing his handsome smile. Walking up to Thelma's window, he'd slide his hand into the front pocket of his overalls and open up that big paw of a palm to reveal the exact amount of change his mother had counted out for him.

Thelma Louise sometimes added an extra scoop of ice cream when no one was looking.

During her break, she'd sit with Petey beside the pond behind the store, where they'd throw bits of hot-dog rolls to the mallards that waddled toward them. To hear Thelma tell it, there was this one duck, a smallish female with a brown-speckled breast, that always seemed to hang back, while the others, a few larger females with plumage similar to that of the smaller bird and males, their glossy green necks iridescent in the sunshine, hogging all the food. Thelma taught Petey to aim his throws toward the diminutive duck, and though many times the other waterfowl would scramble to gobble the bread, the two of them would cheer whenever the little female was successful.

One afternoon, Thelma Louise was taking the order of a guy wearing a Six Flags T-shirt when she saw Petey balancing on his training wheels while pedaling his bicycle down the block. It was an especially hot afternoon and, when telling me the story, Thelma Louise described how the man's shirt was unable to contain his stomach.

"Do you want fries with that?" she asked while staring down at the "outie" protruding from a hairy belly that hung over the band of the man's baggy shorts.

The sun had risen high in a cloudless sky. Thelma had been on her feet since nine that morning. The tennis sneakers she wore gave little support to her aching arches. It was the second week of that rain-starved August and the crowd that morning had begun to collect in front of the Pine Tree Frosty as soon as it opened. Customers filled a number of picnic tables outside the little storefront. The tables' forest-green paint had long since faded. Folks also stood in lines in front of the ice cream stand's two windows, where Thelma and another girl were taking lunch orders.

Sliding a paper plate containing a lobster roll and onion rings toward a tall man wearing mirrored sunglasses, Thelma peeked out at a handsome boy that reminded her of Ashton Kutcher. A couple of minutes earlier, the boy, a few years older than Thelma, had chatted her up while waiting for his order. She now watched him push back a few strands of hair that fell down over his eyes as he joked with four or five other teenage boys and girls seated around one of the tables outside the storefront.

The good-looking teenager called out to Petey as he pedaled to a halt. Looking past the line of people waiting to give their orders, Thelma Louise watched the other kids around the table break into laughter when the boy said something she couldn't make out to Petey.

"A cheeseburger with ketchup, mustard, and relish, and a large order of fries."

Thelma looked down at a woman wearing a blouse with yellow-and-white daisies painted on it. The brightly colored top was barely able to confine two enormous breasts that threatened escape as the woman searched through her purse to pay for the order. When telling the story, Thelma Louise likes to point out how she feared for the lunchtime crowd's safety, should the woman's black spandex pants lose the struggle to hold an avalanche of flesh in check.

"Anything to drink with that?" Thelma asked. Her attention had shifted back to the handsome teenager, who now held the handlebars of Petey's bike. Another boy guided our friend toward the table while the other teens called out something she still couldn't hear.

"I said a diet coke," huffed the woman when Thelma slid her order forward.

Thelma bit her lip rather than reply.

Petey was smiling, although Thelma Louise was pretty sure he didn't understand why the other kids were laughing.

As the woman carried away her tray of food, a man stepped up to Thelma's window. He wore a porkpie hat, plaid shorts and tan socks under leather sandals. Three young girls orbited around his legs.

"Three hot dogs and a lobster roll, please." The man's voice drifted away as he bent down to pick up the youngest girl. He ordered drinks while fighting off a duck feather that the toddler shoved in his face.

Distracted by the father and his daughters, Thelma did not see a second teenager climb on the bike while two of the girls at the table slid down to make room for Petey Boy.

When she looked up again, he was wedged between the handsome kid and the girls. Another boy and girl were seated across from them on the bench attached to the side of the faded-green picnic table. Thelma didn't recognize any of the kids. She could see that Petey was still smiling, but didn't like how the others at the table were acting toward him. Then, Thelma saw that they were looking past Petey Boy at the good-looking guy, who twirled a finger pointed to the side of his head while crossing his eyes.

She watched the guy on the bike begin to ride around the table. With his legs out to each side and his arms in the air, he reached over and grabbed Petey's baseball cap and placed it on his own head. Underestimating Petey Boy's strength, the good-looking teenager was forced backward when the towhead rose in an attempt to retrieve his cap.

As the line grew in front of her window, Thelma watched Petey, running a step behind the bike's rider, who was now weaving in and out of the picnic tables while the other teenagers egged him on.

When Thelma heard one of the kids call out the word "retard," she turned from behind the counter and strode past the long line in front of the windows. As the bike swept past, Thelma Louise stuck out an arm and clotheslined its rider.

"Enough!" she yelled.

"He took my hat," Petey panted. Still breathing hard, he now stood over the fallen boy, whose legs were tangled in the spokes of the bicycle.

Thelma grabbed the cap from the guy's head and handed it back to its owner.

"We were just kidding around." The handsome boy strode toward Thelma. The kids at the table had stopped laughing as they rose from the table. The people in line as well as those seated at the other tables had also grown quiet.

"I don't want any trouble," Thelma Louise stared back at the handsome boy, who had reached her side. The kid on the ground rose to his feet.

The man with the plaid shorts stood up from the table where his daughters were eating their lunch, but when one of the teenagers called out for him to mind his own business, he looked around at the other patrons and then sat back down.

The kid who had fallen, attempted to jostle Petey's bike from Thelma's hands. When she wouldn't let go, the handsome teen grabbed for her wrist. Thelma Louise responded by throwing a haymaker that landed squarely on a jaw that appeared as fragile as a glass vase. A red smudge appeared on the faded green paint along the edge of the picnic table where the good-looking teen struck his head. The bike rider took a step forward, but thought better of it when he heard his friend groaning on the ground.

Everyone in the crowd looked toward the street when they heard a siren. The man in the plaid shorts hurried over to the fallen teenager. The man with the mirrored-sunglasses followed his example.

Turning to Petey, Thelma whispered, "Ride home. I'll see you there in a little while."

Petey's eyes grew wide with fear. He stood motionless, as the sirens grew louder.

"Now, Petey!" Thelma Louise screamed.

As two policemen pushed forward, Petey pedaled back the way he came, while Thelma disappeared into the crowd.

Thelma Louise found her friend seated on the steps of his home. He was rocking back and forth. Petey's father worked for the Building and Supply while his mother sorted mail at the post office. Finding the key under a flower pot beside the front door, Thelma led Petey inside the saltbox style house. After pouring a vanilla coke into a Sponge-Bob jelly jar, she made him a baloney sandwich. It took her a long while to calm him down. His mother was the first to return. Thelma Louise explained what had happened and that none of it was her son's fault.

Later that afternoon, Patti Shannon answered the knock at her door. Thelma Louise's half-brothers stood, with fists clenched, on either side of their mother as she stared up at two police officers. Patti told her sons to stand down, and after a brief conversation, she accompanied her daughter on the short drive to the town's police station where Thelma was charged with assault and battery.

A public defender explained that Thelma would have gotten off with a slap on the wrist, but in this case the kid she hit was the son of a Boston judge, and although his son was not seriously hurt, the father was out for blood. Even so, because of her young age, Thelma Louise was sentenced as a juvenile. A few months later, following the advice of the attorney assigned to her case, she pled guilty, and with her mother and two half-brothers seated behind her, Thelma stood before the judge who sentenced the twelve-year-old to eighteen months on probation.

In the weeks following the incident, Gilroy and I tricked out Petey's bike with banana bars, a rubber horn, and a shiny metal bell. Gilroy found an antenna that he fastened to the back fender and added a skull-and-crossbones flag. I had picked up an old wicker creel at a yard sale and secured it to the front fender. No longer employed at the Pine Tree Frosty, Thelma Louise helped us paint the bicycle black with red lightning bolts along the sides.

"No one's going to bother you on this badass riding machine," proclaimed Gilroy.

"It needs a name," Thelma Louise decided.

"How 'bout Rolling Thunder?" I volunteered.

"Awesome!" Gilroy and Thelma cried out at the same time.

"Awesome," repeated Petey.

In the years that followed, I realized that although we might not have much and could depend upon even less, we'd always have each other. On that bond, the four of us would hold tight.

· *Chapter Eleven* ·

June is a moody month in western Maine. It is a month prone to overcast skies and sudden downpours that roll over the Magalloway Valley, preceded by shards of lightning and cracks of thunder echoing over the ridges and rills surrounding our lakes and rivers. Storms sometimes roll upward through New Hampshire's Presidential Range, other times they sweep down from the north, swirling off of the Boundary Mountains that separate Maine from Canada. It's a time when black flies hatch from their eggs and disperse through the forests like tiny vampires swarming over anything that moves. It's also when the brook trout and landlocked salmon look to the surface for their food.

The fish remain active throughout July, and although the heat of high summer slowly decimates the gangs of black flies, mosquitoes continue to plague the angler during the day, with no-see-ums taking their turn at dawn and dusk.

By imitating the different color caddis that hatch throughout the summer, sports willing to suffer biting insects can take fish. Beginning in June, terrestrial patterns also work well. My great-uncle taught me how to tie a pattern, which imitates the little mahogany-colored flying ants that hatch sporadically during this part of the fishing season. I've been successful casting this fly, as well as another tied on the smallest of hooks that works mostly at dusk when the fish key on very tiny midges while refusing anything attached to a hook bigger than a #22.

As the sun went down over Big Boy Falls, we packed up our empties and piled back into Thelma Louise's Jeep. After she spun the red Wrangler into old man Fogerty's station, Petey climbed onto Rolling

Thunder and pedaled toward home. His smile was as bright as the sun
had been all that afternoon. Although Donnie suggested we continue the
party, Thelma Louise wanted to take a shower before beginning her shift
at the tavern. Scheduled to meet a sport the following morning, I also
begged off.

The first sign of sunburn prickled against the back of my neck as
I watched Gilroy pull away from the diner in that broken-down, rust
bucket of his. Driving the short distance to my apartment, my mind
turned to Thelma.

The woman drove me crazy. Pretty much did for as long as I could
remember. She was forever trying to convince me to leave town, go back
to college, telling me I could be a writer; that I should put all the reading
I did to better use. As if a fishing guide wasn't good enough for her. I
mean, we'd been seeing each other on and off since we were kids. She was
the first girl I kissed, although to be fair, Gilroy could say the same and if
being really truthful, so could a number of other guys from around town.
You might say we were friends with benefits, but we truly cared for each
other. She's always been there when I needed her, and I suppose, when it
comes down to it, I'd do most anything for her.

Still thinking about Thelma in that black bra and panties, water dripping off those tan legs, I entered the Thai restaurant below my apartment. My landlady, Mrs. Mookjai, called, "*Sawatdee Kah*," from where
she stood near a large rectangular aquarium set atop a mahogany counter. While waiting for my dinner, I watched an assortment of blue, yellow, and purple tangs, along with a few damselfish, swim in and out of
multi-colored coral. Thanking Mrs. Mookjai when she handed me my
order of Pad Thai, I turned to watch an orange-and-white clown fish fin
toward the glass. Its eyes reminded me of one of those children painted
by Margaret Keane.

After climbing the stairs to my apartment, I kicked off my boots and
slipped out of my jeans. Between gulps of Long Trail, I lowered wooden
chopsticks to sweep the stir-fried noodles, bean sprouts, scallions, and

peanuts into my mouth. The breeze that kept us cool while on the river had settled down as the sky began to darken. The temperature outside the apartment's open windows remained about the same as that of the stale air inside the small space I called home.

Having stripped down to my BVDs, I squatted on a stool beside the kitchen counter. The "kitchen" was an alcove across from a main room, which, with a small bathroom, comprised the entirety of the apartment where I'd lived since leaving my father's house. In addition to a few stools and a chair, my furniture consisted of a bed and a couch I bought from Gallant's Discount House in Roxbury, a bureau for my clothes that Thelma donated, and a desk that Gilroy rescued from the Rangeley "Walmart," a building located adjacent to the town dump where we locals exchange hand-me-downs.

After clearing away the Styrofoam box that contained my dinner, I took a seat at the desk. Opening one of the three deep drawers running down its side, I pulled out a bag of feathers and another of fur. From the narrow drawer that spanned the front of the desk, I removed a pair of scissors.

In shop class, I think it was during my second year of high school, I had built a workstation out of a twelve-by-eighteen-inch pine board. I glued spindles across the back that could hold spools of silk and thread. Next, I carved out a place where a bottle of glue would fit snugly and drilled holes to hold various tools.

After draining my second bottle of Long Trail, I decided the four or five coats of varnish on my tool caddy made it look as good as any found in the L.L. Bean catalogue.

I'd meant to tie up the imitations needed to supplement my caddis patterns months ago, but throughout the winter and into this spring I'd told myself there was time enough to do so. Now, with caddis season upon me, I could no longer procrastinate.

The smell of the Thai food hung in the stale air. I pulled another bottle of Long Trail from the refrigerator that old man Fogerty had brought back from the dead after Gilroy and I liberated it from the dump. Seated back at the desk, I took a long pull of beer while staring down at a Thompson vise that had been my great-uncle's and was nearly as old he was. When working at the sports shop, I made use of a much newer model, one sold by the Regal Company, that stood on the shelf behind the store's counter. It's a vise I coveted, but one I couldn't afford to own.

I can always count on my great-uncle's soft-hackled flies to take fish under the surface, and although it has a fixed wing, the Gold-ribbed Hare's Ear, a traditional wet fly no longer stocked in the town's sport shop, remains my go-to fly to take fish feeding on bugs emerging from the surface film. But since many of my sports prefer casting patterns that bring trout to the top, I was compelled to fashion a dry fly that imitated the adult phase of the various genus of caddis periodically hatching throughout our region during the summer months.

By my junior year in high school, I no longer used rooster hackle tied palmer style on the elk hair flies favored during my childhood. I continued to cast these stiff-hackled, high riding patterns on the headwaters of the Cupsuptic and Kennebago Rivers, where the brook trout are opportunistic and less picky, but I found that selective fish required a more precise imitation of the natural insect. Over the last few years, I'd experimented with various patterns, trying to more closely match the hatches of these aquatic insects, whose wings remind me of a pup tent when folded against their bodies.

Gilroy claims that black caddis fluttering over the water remind him of helicopters that the U.N. uses whenever it takes over a country. I've tried to explain to him that to my knowledge this has never happened, but he's convinced that Canada is a U.N. stronghold waiting for the right time to invade from the north. Confident that the Canadians are still pissed over the Revolutionary War, he warns that like Attila and his horde of Huns, masses of French Canadians are preparing to descend upon us from across the border. "And don't think the Brits won't be right by their side," he often adds to emphasize the danger. This, notwithstanding my explanation that it was the French who helped us back in 1776.

Now, I know, because my grand has told me, that at least one member of my family, I don't recall how many grands back, came over the sea with the Highland Regiments to fight against the rabble. But I've always thought it prudent not to provide this information to my best friend, fearing he might out me as a spy for the U.N.-led Franco-British Coalition that he is so convinced is amassing only a few miles away on the other side of the border.

Lighting a cigarette, I opened the bag of CDC feathers I'd taken from the desk drawer. CDC is short for *cul de carnard*, which is French for a duck's bottom.

I first learned about CDC from an article in a fly-fishing magazine that Gilroy showed me while we were hanging out at the sports shop. The article espoused the use of these feathers located near the rump of a wood duck. It explained how they were naturally water resistant while describing an imitation called the F fly created by some Slovenia fly tyer whose name I can't pronounce. I was intrigued. If the fly proved to be successful, we'd have an infinite amount of material at our disposal, since just about everyone in town hunted.

Seated at my fly-tying table, I took a deep drag on the cigarette. Adjusting the headphones connected to my iPod, I began wrapping dun-colored thread around the hook while listening to Clarence "Gatemouth" Brown break into his version of "Midnight Hour."

Over the years, I'd followed the instructions that were as simple as the pattern's name, learning how to tie flies using a few fluffs of the stuff so that they lay longways over the hook, while improvising by adding a smidge of fur dyed the appropriate color to match the body of whatever caddis might be on the water.

I was surprised to learn that anglers had been using the material in Europe since the nineteen-twenties, having quickly discovered the lifelike quality of the CDC feathers that naturally repel water. Flies tied with these unique feathers drift flush with the surface unlike those using lifeless rooster hackle. Once, while fishing above Lower Dam on the Rapid River, I commented to Gilroy that this simple, but effective, imitation was every guide's wet dream. Gilroy, who was always looking for a new and better way to attract big fish, agreed. "Besides," he joked, "ya gotta give props to a fly that uses feathers from a duck's ass."

Over the next few seasons, we found that the dry flies tied with CDC feathers took fish in pools below Aziscohos Dam, pools where the trout and salmon are more educated because of the volume of anglers tramping along the river's banks. The flies also did well on still water, where fish are able to take their time inspecting a fly fisher's offering, such as the pond I intended to hike into on the following morning.

Sonny Boy Williamson's blues harp filled my ears, as I rose from the desk to grab another Long Trail from the fridge. Sitting back down, I dubbed a touch of beaver fur dyed the same color as the thread to create a thorax and then tied in a feather over the shank of the hook.

When I woke the next morning, my skin was damp from the humidity that crept through the open window. The air inside the apartment smelled of a fetid combination of garlic, spicy peanuts, stale beer, and cigarettes. Throwing off the sheet, I stretched my arms toward the ceiling. After a moment, I turned to gaze at the desk, where a caddis fly remained fixed in the Thompson's jaws. A few dozen more loitered around the vise's base. Pulling a cigarette from a pack on the bed stand, I grabbed my lighter and staggered to my feet. Taking a long drag, I decided to sit back down on the side of the bed. Smoke spiraled toward the ceiling. The gray cloud that hung above my head slowly slipped toward the open window. I drew in the tobacco with another deep breath and did not rise again until the cigarette burnt down to the filter.

Before leaving the apartment, I swept the caddis flies into a plastic container and, as an afterthought, threw the half dozen empty Long Trails into the trash.

I stopped at the diner and purchased three sandwiches and a few bottles of birch beer. The clock in Fogerty's office clicked just past six o'clock as I rolled into the station. Another few minutes passed beyond my grasp while I gassed up my truck. After taking time to help Petey Boy oil the chain on Rolling Thunder, I drove out of town and headed west on Route 16 while sipping my morning coffee. It was half past six when I pulled into the turnoff for the Lincoln Pond transfer station.

The middle-aged man leaning against a Toyota Highlander wore a cap that had the words FEAR NO FISH embroidered on the front. The cap had an extra long brim drawn down so that the man's face remained in shadow. An Orvis tag was sewn onto the breast pocket of his tan shirt. Although it was shaping up to be a warm day, the shirt was buttoned at the wrists and collar. His pants, made of the same lightweight material as the shirt, were tucked into socks he wore under a pair of hiking boots.

The man grunted when I gave him a half-hearted apology for being late. While transferring his gear to my truck, I assured him that the fishing would be excellent. It was a statement I made as if a matter of fact rather than opinion, one I gave to each of my clients, rain or shine, warm or cold, whether true or not.

He said nothing during the short drive to the two-track that leads to Little Beaver Pond and remained silent while we loaded our gear into a canoe I'd stashed along the spruce shoreline.

While peeing out the coffee, I stared out over the pond. A fog that had developed overnight was breaking up. A number of spiral-shaped funnels rose above the water. Roughly oval-shaped, the natural impoundment was small enough that I could see across to the far side. A few black boulders protruded through the surface near the middle of the pond. A loon floated not far from the rocks. The comely bird's call echoed against the surrounding hills. Hidden under the shadows cast by the ascending sun, its mate returned the call.

I have never tired of the forest, its sights, sounds, and smells. I don't think I ever will. In town, when around people, I'm on my guard, fearing that someone will see me for who I really am—uncertain about my future, unsure of my place in the world.

I have this recurring dream. The sidewalk is constantly shifting while Thelma Louise begs me to hurry. She screams to me, calling not to look down, but I'm paralyzed. In a panic, I know that a single false move will cast me into the abyss. But here, under the evergreen canopy, I have no such fears. There is no past or future—only the present as I paddle a canoe across the dark surface of a pond or motor across a bright lake in my refurbished Rangeley Boat. Red squirrels, chipmunks, and the occasional kingfisher are the only ones to judge me while I wade up a tiny headwater stream or work my way down a fast-running river.

At ease under the boughs of spruce and pine, I zipped up my jeans. Walking over to my sport, I clapped him on the shoulder.

"Ready to catch some brook trout?" I asked, as he stared out onto the surface of the wilderness pond.

A pair of wood ducks floated noiselessly from the reeds as I used my paddle to push the canoe from shore. The air, damp with humidity, held the scent of balsam. A few patches of blue sky appeared above the fog that had nearly burned off. While my sport settled into the bow, I asked how he had come to book time with me. He explained that a guy I'd previously guided gave him my card.

Although I'd rolled up the sleeves of my shirt, the sport left his buttoned both around his neck and wrists. His face remained sheltered under the long brim of his cap. He accepted one of the caddis flies I'd tied the previous night, and while I paddled around the eastern edge of the pond, he cast the little pattern with the CDC wing toward the shoreline.

During two circuits around the shoreline, Roger Wright explained that he had been a teacher in a Rhode Island grammar school. He was married to a woman, also a teacher in the same school, who he'd met ten years earlier. She had two children from a previous marriage while he had none, having divorced his first wife after only a year. The two of them found this second time around very much to their liking.

Disenchanted with the federal mandate that required educators to be test-givers and paper-pushers (his words not mine), they had retired early, which allowed the couple to pursue their passions—hers playing the harp, his fly fishing.

The caddis imitation had enticed three fish to rise to the surface. The retired teacher missed a fourth when he struck too soon, the rod tip nearly knocking his cap from his head. As he adjusted the brim, I saw that his face was as pale as his hands. He had red blotches on his cheeks that were similar to one I'd noticed above his shirt collar.

Paddling over to the far side of the pond, I slid out of the stern and pulled the canoe onto shore. After breaking down our rods, I secured them in two tubes fastened to the sides of the pack that held our lunch and strapped the pack to my back. Lifting the canoe onto my shoulders, I turned into the wood. A few minutes later we came upon a large deadfall. For the next ten minutes we humped over the pile of limbs, branches, and scrap wood that had been left after a logging operation had worked through that part of the forest sometime during the nineties. Although a short portage, we sweated profusely. My sport swatted at a mixture of black flies and mosquitoes that had descended upon us like a gang of New York City teenagers on a "wilding" spree.

Bloodied by the time we broke out onto the shoreline of Big Beaver Pond, I took a few minutes to dip a neckerchief into the water, wringing it over my head and wiping my face. Some sports enjoy such small adventures, but the welt on the retired schoolteacher's neck appeared inflamed. The skin on the backs of his hands had begun to peel where he'd scratched them. At fifty-seven years of age and with a bit of belly acquired during years of sitting at a desk, he had quickly lost his breath. A stain dampened his shirt between the shoulders by the time I pushed us off onto the bigger pond that received less fishing pressure.

Under the shadow cast by the long brim of his cap, a smile, this time genuine, spread across the angler's lips as one trout after another began taking notice of the little fly with the CDC wing. The biting insects were not so bad now that we were on the water, and although the humidity remained high, it didn't seem to bother the brook trout that remained active for the next hour or so.

As often happens, the fish turned off as quickly as they had turned on, but by then the sport from Rhode Island appeared quite content with the half-dozen more trout he'd released. Paddling along the far shore, I slid the canoe beside a long, flat boulder. I set our lunch out on a tarp while my sport sat, with his legs dangling over the water's surface. His socks remained tucked into his boots. As we ate our sandwiches, I explained how the brook trout of the region descended down through the ages.

"Kinda cool playing tag with fish whose ancestors lived here before ours, don't ya think?" I remarked, handing him a bottle of birch beer.

I also told him that unlike brook trout, landlocked salmon were introduced to the region in the late eighteen hundreds, as were smelt. Both fish were able to reproduce naturally, quickly going native. Today, the descendants of those stocked fish are just as wild as the trout with which they share the water.

After lunch, we began to talk about the books we'd read. I explained about my great-uncle's extensive collection that covered a variety of topics and how as a kid, I'd read almost every one. Roger told me that, as a child, he had been bullied because of the eczema that had developed while he was still very young. He said that books had been his refuge and also the reason why he became a teacher. I told him about my aborted attempt to go to college and how Thelma Louise was always nagging me to return. He said it was never too late.

Sometime during our conversation, the retired schoolteacher felt comfortable enough to remove his socks and boots. Pulling up his pants, he lowered his pale feet into the water. I found the trunk of an enormous birch tree to lean against. With my face lifted to the sun, I closed my eyes and tried to remain in the present, but Thelma Louise wouldn't allow it. I knew she wanted to leave town. Her biggest fear was winding up like her mother, while mine was that I'd become my father.

I must have dozed off, because I was awakened by a whoop that came from around a bend in the cove. Grabbing the net from the canoe, I trotted along the shoreline to where my sport stood knee deep in the water. The schoolteacher had a nice bend in his fly rod.

"Good fish," he grunted.

"Keep pressure on him," I instructed. "Give him line when he wants it. We're in no hurry."

A few minutes later, I used the sport's phone to take his photograph releasing a brook trout measuring just shy of sixteen inches. Just as I snapped the photo, Roger Wright raised the long brim of his cap to reveal another wide grin.

Afterward, the sport worked over the pond while I paddled the canoe along the shoreline. Over the winter, I'd been working on a streamer pattern of my own design, playing around with different materials and various colors. I decided upon a body comprised of green silk ribbed with silver tinsel, adding a few pink-and-olive marabou feathers for a wing. After replacing the caddis pattern with the streamer, I instructed Roger to cast toward the shoreline, where shadows had grown now that the sun had slipped toward the west. With the heat of the day behind us, I hoped that a large trout might take an interest in an injured baitfish or perhaps a crayfish crawling along the pond's edge.

After an unproductive hour, I snipped off the streamer and knotted on my go-to pattern, a Hare's Ear wet fly. On the second cast, a big fish splashed, my sport pulling back an instant too soon. The flash of crimson and gold would be a memory he wouldn't soon forget. While still shaking his head over the loss of the fish, Roger Wright pointed into a dark cove. A trio of black bears, each no larger than a mature Labrador Retriever, were rolling around in the summer grass that had grown high in a small clearing beside the edge of the water.

"Can we get closer?" Roger whispered as he pulled his phone from a pocket in his fly vest. The three cubs continued their playful antics as I dipped my paddle into the water. One of them stopped as we drew closer, the others following their sibling's gaze in our direction. Knowing the mother must be nearby, I held the canoe about ten yards out from the shore.

I spotted her a moment later. She was a good-sized sow. I estimated her weight to be just under two hundred pounds. She remained on all fours, staring out with suspicious eyes from behind a stand of spruce. I noticed a bit of gray above her brown muzzle and a hitch in her stride when the old girl lumbered out into the clearing. The big bruin kept her eyes fixed on us. Playing it safe, I slowly backstroked the canoe farther out into the pond. Satisfied that we were no threat, mama grunted her displeasure before turning back into the forest. Two of her brood followed while the third rose up on its back legs. After sniffing the air, the third cub followed his family into the forest.

Not long after our encounter with the bears, we tramped back over the deadfall. Paddling across the smaller pond, I slipped out of the stern and stood ankle deep in the shallows while pulling the canoe onto shore. As I climbed onto the bank, my sport appeared more at ease than I'd seen him at any time during the day. Bending forward, he dipped his cap into the pond and slipped it back on his head. Water dripped down his neck and wet his shirt.

When the retired school teacher from Rhode Island turned in my direction, he said, "It's really never too late."

· *Chapter Twelve* ·

"HAND ME THAT BOX OF NAILS." GILROY'S DAD CLIMBED DOWN the ladder he'd brought with him and was pointing to a big blue box beside his older son's feet.

Frank Gilroy had his own business, working as a plumber. He drove a truck with his name scrolled across the side. When he wasn't fixing toilets and sinks, he set up and broke down summer camps for vacationers. Although I suppose he worked hard, Gilroy's father always made time for his sons. He'd throw the ball around and take them fishing. It seemed as if he had Gilroy shooting a rifle no sooner than Donnie could walk.

He had this sixteen-foot Grady White with a big ass Johnson outboard on the back that he'd cruise up and down Rangeley Lake. The previous spring, he took four of us kids out on it. We motored up and down Mooselookmeguntic Lake while a storm developed, first rain and then snow spitting down. The big lake's waves crashed against the boat's bow while we huddled under the Grady's fiberglass top. Mr. Gilroy just laughed, exclaiming that it was salmon weather. Sure enough, we took four fish that afternoon.

Gilroy's dad also had a couple of old snow machines that he kept tuned up and ready to go as soon as the first flakes hit the ground. Old man Fogerty once described him as a real man's man. That's why it was no surprise when I saw Frank Gilroy up on that roof helping Tom Rider fix up the sporting camp Rider had purchased the previous spring.

Beaver Den Camps was built in the early nineteen hundreds when the Magalloway River was dammed and Aziscohos Lake formed. The camps hadn't changed much through the years. They were the same when Tom bought them as when they were first built—a main building flanked on either side by a number of one-room cabins. Located under the shadow of Bosebuck Mountain, the traditional Maine sporting lodge was situated along the northwestern shoreline of the lake just below the confluence of the Little and Big Magalloway Rivers.

The air was crisp on that October morning, a bit of frost on the ground. The fishing season had ended the previous week, and as they do each year, the trees had turned color weeks before the rest of New England. The hills surrounding the camp were ablaze with scarlet, bronze, and gold that reminded me of a bowl of Trix, a cereal I favored back then. The sound of an occasional shotgun reminded the men that grouse season had opened.

It seemed to me that half the town had shown up to help refurbish the old sporting camp that had fallen into disrepair. Although my father was away at a banking conference in Bangor and my grandmother had come down with a cold, the remainder of my extended family had jammed into my grand's open-roof Jeep to make the long ride to the camps. With my mother and her father seated up front, I squeezed between Angus and Matilda, who had draped a woolen blanket across our laps. The three of us hung on for dear life during the forty-five minute bumpy journey up the logging road along the western side of the thirteen-mile lake.

Before Tom purchased the camps, a number of absentee owners had tried to make a go of them. The guide used his life savings for the down payment, hoping he could carry the hefty mortgage that encumbered the land. He planned to build back the reputation that had been lost as the result of leaking roofs, mice-riddled cabins, incompetent guides, and poor food. That first season, Tom had hired a new chef and a few local men he trusted to be his guides. With the help of his friends, he hoped to refurbish the cabins and main lodge in time for his second season.

Four months had gone by since Gilroy lost that big fish. Still too young to be of much use, he and I spent the weekend getting in and out of trouble. By Sunday afternoon we became bored, and our mothers exiled us to a bench between the main lodge and one of the camp's twelve cabins. We were playing checkers while Donnie's father and big brother worked on the roof.

Gilroy's older brother had spent that weekend helping his father and two or three of the other men from town as they worked to replace leaky shingles on each of the little cabins. From where Gilroy and I were seated, we saw Thelma Louise's two half-brothers unload lumber from a pickup and carry it down to the lake where other men were repairing the dock. A number of old Rangeley Boats were hauled up onto the shore. Two guys were hunched over an Evinrude engine attached to the back of one of the boats. Between them, a tool chest lay open with wrenches, pliers, and screwdrivers strewn along the sandy shore.

I recognized Rusty Miller, who with his wife, Jeanne, owned the sporting goods store in the neighboring town of Easie. The couple guided sports and were well known throughout the region. The orange mustache that hid Rusty's upper lip was as bright as the changing leaves. The other guy had a dark complexion, darker than most of the men from town. Flecks of gray dotted his bushy black beard and unlike Rusty's unruly red mop, his hair was sparse.

"Who's the guy working with Mr. Miller?" I asked Gilroy, who was loopy about fishing even back then and knew most of the guides in town.

"Bought a camp on Otter Pond. Old man Fogerty says he's I-talian."

I was thinking about how much fun it would be to mess about with one of the Rangeley Boats when Gilroy shouted, "King me!"

My grand trudged past while I was mulling over my next move. Opening a metal box attached to the outside wall of the main lodge, he pulled down on a lever. "Try it now!" he called into the open door of the kitchen.

A moment later a hand appeared, its thumb held upright. My grand grunted and then turned around as Fogerty approached him. After a brief discussion, the two men tramped toward a grove of spruce trees.

Earlier that morning, Petey's father came in by boat carrying supplies Tom Rider had ordered from the Rangeley Building and Supply.
He now was helping my great-uncle paint the little boat house at the
foot of the dock.

Most of the women, my mother among them, cooked meals and
handed out coffee and beer. Dressed in jeans and work boots, a few, like
Jeanne Miller and Patti Shannon, worked side by side with the men.

With a pair of pink Keds on her sockless feet, Thelma Louise skipped
out of the kitchen door. I remember her wearing pink shorts and a pink
blouse with glitter along the edges. Patti Shannon followed her daughter,
doling out jelly donuts to the three of us.

"Whatcha doin'?" Thelma Louise asked. Red jelly gushed out of the
corners of her mouth after she took a big bite of her donut.

"Nothin'," Gilroy answered for the two of us.

"Did ya see the sign Harry's mother painted?" Thelma Louise pointed toward the kitchen door.

My mother had been doing well that summer. She remained up and
around most days and appeared to take an interest in things while taking
the pills Doc Woodward prescribed.

Thelma grabbed my hand and pulled me into the lodge. Her fingers
were sticky. Gilroy followed, the three of us running past huge pots, pans,
and cooking utensils hanging from hooks screwed into the ceiling. We
bolted through a swinging door on the other side of the kitchen and into
the dining room where a number of adults were crowded around the
middle of the room.

We had heard that Koos Kynfd, the man who used a chainsaw to
carve a twelve-foot wooden bear outside of the town of Easie, had spent
the previous afternoon working inside the camp's workshop, a small
building set back from the lake and located a few steps away from the
shack that housed a generator. A few minutes earlier, Tom Rider had
dragged two tables across the floor of the lodge's dining room and with
the help of another man, lowered Koos' latest project on top of the tables.

Hidden under a gray blanket were five pine boards the old Swede had cut from a conifer. After shaving and planing them, he'd doweled the boards together and created a smooth surface with a flat bottom and beveled top that was roughly rectangular in shape and measured approximately six feet by four feet.

One of the people gathered around the tables told me that Tom had asked my mother to come up with a logo for the camps. Although at first protesting, she worked through the night to complete the sign.

With a flourish, Tom removed the blanket revealing a painting of a fat beaver grasping an aspen branch between its teeth. A second beaver swam beside the first, while in the background three kits peeked out of the branches that formed the family's den. Below the beavers, my mother had printed the name of Tom's sporting lodge in big block letters.

The crowd of local people applauded when Tom, with the help of another man, raised the sign upright. Afterward, we followed the adults outside. Gilroy headed for the stand of spruce that my grand and Fogerty had entered while Thelma and I watched three men haul the large sign onto two enormous metal hooks that had been screwed into the outside of the building.

A few minutes later Donnie called out from the tree line, "Want to see something cool?"

Before either of us could answer, he pointed toward a dirt drive that stretched from the logging road above the camps to the cabins alongside the lake. With Gilroy in the lead, we crossed the wide lawn above the main lodge and followed the dirt drive toward a cabin built on a high knoll that set it apart from those down by the lake. Gilroy said that Tom Rider had lived there during the previous winter. Word was that having spent every last dollar on the camps, he could not afford to rent an in-town apartment during the off-season.

Scurrying past the lodge-owner's cabin, Gilroy stopped to allow Thelma and I to take in the wonderland of mystery that he had discovered. We scanned an open yard above the cabin that was roughly oval in shape and flanked by various out buildings masked from the lodge by the stand of spruce trees.

Thelma Louise and I scrambled up the steps of the nearest building. We stood back as Gilroy pushed on a door that creaked open. Bunk beds lined two walls. A shaft of light slipped through a torn curtain on the single window. A few old newspapers and an out-of-date Maine Sportsman magazine littered the floor around a potbelly stove. Gilroy knelt beside the metal frame of a bed while explaining that this was most likely the guides' cabin. Sliding his arm under the dirty mattress, he whispered, "Look what I found."

Plastered across his face was that shit-eating grin he sometimes gets when he's about to do something stupid.

After unscrewing the cap, Donnie handed me a nearly empty pint of Jim Beam. When I hesitated, Thelma Louise grabbed the bottle from my hand.

"Yuck!" After taking a sip, she nearly dropped the bottle onto the floor.

With her face scrunched up in a sour expression, she offered the pint to Gilroy, who followed her example. With watery eyes, he flashed a contorted smile in my direction. I did what they expected of me, the few remaining drops of liquor burning their way down my throat.

Not far from the cabin stood another building, where old man Fogerty was using a large wrench to bully a recalcitrant nut fastened to a water pump. He was in the middle of some choice curses when we walked inside. "What're youse kids doin' back here?" he growled.

Ignoring the mechanic, Gilroy brandished a long portion of pipe as if it were a light saber while I picked up another. Thelma walked over to a series of shelves filled with tools and equipment needed to maintain the lodge. She pulled down a box of plastic plumbing fittings and slid one after another onto her wrists, examining each for possible worth as jewelry.

After Fogerty shooed us away, we found my grand tinkering with the camp's ancient generator that was housed in a nearby shack. Finding little of interest in the big noisy machine, we turned our attention to a large lean-to structure that was partitioned into three sections. In the first, we climbed up and slid back down an enormous pile of dirt that Tom Rider used to grade parts of the logging road leading to the lodge. After doing this several times, we moved past the second compartment that contained a mountain of split stove-wood and devoted our attention to the adjacent section, where we stared up at a truck with an enormous snow blade. Parked on one side of the huge truck was a Dodge pickup that had lost its doors. On the other side, an excavator and skidder stood in mid-motion.

The three of us were scrambling over the vehicles like ants on a pile of crumbs when we heard men shouting followed by a woman's long shrill wail. I thought I recognized the woman's voice, but was too scared to say anything. We watched Fogerty hobble toward the grove of spruce. A moment later my grand followed. The three of us overtook the two men before they reached the lodge. I suppose we'll never forget what we saw there.

· *Chapter Thirteen* ·

"THERE'S ANOTHER ONE." GILROY POINTED THROUGH THE HAZE of smoke that unfurled from a joint he clasped between his lips.

"Geronimo!" Petey Boy yelled from where he sat beside Thelma Louise. Thelma lay with her head on my stomach, knees bent upward. She smiled into the darkness. I was finding it hard to keep my eyes open, feeling a bit too high from the wine we drank with dinner and the grass Gilroy was passing around. Thelma and I were warm under the wool blanket we'd tucked around us. I stroked her hair that she'd dyed red with pale green streaks running down one side.

Thelma Louise whispered that she felt herself floating toward the stars that drew closer as her body rose higher and higher. After describing her ascent into the nighttime sky, she rose to her feet with her hands raised outward and began to turn round and round. When Gilroy asked what she was doing, Thelma replied, "Don't you see it?"

"It?" Gilroy passed the joint to me.

Thelma Louise pointed toward a star in the southern quadrant of the sky that was shining bright blue. "Doctor Who's Police Box," she proclaimed.

A few minutes into a discussion about the iconic Time Lord, Thelma confessed her fear that the only way she was getting out of Rangeley was to accompany the Doctor on his adventures. I raised my hand to pass the joint back to Gilroy while Thelma Louise told us how she'd gladly spend her life exploring the stars.

"I'd glide from one galaxy to the next. Cruise past the Big Dipper. Slide down Orion's belt. Explore the universe as the Doctor's companion."

Taking the joint from Gilroy, she giggled, "No, that isn't quite right. I mean the Doctor Who part would be fun, but only if I could bring you guys with me."

"Me too?" Petey looked over from where he sat.

"Especially you," Thelma assured him.

"Don't know about that newest Doc. He might not like the idea of you inviting your friends along for the ride," Gilroy played along.

"I don't know. You ever watch the older episodes? Back then there was more than one companion."

We stayed on this jag until Thelma Louise reached out a hand. She extended her fingers toward the night sky, but the blue star remained fixed above us. When she suddenly began to sob, the three of us came to her side. As we tried to console her, Thelma Louise explained that we were about the only people she could trust either in this world, or any other that the Doctor might explore. Oh, she loved her mother, and her two half-brothers tried hard, but through her tears Thelma Louise said it was only Gilroy and I that she could depend upon in a pinch. Throwing her arms around Petey's massive frame, she sighed, "And for you sweet boy, I'd do anything." Thelma concluded her little pity party by declaring, "The Doctor will just have to understand."

A few moments later Thelma Louise willed herself back to earth. Wiping away the tears, she raised her hands to my face and drawing me close, kissed me on the lips.

"Thelma kissed Harry," Petey giggled.

"What was that for?" I whispered.

But she had once more ascended toward the stars.

Turning my attention back to the sky, I pointed at a fading streak of light that passed through Cassiopeia, the constellation that looks like a drunken W in the northern sky.

Thelma oohed while Petey aahed.

"Geronimo," said Gilroy.

Earlier that evening, the four of us had driven east on Route 16 in

Thelma Louise's Jeep. Heading toward the ski town of Stratton, we turned right onto Oddy's Road and motored up Quill Hill, where each year, we spent a night watching the Perseid Meteor Shower.

That afternoon I'd guided an older guy from Virginia up a little-fished brook that was a headwater of a larger river and where brook trout can be found throughout the summer months. My sport was happy with the outing and he offered to buy me a beer at the Wooden Nickel. One beer led to two and then three. A very pissed-off Thelma Louise answered when I knocked on her apartment door more than an hour behind schedule. Although I explained that the mid-August shower of shooting stars never gets under way until after midnight, her shoulder did not begin to thaw until we turned off Route 16's macadam and began driving up the dirt road to the top of the hill that is well known by us locals for its three-hundred-and-sixty-degree views.

We parked beside some flat boulders. In the waning light, we could make out the wind farm across the border in Canada. The long blades on the tall white towers had slowed as the afternoon breeze died down. Looking east we saw the ski trails running down the sides of Saddleback Mountain. To the south, New Hampshire's Presidential Range was visible, the top of Mount Washington lost in a passing cloud. While Thelma pointed out Rangeley and Flagstaff Lakes to Petey, Gilroy and I began unloading our stuff from her vehicle. After removing two large rucksacks containing extra clothes, sleeping bags, and blankets, I untied the heavy tarp we had rolled up and secured to the roof of the Wrangler. Although the temperature had bumped against eighty degrees earlier in the afternoon, we knew it could fall into the low forties by early morning. Gilroy had unstrapped an aluminum lounge chair he had tied to the back of the Jeep's spare tire while I pulled a banged-up metal cooler out of the roof-carrier.

Petey Boy's father had packed his son's canvas backpack, the one with the Boy Scout insignia stenciled on the flap. It contained the essentials for a night in the Maine woods—a pocket knife that Petey's mother permitted him to carry only if he promised not to open it unless either Thelma Louise, Donnie, or I said it was okay; two cans of vanilla coke; the picture book of King Arthur and his Court that I had lent to him; his yellow-and-black Bruins' ski cap; and most importantly, a big bag of marshmallows.

I hung the backpack on a branch of a nearby tree while Donnie unrolled the plastic tarp and laid it in front of the flat boulders. We spread the sleeping bags over the tarp and added the wool blankets to insure our comfort as the temperature dropped.

"Be careful," I yelled to Petey, who had followed Gilroy to one edge of the hill.

Thelma Louise unpacked the cooler that contained two large steaks her mother had brought back from the IGA, six cobs of corn, and two bottles of cheap red wine that were jammed into ice beside a six-pack of beer.

Gilroy and I knelt on either side of Petey while showing him how to build a campfire. After he gathered a number of stones, we laid them out in a semi-circle around one of the flat boulders. I placed a number of sticks over a few strips of birch bark and added a couple of larger branches. When the second match failed to ignite the wood, Donnie walked toward the Jeep.

Returning a few moments later, he said to Petey,

"Watch closely." After squirting a thin stream of lighter fluid onto the wood, Gilroy handed Petey a lit match.

"Old Ingun trick," he grunted when the flames rose upward.

Thelma Louise sprinkled seasoning on the steaks. Once the fire burned down, she placed them on a metal grill that Gilroy had brought with him. Next, she wrapped the corncobs in tin foil and dug them into the glowing embers.

After dinner, we swapped stories we'd all heard before, but liked to tell when we were together. Thelma pulled out the one about the afternoon when her half-brothers decided it was time she learned how to swim, Petey Boy crying out, "Geronimo!" when she described how they tossed her ass first into Dodge Pond.

"They stood on old man Crocker's dock while I went under. I can still hear them laughing."

Thelma Louise swung her arms from side to side as she described breaking back through the surface, anger like a life vest holding her up as she managed to doggy paddle back to shore.

Then there was the old chestnut Gilroy remembered about Daniel Fogerty. The four of us laughed as he recounted how, for a year after nine-eleven, the old man wore sneakers wherever he went, telling anyone who would listen that he might have to run for his life should the terrorists decide to strike Rangeley, insisting that among other targets, the Aziscohos Dam was ripe for attack.

"Those white Chuck Taylors he wore on Sundays." Tears ran down Thelma's cheek.

"And the tired old black ones when he worked at the gas station." Gilroy rolled onto his stomach.

When it was my turn, I described a morning a few years back. It was in late May and I was alone in my Rangeley Boat. Seated in the stern, with one hand on the outboard and the other on my trolling rod, I discovered that my thirty-foot-long leader was hopelessly tangled in the reel. Petey grimaced as I related how a large salmon struck soon after I cut the tag end of the monofilament from the rat's nest of a fly line. While the fish tail danced no more than ten feet from the boat, I was forced to grab the loose end of the leader playing the fish by hand as if from a drop line.

"What happened next?" Although it wasn't the first time I'd told this story, Petey's eyes grew wide across the flames that danced between us.

"The monofilament cut me pretty bad, but I brought that salmon to the boat. It was the best fish of the season."

"I can beat that." Donnie rose to his feet. He leaned over the fire and passed the bottle of cheap Red to me.

"Remember the evening we were out on Upper Richardson? It was the first summer after you and Angus restored that Rangeley Boat of yours. I had to pee and you passed me that tin can."

"Donnie had to pee!" Petey fell back onto the tarp we were sitting on.

Gilroy grabbed a long stick from the pile of firewood he had gathered and held it to his crotch.

"So, there I am with my wiener out, watching this empty can of corn fill up." Shaking the stick up and down, he looked over at Petey. "You know what it's like. I mean, I hadn't pissed all afternoon and no pint-can was gonna hold what was pouring out."

"Gilroy wet his pants!" Petey screamed.

Donnie continued, "Well, all of a sudden my rod bends over the side of the boat." Leaning forward, he said to Petey, "My trolling rod not my ding dong."

I looked over at Thelma Louise, who rolled her eyes.

"Well, when I go to grab the rod, the can spills all over the bottom of Harry's new boat. My pecker is swinging in the breeze and piss is still streaming out, but I got that fish. A nice brookie too!"

"Was Harry mad?" Petey looked over at me, wiping his face with the sleeve of his flannel shirt.

"You bet I was. Washed that damn boat out for three days before putting it back in the water. Wouldn't let Donnie aboard for a month." I passed the wine to Thelma Louise.

As the fog from the wine and weed slowly receded, Gilroy added some larger branches to build up the fire. For a while we stared silently into the flames. A fat marshmallow hung precariously from the sharpened point of a stick that Petey held out.

An infinitude of suns blinked down on us. I pointed toward a nebulous band that stretched across the sky.

"That's the Milky Way," I said to Petey.

"Like the candy bar?" he asked.

"It's our galaxy," Thelma Louise corrected him.

Petey looked confused.

"The universe is comprised of all the stars in the sky," I explained. "The stars are so far apart that you need a space ship to get from one to another."

"Or the Tardis."

I frowned at Thelma.

"Like in Star Wars," Donnie added.

"The stars that are closest together we call galaxies," I continued.

"Like a town of stars?" Petey Boy smiled.

"Exactly. And our town is the Milky Way. It's our little patch of the universe."

Although it was the second week in August, a chill had crept across the ground. Gilroy unfolded the metal frame of his lounge chair and lay horizontal to the star-studded dome.

Our conversation slipped from the latest movies to music and from there to the top five best video games, eventually turning to the weather. The four of us watched the dying fire briefly rise when I placed the empty bag of marshmallows onto the embers.

"There's one," Gilroy called.

We followed his gaze.

"There's another," Thelma Louise pointed toward the handle of the Big Dipper.

"It won't be long now," I reassured Petey.

"C'mon Bubba," Gilroy called to Petey Boy as he trudged into the darkness that surrounded our fragile circle of light.

A few moments later Petey called back, "Donnie's peeing!"

· *Chapter Fourteen* ·

I SUPPOSE IT'S TIME I TELL YOU MORE ABOUT MY FAMILY. MY GRAND and his brother were inseparable. As teenagers Harold and Angus Ferguson accompanied their parents when they departed Scotland.

After the ocean voyage, they resided with their family in Boston until Harold, at age nineteen, enlisted in the army. That was shortly before the outbreak of World War II, at a time when Germany was pounding London. Only sixteen, Angus lied about his age and followed his older brother across France and then Germany.

Harold met Emily Ryan while on leave. He'd walked into a USO dancehall with a few friends, and while the others found girls willing to dance with them, he accepted a cup of tea from a pretty girl with hazel eyes and an Irish brogue. After speaking for a while, she gave him her address. As Harold fought his way through Europe, they wrote to each other. Six months after his return to Boston, they married. Crazy, huh? Well, I guess that's how it was back then. Anyway, Angus married Matilda a few years later. By that time, Emily had given birth to my mother, who they named Clementine.

When Harold announced that he'd secured work as a logger and would be moving to Maine, Angus decided he and his wife should accompany them. The brothers eventually settled in Rangeley. Harold and Emily raised their daughter a few doors down from Angus and Matilda, who, although devoted to one another, never had children.

By the time the Ferguson brothers arrived in Rangeley, Roger Duncan had inherited the pharmacy that had been owned by his father and located beside Rangeley's hardware store, a short walk from the

Duncan family home, with its wraparound porch on the corner of Main and High Streets.

Roger's father was a descendent of Breannan and Abigail Duncan, who had emigrated from Scotland to North Carolina before the War Between the States. The Duncans traveled north a few years after Robert E. Lee stepped out of the Virginia courthouse to formally conclude the bloodletting. The family settled on a small farm on the outskirts of the town named after its founder, Squire James Rangeley, Jr.

The latest generation of the Duncan family to prosper under the shadow of Maine's pine forest, Roger and his wife, Effie, had two children, a girl, Doris, and a boy, Edward. Effie sang in the choir of the Presbyterian Church while her husband sat in the front pew, his back to the rest of the parishioners. After their arrival in Rangeley, the Fergusons attended services at the same church, although they rarely had occasion to speak with the more affluent Duncans. Roger spent his days working at the pharmacy, while each Thursday evening he and his wife engaged in games of cribbage and bridge with other members of the small-town elite. The Ferguson men spent six days a week felling timber with one of the logging crews that worked in the region, venturing back into the forest after Sunday service to hunt or fish.

Roger Duncan had received his pharmacist degree from Boston University. The Duncan's daughter moved to Portland after marrying a young man she met while at the same college her father had attended. Roger had expected his son to also attend Boston University. He hoped that when Edward returned, he would take his turn at the pharmacy. But never one to trust others, especially those living outside of his town, Edward chose to remain home. Instead of taking the trail blazed by two generations of Duncans, he obtained an entry-level position at the newly established Rangeley branch of The Camden National Bank.

It was a surprise when Edward and Clementine married. The groom's parents were not pleased with the union. A year after the wedding, Roger Duncan collapsed behind the pharmacy's counter. He died of a heart attack before his sixtieth birthday. According to my mother, that's when my parents learned that her father-in-law had revised his will to disinherit his son.

Named after my grandfather on my mother's side, I was born the year after Roger Duncan died. I suppose you could say Effie Duncan mellowed with my birth, because shortly afterward, she lent my parents enough money for a down payment on a small house. Set beside the pond that lapped against the south side of our town and located around the corner from the homes of my grand and his brother, it was where I was raised. A few years later, Effie moved to Portland to live closer to her daughter. Before doing so, she sold the pharmacy to a chain that eventually went bust. Since then, the people of our small town have had to drive an hour to fill a prescription.

Edward Duncan was a man of few words, more so after my mother left us. It's from my mother and her family that I've pieced together what I know about him. My father worked hard, I'll give him that. My mother told me that he was promoted to assistant manager after only a few years and not long afterward to manager of the bank's local branch. My grand once said my father worked so hard to prove he could succeed despite disappointing his father. After being promoted to the position of senior loan officer, my dad transferred to the bank's Lewiston office, making the hour-and-forty-five-minute commute back and forth each day.

Some of my favorite memories are those evenings when my mother tucked me into bed. Pretending not to be tired, I'd hope to prolong the private time we shared. At night, my mother often read to me from books, like the one about King Arthur. Most of all, I enjoyed stories about her father and his brother. Seated on the edge of my bed, my mother often would say how the two of them were mad about fishing.

"What about dad?" I'd sometimes ask.

"Your dad works hard to support us," she'd say and then tell me another story about the Scottish Highlands.

She repeated the tales told to her by her father, describing how his mother's parents and theirs before them, worked for a wealthy landholder. How the family lived on the Lord's Derbyshire estate while the land's owner spent most of his time in England. My mother explained that Harold's grandfather and his father before him, maintained a river that ran through the Lord's vast holdings. She described the river as a rough-and-tumble stream.

"Like the Magalloway?" I would always ask.

"Like the Magalloway," she would always reply.

My mother once described the grief her great grandparents experienced upon the loss of their oldest son, my grand's uncle. It was during the First World War at the Battle of the Somme, when the Scots Guard was called in during the British offensive of September 1916. She explained how the family carried on, and how, not long after the war's end, Harold's two aunts and his mother married men returning from the conflict that had defined their lives.

Molly, his youngest aunt, died in childbirth. Shortly afterward, Harold's grandfather passed away. The following year his grandmother decided to move to Ireland to live with her brother and sister-in-law. Harold and Angus's parents remained in Scotland until they booked passage on a freighter bound for Massachusetts the year before England entered a war that for a second time would engulf the world in flames.

My favorite stories were those about fishing in Scotland. My mother recounted how as small boys, her father and uncle accompanied their grand on his trips "astream," watching and listening while playing beside the river where trout could be found behind each boulder and in every wild riffle and run.

"Your grand says the brown trout of those highland streams had spots the color of pumpkins," my mother would tell me.

My father, on the other hand, never seemed to have time for sport. I remember pestering him to take me fishing. It was the summer before Gilroy lost the trout of his dreams. My mom had gone through a bad patch, but had been doing better. I recall the three of us seated at the kitchen table. While my mother served us pot roast, I begged my father to take me out on the water.

"But dad," I moaned when he explained that the stack of paperwork in his briefcase would not get done by itself.

"Pass the potatoes, please." Trying to change the subject, he turned toward my mother for support.

"Your father is very busy this time of year." Sliding the big bowl of mashed spuds in my father's direction, she looked over at me and said, "Finish your beans and I'll call your grand and see if he'll take you out with him."

Not long after dinner Harold opened the screen door, followed by Angus, who limped in after him. The two men wore tattered vests, with pockets running down the front. Harold wore khaki pants and a tan shirt. Like bugs caught on a strip of sticky tape, trout flies were hooked into a felt band around his wide-brimmed hat. Angus's green work pants were the same color as his cap and a shirt that he wore with the sleeves rolled up to his elbows. My great-uncle gripped a corncob pipe between his teeth. Harold puffed on a cigarette.

Piling into the back seat of my grand's open-roof Jeep, I asked my great-uncle where they'd be taking me.

Turning around in the passenger seat, Angus allowed a sly smile to slip over his lips. "Tis a secret."

"Aye, laddie. A secret i' tis." Harold looked back at me from the rear-view mirror. "N' ye cannae tell anyone. Not even yer maw."

As my grand backed out of our driveway, Angus pulled a pouch from his hip pocket. The tobacco inside filled the open vehicle with its fragrance as he tapped the strands into the bowl of his pipe.

Ten minutes later, we were bouncing along a logging road as dust billowed up behind the Jeep. The scent of freshly cut softwood rose through the open top each time we passed a stack of felled trees. I was nearly propelled through the windshield when my grand careened around a bend and applied the brakes, bringing the vehicle to a sudden stop a few feet in front of a massive moose. I'd seen a few cows while driving with my parents along Route 16, but never a male. To me, the bull appeared as tall as an elephant, his rack nearly as wide as the road. The animal didn't budge until my grand leaned hard on the horn.

After a number of turns, the logging road narrowed into a two-track cluttered with boulders and pocked with holes. My body threatened to bounce out of the Jeep's open roof whenever Harold rolled over a particularly large crater. We pulled to a stop twenty minutes later. High grass and ferns made it difficult to see an opening in the forest, but after collecting their gear, the two men ambled toward a narrow trail.

We walked single file down the muddy footpath flanked by spruce and balsam. A few moments later we looked across the hills that rose along the far shoreline of a little pond. The sun cast a golden glow upon the water's surface that was lapping up against low-growing blueberry bushes. Angus pulled a long canoe from among the conifers. While the two men set their rods in the wooden craft, I remember seeing a plethora of tiny rings that radiated outward upon the water's dark surface. Harold removed two paddles from the canvas pack slung over his shoulder while he explained that each set of rings was a trout feeding on tiny insects rising from the bottom of the pond.

After helping me into the center of the canoe, they took their positions—one in the bow and the other in the stern. Angus used his paddle to push the sixteen-foot Old Town into the pond.

Only inches from my face, a dragonfly interrupted its flight. I could hear the sound of the flying carnivore's wings as its big eyes stared directly into mine.

"Gonnae swallow a wad o' bugs, keepin' yer gob open lik' that," my grand joked.

As the evening progressed, the two men answered my many questions. They patiently explained the difference between mayflies, caddis, and stoneflies and how and when these insects came to be on the water. My grand was the more talkative of the two men. My great-uncle chose to point things out without comment such as a large hump of branches and mud that formed the top of a beaver's lodge, or the two cedar waxwings that flitted over the surface taking mayflies on the wing. I remember the graceful arc of their silk lines floating through air heavy with humidity and the tiny flies at the end of their tippets barely touching the surface before a trout would rise to snap at them.

I had caught sunfish and perch in the pond behind our house, but at that age had seen relatively few brook trout. Unable to look past the pond's surface, I was surprised when the first trout rose to grab my great-uncle's fly. When I asked why he slipped his hands into the water before holding the fish, his brother explained that it was to avoid damaging the slime that covered the sides of each trout, without which the fish would succumb to disease.

I promised myself never to forget a single detail of those wild brook trout that appeared to rise at each cast of the old men's flies. I was fascinated by the cloak of yellow trails that twisted wormlike over the dark green shoulders of each fish and marveled at the crimson spots, each one enclosed in a light blue halo that were interspersed among yellow dots splashed across their flanks. Then there were the bellies of the few trout bigger than nine inches that appeared dipped in butter and the thin white line etched below a dash of black along their blood-red fins that reminded me of the eyeliner the waitresses at the diner liked to use.

Harold killed a palm-sized trout with a quick twist of the head while saying I should never kill more fish than I could eat. Watching him hand the fish to Angus, I noticed how quickly the trout's color faded. The brilliant reds, blues, and yellows grew pale by the time my great-uncle lowered the fish into a wicker creel layered with ferns he'd previously gathered from the edge of the pond.

As Harold released a trout no longer than his pinkie, he pointed to the dark bars running vertically down its sides. He called them "parr" markings and explained that they signified a juvenile fish. When I told the two men that I expected the brook trout to be larger, my mother's uncle chuckled. His brother explained that the ancestors of the little fish in that pond had inhabited waters throughout western Maine. He said they'd been living and dying there since the beginning of time. Harold told me that unlike most strains of fish throughout the eastern part of the country, the trout of western Maine remain native to the region.

My grand said that some brook trout grew as long as a man's arm, but that it was not the size of the fish that mattered. Years later I'd chuckle, remembering Harold's comment and wondering what Gilroy might say about it.

After running out of questions, I recall spending the remainder of that evening seated cross-legged between the two men. As a crescent moon descended through a star-lit sky, we said little. At times the only sound was that of the paddles gently dipping into the pond and later, that of the men's casts slipping through the still of the summer evening.

Sometime during that night, I reflected on my father. I was unable to understand how he could prefer spending his time behind a desk, rather than floating in a canoe on a pond surrounded by spruce and pine. I could not comprehend how he could count numbers rather than the stars in the nighttime sky, or stare at files instead of casting bits of feather to trout that Harold described, in words he attributed to Henry David Thoreau, as "bright fluviatile flowers."

After that first evening, when not in school and at times when I should have been, the two men would take me with them on their excursions to the streams, rivers, lakes, and ponds surrounding my home.

During the years that followed, Harold taught me how to cast against the wind while Angus demonstrated how to tie each of the flies depicted in the leather-bound notebook that he'd inherited from his own grand. I learned when the different aquatic insects hatched and where to fish the spring and fall runs of brook trout and landlocked salmon. The two men pointed out pools and runs that fished well during the summer months, and they shared with me places few anglers had ever seen. Most of all, they instilled in me a reverence for the lakes and ponds, rivers and streams, and the wild fish that lived under the shadows cast by the surrounding forest of spruce and pine.

Preoccupied with my initiation into the Brotherhood of the Angle, I failed to notice my parents growing apart. More and more my father gravitated toward his work at the bank, while my mother slowly slipped away to a place from which she would eventually find it impossible to return.

· *Chapter Fifteen* ·

IT WAS THE LAST WEEK OF AUGUST, A MONTH OF FAIR WEATHER FREE
from black flies, mosquitoes, and no-see-ums. During the latter part
of the previous week, the New England stations had had a field day predicting the advance of a tropical storm. The forecasters debated whether
it would intensify into a full-fledged hurricane. A sport from New Jersey
canceled his reservation. Two others, one from Boston and another from
Albany, rescheduled their time with me and with the lodge where they had
intended to stay. A fourth, an older guy living in Manchester, sent me an
email explaining that his wife was afraid to leave home on account of the
predicted bad weather. I emailed back, telling him that he might miss out
on some outstanding fishing if the storm dumped enough rain to bring
the rivers up and the big fish out of the lakes. When the sport declined,
explaining that he couldn't convince his wife otherwise, I called Gilroy to
tell him I'd be free for some fishing as soon as the weather blew through.

The town's marinas had spent the previous afternoon hauling boats
out of harm's way. Fogerty, on those old legs of his, pumped gas to disap-
pointed vacationers, who waited in line before heading out of town. By
the twenty-eighth, those who owned camps were lining up at the Building
and Supply to purchase plywood and tarps to weather the blow, while
others converged on the IGA to stock up on water and other essentials.

Gilroy, on the other hand, insisted that the hurricane would do little
damage, while dropping enough rain to provide us with excellent fishing. Although Donnie relied on his gut to predict the weather, I spent
the afternoon in my apartment scanning my laptop, switching from The
Weather Channel to Accuweather.com, both of which were predicting

the storm of the century.

After battering New Jersey in the early morning hours of the twenty-ninth, the hurricane morphed into a tropical cyclone, veering farther west than anticipated by most computer models. By the next day, it dropped a cataclysmic eleven inches of rain in some parts of Vermont and New Hampshire. While causing some of the worst flooding in those states in over eighty years, only the edge of that extreme weather reached the Lakes Region. The rain we received was pretty much as Gilroy had predicted.

Donnie and I spend most of each summer working hard to find fish in low water, some years doing so through the better part of September. When it doesn't rain, the fall run of brook trout and landlocked salmon won't begin until October, which is after the fishing season closes on most rivers throughout the region. Until the spawning run, I earn my money by putting sports on fish in skinny water.

Although I learned most of what I know about fishing from my grand and his brother, my knowledge of psychology has been acquired during the relatively short time that I've been guiding anglers, many of whom go to sporting shows held each year throughout the winter. While there, they stop at booths manned by western guides wearing battered Stetsons and Tony Lama boots.

Speaking through handlebar mustaches that droop over their upper lips, these twentieth-century cowboys spend more time working the oars of guide boats than atop saddles. They tout the rivers of Idaho, Montana, and Colorado that contain trophy brown and rainbow trout. In other booths, eastern guides are dressed in khaki shirts and pants, with olive baseball caps on their heads while Canadian outfitters with French accents boast of tremendous brook trout north of the border.

A few Januarys back, Gilroy and I made the six-hour drive to Marlborough, Massachusetts to attend one of the bigger shows. We were surprised to see so many young women among the guides and lodge owners. Their fit bodies and good-natured smiles are as enticing to the mostly middle-aged men who frequent these shows as were Persephone's handmaidens to the ancient sailors who heard their songs. Although Gilroy mumbled something about eye-candy, I figured this modern version of the Greek myth was preferable to losing one's life along some barren shoreline. Besides, the few female guides I know, tend to outfish their male counterparts.

Walking down an aisle filled with New England lodges and fly-fishing stores, we came upon Tom Rider seated under a banner for Beaver Den Camps. Tom nodded as we approached and offered us a seat behind his table. It was there that I spent the remainder of the afternoon booking trips while he wobbled back and forth to the hotel bar. Gilroy lasted about twenty minutes before walking across the aisle to talk up a pretty young thing wearing a pink cap with the words **Got Trout?** stitched across the front.

Despite the Sirens standing behind the Canadian booths, Tom did well at the shows since many sports preferred western Maine as an economical alternative to plunking down a few thousand dollars for a week in one of the Labrador or Newfoundland fly-in lodges.

That afternoon, I spent my time speaking with prospective customers as they leafed through photographs of smiling anglers holding brook trout as large as any you'd find south of Labrador.

I wanted to tell them that when traveling to the Rangeley Lakes Region, they shouldn't expect to find hills manicured by black-and-white Holsteins, or white clapboard homes surrounding a town square like those scattered throughout Vermont. Missing will be the snow-capped peaks of the Rockies and the larger-than-life western rivers like the Madison or Gunnison. But I didn't.

I could have told them how the western side of Maine is painted in dark, almost morose colors that are more reminiscent of Winslow Homer's Adirondack art than that of a Norman Rockwell illustration or an Ansel Adams photograph, but I knew they would not understand.

I've never been able to find words to adequately describe the wild beauty found in our swiftly passing storms, with their sudden downpours and enormous thunderheads; or in the bogs and backwaters, where under the shadows cast by a rising moon, moose graze waist-deep in the ooze and muck. It's hard to explain my attachment to the tiny streams winding through forests of conifers, streams containing little brook trout that fight with a fury of fish twice their size. Then there's my fondness for the spruce-covered hills and mountains with names like Green Top, Bosebuck, Burnt, and Saddleback. How do I recount the scent of balsam and bark drifting up from massive piles of timber or the sound of the big rigs rumbling over dirt roads to carry that timber to the mills across the border in New Hampshire?

Rather than describe the rugged, no-nonsense beauty that is as hard and unforgiving as it is fragile; instead of explaining how this heart-breaking beauty can be lost if the corporations, aided by the politicians they retain in their pockets, have their way; I discussed the size of our trout and salmon, the pools and runs where they can be found, the clothes that must be packed, the bug spray that should be carried, and the lodges and camps where sports can stay.

After a few years of guiding, I learned that most sports pay only lip service to the sights, sounds, and smells that surround them, looking up from the water only after they release the fish of their dreams.

There are certainly those sports who stop along the water's edge long enough to catch sight of an otter or mink, or those who set aside their rods to pick a handful of blueberries. There are anglers who take a moment to appreciate the delicate beauty of a single painted trillium, or who chuckle over the antics of a line of baby mergansers as they follow their mother in single-file formation. There may be such anglers, but they are few.

Such sports as these are more interested in the splendor that is a brook trout's flank than its size. They are the type of man or woman who might cheer at the sight of a salmon slipping the hook as it tail-dances across the surface of a sun-splashed lake. It is to these few sports that I may reveal a secret pool or run first shown to me by my grand or great-uncle, but only after I'm satisfied that the angler is worthy of admittance to such hidden places.

But I'm way off the trail here. Like I started to say, there were a few blown-out culverts, but otherwise the Lakes Region was spared the devastation experienced by those living no more than sixty miles to the south of us. We woke on the morning after the storm to find that the rain had raised the rivers to a level the big fish could not resist.

With Gilroy seated next to me, I pulled my pickup beside the gas pumps in front of Fogerty's station. Petey Boy was fussing with his bicycle outside the office where Fogerty was talking to a customer. When Petey saw the Rangeley strapped to the trailer, he dropped Rolling Thunder to the pavement. We had only packed a lunch for two, but Petey loved riding in my boat. Although worried that he might get bored halfway through the afternoon, I relented when Fogerty agreed to let Petey's mother know he'd be late for dinner.

After making a stop at the diner to add a peanut butter and jelly sandwich and a couple more bottles of pop to the day's menu, I paid Bernice, who slipped something into my bag.

Pointing toward my truck, she rasped, "A treat for Petey."

Thirty minutes later I backed my Rangeley Boat down the ramp at the southern end of Aziscohos Lake. While we motored north, Petey munched on the Three Musketeers bar the waitress had tucked into the bag. A washed-out orange life preserver hung loosely over his broad shoulders. I had fastened its rusted buckle around his waist. Polyethylene floatation flowed out of a tear in the stitching. With one hand on the outboard, I leaned forward to wipe a smudge of chocolate from a corner of his mouth.

Gilroy sat in the bow. He turned the brim of his baseball cap backwards as the Rangeley's cedar hull cut through the water's surface. The sound of the outboard's six horses filled our ears as we motored under a cloud-free sky.

On our way up the lake we saw a few younger loons amongst the pairs of adults. Hatched in July, they had survived the Lady of the Lake, who, despite her age, sought food for her own brood that had also hatched earlier in the summer. After passing a set of private camps built along the bluffs on our right, we saw a mottled bird, one of the Lady's two eaglets, glide over the hills alongside the lake.

A few minutes later, I pulled up to an eighteen-foot Glastron that was drifting over a deep hole known locally as The Ledges. The man at the controls wore his black beard long and his hair short under a Boston Bruins cap.

"Still keeping up that Rangeley of yours?" Wally Hancock called as I cut my engine.

The guide in the fiberglass bowrider worked out of Beaver Den Camps. I figured the average age of the three sports in the stern of his boat had to be over seventy. They held trolling rods with sinking lines. Wally was trying to put them on salmon that would remain near the bottom until they made their spawning run.

"You check out the river?" I pointed up the lake.

"Fish should be there all right, but the water's really running fast and high from the storm. Could be tough wading." The guide motioned to his older clients with a quick flick of his head.

While we spoke about the weather and the latest reports of fish caught and lost, Gilroy began to fuss, first checking his rod and then his flies. He opened a plastic box and stared inside at the streamers set one beside the other.

"What's with him?" Wally asked. More than once the older guide had maneuvered his sports into a run fished by Gilroy, resulting in words said over beers at Sparky's.

"You know Donnie, it's all about the fishing." Seeing that Gilroy was becoming increasingly impatient, I pushed away from the bigger boat before pulling on the cord of the Johnson outboard.

"Geronimo!" Petey called, as the Rangeley sprang up on its stern.

It took another ten minutes before Beaver Den Camps came into view. Its one-room cabins spread down to the lake. Although weathered, the large sign my mother had painted continued to hang from the outside of the main lodge. An American flag fell limply from a tall pole in front of the long wooden dock where a few aluminum Lunds bobbed up and down.

I looked over at Gilroy, but he was facing forward. I wondered if he was thinking of his father.

"Won't be long now!" I shouted over the sound of the outboard.

"Won't be long now," Petey repeated.

"Water's up all right." Gilroy had turned in my direction while wiping a sleeve across his face. A moment later we could hear the river. Camp Ten Bridge came into view as we cleared the final turn. The swollen current was indeed running high and fast.

Two rivulets cut through the western shoreline, where the previous week there had been only shallow trickles of water. We watched two anglers. With water up to their waist and their arms interlocked, they struggled to ford the fast rip.

Tying up at an old stump, Gilroy pointed to a number of men who lined the sides of the river.

"Seems like everyone in town had the same idea," he grunted while helping me pull the boat onto a spit of land between the river's main channel and the lower of the two rivulets.

We had slipped on our chest waders earlier in the morning. Gilroy handed me my nine-foot Leonard, the fly rod I prefer when casting to big fish. Looking over at Petey Boy, I made him promise to keep his life vest on and stay away from the water.

Petey raised his right hand and promised, "Cross my heart and hope to die." He bore a serious expression on his face while drawing a cross against the bulky preserver.

Leaving Petey Boy to examine the cobble along the edge of the island, I followed Gilroy, who was already laboring up the river. He'd knotted a streamer to his line by the time I caught up with him.

Although most of the anglers remained clustered on either side of the bridge, the two men who had forded the first rivulet were working the lower run that flowed between the island where we had beached the Rangeley and the western shoreline.

"Son of a bitch," muttered Gilroy as the two men waved. When I looked in their direction, the town's retired doctor gave me a thumbs-up while its most reliable mechanic merely shrugged his shoulders.

Like the men on either side of the bridge, Doc Woodward and old man Fogerty had traveled the logging roads that crossed over Green Top Mountain to get to the river.

By the time I'd rigged my rod, Wally Hancock had motored his Glastron into the main channel fifty feet or so below the island. The three septuagenarians stood on either side of the fiberglass craft, chucking weighted nymphs that their guide had chosen for them.

"He should know better than to crowd us like that," Donnie had shouted, but by then I'd tromped down to the end of the island where his words were lost in the Magalloway's heavy current.

Gilroy and I prefer the tranquility of fishing in unspoiled country. We rarely cast our flies within sight of another angler, and at first I found it disconcerting to see so many people lining the banks on either side of the river. I knew that Gilroy had little tolerance for guides who stalked his favorite pools, or for that matter, any angler whose first name he did not know. He was not predisposed to giving up what he considered his birthright to outsiders. Donnie figured those from away had pretty much taken all that there was to take. In his mind, the region's water was his domain. He'd share the streams and rivers, however begrudgingly, with those few locals he knew, but never with wealthy camp-owners who lived out of state. In my friend's opinion, they were part-time sports at best. Gilroy had even less tolerance for the hoards of Orvis-clad yuppies who were finding their way north in ever increasing numbers.

While still flinging expletives at the fishing gods, Donnie Gilroy swung a Ballou Special through the air. After a moment or two, the pattern's marabou wing sunk under the current forty feet across the river. Using a jerky motion to imitate an injured smelt, he stripped the streamer back toward shore. A fish struck on his first cast. I stood twenty or so yards downstream, a salmon taking my line after a hard strike. The fish erupted through the surface thirty feet out in the current before slipping the hook. Gilroy looked over his shoulder, his rod vibrating as he continued to play his salmon.

Up and down the river others took fish after fish. We lost count of the number of salmon and trout released in the next few hours. Our arms ached from the strain of one good fish after another, and at some point I set aside my rod, sitting on the cobbled shoreline while watching Gilroy, who was unwilling to quit.

After a while, Petey Boy stomped around the bend of the island and plopped down by my side. He emptied his pockets, showing me different shaped stones and a number of feathers, including one from a duck and another from a seagull. While I examined his treasures, a tiny man hobbled out of the forest along the far side of the river. The slender elf with the stitch in his gait wore the same hip waders he'd worn in June. The tattered bill of his khaki cap hid his hawk-like features. He was too far away for me to identify his flies, but I assumed they were the same tiny wisps of feather and fur that he'd taught me to tie.

By then, every man on the river had taken at least one fish, and many of us reeled in quite a few more. Anything below sixteen inches was released in near disgust, the anglers on that afternoon out for bigger game. Gilroy had taken two salmon bumping twenty inches. The entire crowd applauded when Fogerty released a huge brook trout with a hooked kype as long as any Gilroy and I had seen since that afternoon at Landing Pool. The fish barely fit in his net.

On his second cast my great-uncle pulled back on his rod. The sound of his reel screamed above that of the river's current as the little man backed out of the water while trying to control the fish. A moment later the reel once again cried out as the fish ran for a second time. Some sixty feet downriver there appeared a flash of black and silver.

Petey shrieked, "Geronimo!" while men up and down the river shouted at seeing the salmon's size. I saw the painful look on Gilroy's face when he turned in my direction. If not the fish of his dreams, it was pretty damn close.

It took some time for my uncle to bring the salmon to his hand. By the time he did, a number of guys on that side of the river had assembled around him. When one of them extended his hands out wide, men up and down the shoreline hooted and hollered. A few cried out, "King of the River!"

"Unfuckinbelievable," was all Gilroy could mutter as Angus Ferguson released one of the largest landlocked salmon we had ever seen.

· Chapter Sixteen ·

AFTER MY NIGHT OUT WITH THE OLD MEN, I COULDN'T WAIT TO catch a brook trout. Gilroy and I abandoned the pond behind my house for the streams and brooks where we hoped to catch trout rather than pan fish. During the rest of that season Harold and Angus watched over my efforts, while I passed on their lessons to Gilroy.

During the following winter, I trekked through the snow, spending afternoons at the home of my great-uncle and aunt. While Angus tied his Highland patterns, I sipped my great-aunt's hot cocoa. Nibbling on freshly baked cider donuts, I looked through one after another of my great-uncle's books. That April, I rushed out to the pond each morning hoping for an early ice-out. When the ice finally did break apart during the second week of May, I couldn't wait to try out what I'd learned over the winter.

Through the rest of that spring Gilroy and I cast flies on our hand-me-down rods leading up to the afternoon when Fogerty drove us to the gate. In the years that followed, I accompanied my grand and his brother whenever my parents would allow. When not with Harold and Angus, Gilroy and I would fish some no-name brook or backcountry beaver pond, a few times convincing Fogerty to take us to the Magalloway, where we would fish below the Route 16 dam under the watchful eyes of the old mechanic. We had become brook trout fanatics.

After the warden pinched us, I became a regular at my great-uncle's camp. I remember mornings seated at Angus's kitchen table. While he and his brother drank mugs of coffee as black as a raven on a moonless night, I sipped tea the color of our tannin-stained streams. I would listen

to them debate where we should fish. For my part, anywhere would do.
I was just happy to be above the gates.

Staying overnight, sometimes for the weekend, I cast my flies along-side the old men. I spent my evenings seated by my great-uncle as he tied his strange little flies. Later, I'd pull down one of the many books from the shelves beside the oak table with the short legs, reading by gaslight until my eyes could no longer remain open.

Angus and Harold Ferguson had wandered the forest around Parmachenee Lake ever since moving to the Rangeley Lakes Region. To a young boy, it seemed that they had hiked through each valley and over every hill within the thirty-one-thousand-acre tract. I was sure they'd ca-noed across every pond, waded up every brook, and cast a fly into every riffle, run, and pool of the Big and Little Magalloway Rivers. During the summers that followed, we sometimes camped away from the cabin for days on end. The two men accepted me into their fraternity. Imparting knowledge freely and without pretense, they continued the education I began during that first evening on the moonlit pond.

Once, while hiking on our own, Gilroy and I came upon a cave less than a mile from Angus's cabin. It was no more than a large indentation in a rock outcropping along the side of a hill. Inside, we found the remains of a rusted trap, as well as the lid from a kettle and a few metal utensils. That evening, while my great-uncle served us pork chops, I recounted what we'd found. Shoveling a huge heap of mashed potatoes onto each of our plates, Angus told us about a young trapper only a few years older than we were at the time, a guy named John Danforth. My great-uncle said that Danforth had found the cave in the late eighteen hundreds, having set out from Wilson's Mills to hunt and fish around Parmachenee Lake, which back then was true wilderness. To illustrate his point, the little man limped into the other room, returning with a book he pulled from the shelves adjacent to the oak table. It told the story of resourceful, independent-minded men, who built makeshift cabins to survive the winter while trapping beaver and otter and hunting deer and moose.

The next afternoon, Gilroy and I scrounged around the old man's camp until we found a suitable piece of wood into which we carved the words Camp Danforth. Afterward, he and I hiked back up to the cave to nail the sign onto a nearby tree.

The following summer, my mother fell under another of her dark spells. One day she'd be fine, working in the garden or on one of her paintings, the next, she was too weary to leave the house. Then, unable to dress, she'd remain in bed, a damp washcloth draped across her forehead. This continued until the pills Doc Woodward prescribed kicked in.

Unable to seek my mother's permission, I begged my father to allow me to spend a week at my great-uncle's cabin. I had worked all that summer as a bus boy at the Red Onion. Before returning to school, I hoped to get away from the dirty dishes and garbage cans for a few days. With my mother confined to bed, it was easier for my father not to have to deal with me—the reason, I'm sure, he said yes.

The first part of that week was uneventful, with the river above Parmachenee Lake low from lack of rain. During those first few days, the old men and I took a few trout, but no salmon. In the evenings, we paddled the canoe in and out of the lake's coves, but didn't fare much better. Over dinner on the fourth night, Harold announced his plan to wake early the following morning. He hoped the fish would be more cooperative before first light.

It was still dark when Angus roused me from my bed. Fog shrouded the lake as we walked down to Harold's Jeep. After a brief drive, my grand pulled to the side of the logging road. The fog was so thick it was hard to see, but after collecting my gear, I followed the two men who had hiked down a narrow path that began alongside the dirt road. Before turning onto the trail, I looked back at the vehicle, but it was shrouded in mist. Harold said the path would end at a dark bend in the Little Magalloway River that he called Long Pond. Blackness surrounded us until Angus turned on a flashlight. When he shut the light near the end of the trail, a large pool materialized in the pre-dawn darkness.

Walking out onto an ankle-deep gravel bar, the two men began casting weighted streamers comprised of olive marabou feathers. Harold explained that when dragged along the bottom, the undulating marabou simulated the movement of a leech. I suppose my grand saw me staring down at my hippers because he explained that the blood-sucking worms preferred warm flesh to nylon. He tied a smaller version of the pattern to my line, but I had difficulty casting the weighted streamer and, after a while, put aside my rod.

A half-moon broke through the fog. Its silver shape glowed through the mist. It cast an eerie light that shimmered across the surface of the pool. The murky halo surrounding the moon made me think of Halloween. Even so, seated on a boulder, my knees folded up to my chin, I felt safe between the two old men.

Sometime before the sun burnt off the fog, a fish ripped at my great-uncle's leech pattern. His sleek rod bent forward as the sound of his reel echoed over the pool. Harold estimated the trout to measure at least eighteen inches. Angus released the fish without removing it from the water, as was his way.

We developed a pleasant rhythm over the next few days. The two men sat in their porch rockers, napping during the heat of the day, while I dragged their Old Town canoe from under the big spruce tree.

As I paddled around the lake's shoreline, the Lady of the Lake kept an eye on me. I saw her gliding over the tops of distant hills. More than once, the great raptor would dip a wing as she stared down with her cold yellow eye.

It was during one of these excursions that I spotted a moose. The large cow had emerged from Indian Cove and was swimming across the river's inlet. Paddling close by, I could count the flies buzzing around her head. When the moose reached the far side, she rose up on her hooves and splashed through the shallows. Upon reaching shore, the big cow trotted into the wood, where I could hear her crashing through the tightly grown trees. Paddling back to my great-uncle's camp, I thought to myself that there was no better place to spend my life.

On the Friday of that last week in August, Harold fixed an early dinner of snowshoe hare stew. In addition to the rabbit, we each had a helping of green peas and another of zucchini that had been cooked in butter with little pieces of onion. Earlier that day, I'd gathered the vegetables from the garden Angus kept by his cabin. For dessert, we devoured the last of the blueberries that I'd picked earlier in the season and that Angus had kept frozen, topping them off with big dollops of whipped cream.

Later that night, we fished until the bats swept over our heads. Angus had suggested that we cast our flies in a cove below Black Cat Brook, above a dilapidated wooden dam that no longer held back the water of Parmachenee Lake. By evening's end, we took a mess of small trout.

While I cleaned the fish, Harold and Angus retired to their rockers. I could smell Angus's tobacco and see the tip of Harold's cigarette glow orange whenever he inhaled. The moon cast a soft glow over the lake's surface. A loon called in the distance as I walked back to the cabin. A moment later, another answered.

After dinner, Angus sat at the desk with the short legs while Harold fiddled with the dial of his battery-operated radio. Pulling down a book from the shelf, I lay on the couch reading stories about a fictional Maine guide named Dud Dean. A commentator on the Canadian Broadcasting Company's program was describing a storm due to hit Sherbrooke, the closest city on the other side of the border. He warned of high winds and considerable rain.

The following morning, I woke to a bright blue sky. Walking outside the cabin in my pajamas, I looked out onto the lake that shimmered under the morning sun. A breeze rustled its surface with an occasional gust of wind sweeping down out of the pines. Something had devoured the fish guts I'd left on the stump the evening before. Although it may have been the eagle, it could have also been a raccoon or some other nighttime critter scavenging a meal.

By the time we finished our breakfast of brook trout, the winds had picked up. Clouds rolled in by mid afternoon. Sometime after two o'clock, a few drops of rain began to sprinkle down. By then, the afternoon had turned prematurely dark, the air growing heavy. Angus pulled the canoe away from the shoreline and secured it beside the stump under the large spruce while I set out more scraps for the Lady to eat.

Harold had managed to pull in a station from Mount Washington. A New Hampshire broadcaster was also predicting a major blow. The two men decided it'd be prudent to remain near the cabin, where we spent the remainder of the afternoon filling the generator with gasoline and the cistern with water. I added wood to the pile by the stove and gathered buckets, tools, and other paraphernalia strewn around the camp, storing them in the outlying buildings.

The small fire Harold started in the wood stove removed the dampness that had built up during the latter part of the afternoon. Sometime after four, he walked over to where I was watching Angus tie a pattern called a Dark Needle. Harold stooped over his brother's shoulder. He squinted through a spiral of fragrant smoke that rose from my great-uncle's pipe. As Angus finished the last few wraps of the ancient pattern, I heard a vehicle driving along the logging road below the cabin. Brushing aside the curtain, I wiped away the moisture from the inside of the window to see a green pickup pull in beside my grand's Jeep. I noticed the red-and-black emblem of Maine's Inland Fisheries and Wildlife Service painted on the truck's door.

In the waning light, I watched a tall man unfold his lanky frame from the vehicle. Although he wore rain gear over his green uniform and a hood pulled over his cap, I recognized the same taciturn warden who had taken me into custody the previous season. As the man ambled up the walk, Angus rose from the vise. I accompanied my grand and his brother as they stepped onto the porch of the cabin.

"This one behavin'?" The warden extended his hand first to Angus and then to Harold.

"Th' laddie's alrecht," my great-uncle replied.

We were standing under the eave of the porch. The warden slipped the hood of his rain jacket down. After removing his cap, he ran long fingers over his closely cropped hair and said, "You fellas do know there's weather coming?"

"Planning tae wait it oot," Angus stared up at the sky that was spitting down rain.

"May not be able to get back up here for a while if it gets as bad as they say." The warden wiped a droplet of water from his cheek.

Harold pointed to the little shack that housed the generator. "We'll be braw."

The younger man frowned. "Suit yourselves."

When the warden turned, his rain pants made a swishing sound. We watched him trot down to his vehicle. Back inside, Harold stoked the wood stove. The warmth from the cast iron was comforting.

After dinner, I resumed reading about the fictional fishing guide, who reminded me of the two old men playing cribbage in the next room. The rain intensified sometime around seven that evening, continuing throughout the night and into the early morning, beating against the cabin's tin roof.

I woke early, ambling down to the lake a few minutes after six. Only the slightest of breezes rippled across the surface. The skies above me were once again bright blue. The only evidence that a major storm had passed through was the wet grass beneath my toes and a few fallen branches and clusters of leaves that littered the ground. The humidity of the previous few days had been sucked out of the air. Looking toward the far shore, I couldn't find a single cloud.

Back in the cabin, I found Angus scrambling eggs in a big black skillet while my grand sat in the other room switching back and forth between the New Hampshire public radio station and the CBC station out of Montreal. We soon learned that the damaging winds that had battered Sherbrooke remained on the Canadian side of the Boundary Mountains. Even so, the tail end of the storm had drenched our region with heavy rain for nearly twelve hours.

"We got lucky," Harold called to his brother from where he sat listening to the radio.

Angus limped over to the table where I was seated and slid eggs onto the plates he had previously set.

"Eat," he said to me. "Breakfast is oan th' table," he called to his brother.

Shuffling into the kitchen in the moccasins he favored wearing around the cabin, Harold pulled out the chair across from mine. He removed a slice of bread from the pile Angus had toasted and slathered it with apple butter.

"Efter I eat, I'll take th' Jeep 'n' check oot th' best wey tae git tae th' river," he said.

"Dinna fash yersel. It'll take th' laddie a bit tae eat, so dinnae rush," Angus mumbled through a mouthful of scrambled egg. After he finished a second helping, Harold drained his coffee mug. Offering me the last piece of bacon, he rose from the table. Dressed only in a pair of striped boxers and a sleeveless white T-shirt, he shuffled out to the Jeep. The untied laces of a pair of hunting boots dragged behind him like four trolling lines behind one of the brothers' Old Town canoes. An hour later, Harold returned from his reconnaissance mission. He recounted how the small brooks and rivulets that entered the lake had turned to raging torrents causing many of the culverts to blow out, which made a number of the logging roads impassable.

While I cleaned off the breakfast from our dishes, Angus cut thick slabs of meatloaf leftover from earlier in the week. He placed the meat between slices of French bread and slathered them with ketchup.

"Take this down tae th' Jeep." My great-uncle handed me a pack that contained the sandwiches, three apples and a few bottles of pop.

When I looked puzzled, Angus explained, "Th' paper companies'll have repair crews oot afore we're dressed."

"Those lumber trucks wull be motoring ower brandy fresh culverts by lunch time," added Harold, "'n' you kin bet all th' rain is gonnae bring the big fish tae th' river."

"I thought they didn't spawn until September," I said.

"That's whit th' books say." Angus pointed down the hall toward the bookshelf. "It takes quite a bit o' rain tae git th' river running fleet enough fur they muckle fish tae stairt thair run, bit they'll come oot o' th' lake in August if it does." Harold poured another mug of coffee.

Twenty minutes later I was sitting in the back seat of my grand's Jeep listening to the two men discuss whether they should fish Island Pool or Little Boy Falls. My grand had his left arm leaning out of the vehicle's open window. A cigarette dangled from the corner of his mouth. The sleeves of the old man's shirt were rolled up to the elbows. After countless summers under the sun, his skin had turned dark and leathery. In the seat beside him, my great-uncle grasped his unlit pipe between his lips. He had the bill of his olive cap pulled down tight over his brow to keep it from blowing out the top of the vehicle. The liver spots on the back of his hands reminded me of a set of ponds sunk into the hills south of town, the location of which the old men had sworn me to secrecy.

Angus was pushing hard for Island Pool, which was not as productive as the runs farther down the river, but harder to access. He argued that there would be less of a chance that we would encounter other anglers, which in his opinion was paramount. Harold also enjoyed having the river to himself, but if given the choice between catching fish and isolation, he opted for the former. With this in mind, he lobbied for Little Boy Falls. The scenic run boasted some of the largest salmon in the river. Big fish came up from the lake to hold in the oxygen rich water below the falls, but it was also the first pool that most anglers sought out upon venturing above the gates.

"Besides," Harold pled his case to his younger brother, "we can always move down to Landing Pool, where Harry's mate lost that trout ye been tryin' tae catch for th' last thirty years."

· *Chapter Seventeen* ·

"THERE." The older woman seated in the bow of my canoe leaned forward. Her dark eyes fixed on a set of rings emanating outward on the tea-stained surface of the pond.

"They'll be cruising. You have to lead them," I explained.

A trout once again broke the surface, this time only a few yards from the bow of the canoe.

Diana Russo was a novice angler. A secretary, she made a thirty-minute commute each weekday from her condo on Staten Island to a law office in Manhattan. The previous year, she'd divorced her husband. The same year, the divorcee traveled to Vermont to take a course on fly fishing offered by the Orvis Company. Afterward, she practiced her casts on put-and-take trout streams in New Jersey. This was the extent of her experience with a fly rod.

The woman's long dark hair tumbled out of the back of a wide-brimmed straw hat and down her shoulders. She wore a light blue shirt tucked into jeans that fit snuggly over shapely thighs and around a waist with only a hint of a belly. Her boots were the type with leather tops and rubber soles. They looked newly purchased, perhaps from L.L. Bean. Earlier that afternoon, we'd left her two-door sedan at the motel where Gilroy's mother worked and climbed into my pickup. I'd decided to bring this newest sister of the Angle to the little-fished pond where my grand and his brother had taken me that night more than fourteen years ago. I didn't want to bring attention to the secluded water and parked my truck a half-mile up the logging road. Swinging a canvas pack across my shoulders, we grabbed our fly rods and walked the remaining distance.

On the way, the legal secretary told me she'd decided to spend her one-week vacation in Rangeley after reading an article about the region's brook trout fishing. I remembered Gilroy's rant when he spotted the cover of the well-known fly-fishing magazine in the rack opposite the counter where we sat waiting for a customer to walk inside the sports shop on a cold, damp morning in late April.

"You watch. A bunch of rich assholes, with nothing better to spend their money on, will be mucking up our water!" he exclaimed throwing his hands in the air.

Diana Russo was neither rich nor did she appear to be an ass. Even so, I'd made sure to take a number of unnecessary rights and lefts to avoid any possibility that my sport might be able to find her way back to the pond. Although bumping fifty, the lady walked without huffing and puffing, something many of my middle-aged male sports are unable to do. The leaves on the maples had begun to turn. In another few weeks, the other hardwoods would follow.

After removing the spruce limbs that I'd cut earlier in the season to camouflage the entrance to the narrow trail, we hiked down the path that ended at the shoreline of the little pond. It was a breathless evening without a hint of a breeze, but by this time of year the biting insects that would have plagued us in June and July were no longer a bother. Although the rivers had returned to their pre-storm lows, the backwoods pond always held trout willing to come out and play. Diana Russo had chosen a lovely few days to become acquainted with my home water.

Blueberries from the low-growing bushes along the shoreline had been picked over, but a few remained. I handed a couple to my sport, who popped them into her mouth.

Over the years, I've collected three canoes. Two are sixteen feet long, the other is fourteen. They are pretty banged up, but still get the job done. I've chained each to trees beside different ponds. There is no need to haul them out in the fall since they are aluminum, and there is no problem remembering the combination on the locks, because it is the same for all three—Thelma Louise's birthday.

I dragged my canoe past what remained of the Old Town my grand and his brother had once paddled around the pond. The cedar ribs of the wooden craft had sunk into the moist soil as if returning once more to the forest. While I helped my sport into the bow, a pewee flew over our heads. The flycatcher grabbed a tiny black insect out of the air. After further examination, I realized that we'd come upon a hatch of flying ants. Hoping my sport's afternoon would be as memorable as my evening with Harold and Angus, I paddled out among a squadron of dragonflies that zigged and zagged as they feasted on the unexpected bounty fluttering along the water's edge.

Now, seated in the stern of the canoe, I gently coached the novice fly fisher. "Watch for a trout to surface, then wait until it does it again to gauge the direction of the fish. After that, cast your fly a foot or so in front of the rise." As the woman from Staten Island swung her fly line toward the shore, I continued my instruction while holding the canoe steady with my paddle. "Doing it that way allows you to cast where the fish is headed and not where it's been."

While transferring her gear to my truck, I learned that Diana Russo took up fly fishing on a whim after her divorce was official.

"The new me, I suppose," she had joked when I hit the brakes for an elderly couple crossing the road in front of the Town and Lake Motel. On the drive to the pond, she had been a bit self-conscious, staring out the window the few times I turned in her direction.

In the canoe, my sport tended to look backward when she cast the fly line over her shoulder. When she brought her arm forward again, the wide-open loop formed during her backcast fell upon the water well short of its target. When she turned and shrugged as if to apologize, I told her to relax, that there was no one to impress. I wanted her to have a good time and not be overwhelmed by my instructions. The last thing a sport wants from a guide is to spend the day being told that everything he or she does is wrong. We worked on keeping her wrist straight while

I explained a few techniques to help with line control. Her next few casts were awkward, but better than her first, and eventually the legal secretary was able to lay out twenty feet of line.

After telling her to take a breath, I said, "As the sun sets, fish should start rising everywhere. Have fun. You've got nothing to prove."

On her fifth or sixth attempt, a brookie no bigger than my middle finger took the fly. A few moments later, another trout made us chuckle. The fish was about the same size as the first, its tail clearing the surface in a frantic attempt to strike at the little ant pattern I'd knotted to my sport's line. The divorcee's confidence improved when a third fish, a bit bigger than the first two, rose to take her fly. After that, she seemed to enjoy herself, no longer trying so hard. Although her casts were still erratic, they were accomplished enough for the naive trout of the seldom-fished pond to remain interested.

With the sun still above the hills along the western shoreline, I decided to break for an early dinner. Blueberry bushes grew tight along the shoreline while farther back the spruce and balsam left little room to spread out a blanket. Rather than paddle to shore, we remained in the canoe. After unwrapping the turkey sandwiches I'd purchased from the diner, we twisted off the caps on two bottles of birch beer and stretched our legs out from either end of the canoe. While eating, Diana talked about her decision to divorce her husband. Over apple turnovers, she told me that life was too short to spend in a loveless marriage. Although her husband was a decent enough man, she needed more from life than sitting across a table night after night with nothing to say.

Although rarely discussing personal matters with my male clients, I found myself telling the attractive, middle-aged woman about Thelma Louise's desire to leave Rangeley, and how I found it hard to imagine a life away from the rivers and streams that I loved.

"As hard as it might be, sometimes you have to make a choice. Just don't wait as long I did to make yours." The secretary raised the bottle of pop to her lips.

She had never seen a moose and was hoping to do so before leaving for home. I explained that not that long ago moose could be found most any night along Route 16, but that over the last few years their numbers had declined. Old timers, guys who spend their time skulking around the woods, were finding more dead animals than antlers.

"Everyone has a theory," I said, "but to my mind, a combination of factors is to blame. I know one thing for sure, while I was growing up, we never had ticks this far north. Now, they're all over the place. They certainly plague the moose. Climate change has to have something to do with it."

I promised that on our way back into town, we'd drive down a few of the logging roads frequented by moose.

The sun had slipped behind the hills along the western shoreline of the pond. Fish should have been rising, but instead, they mysteriously stopped feeding. I opened my fly box and stared down at the neat rows of different-colored patterns.

The fly I initially tied to my sport's line had a body of black Antron dubbed to imitate the two humps of an ant's body, with a dun-colored hackle wound in between and a bit of elk hair tied in to represent the ant's wing. It's an easy pattern to tie, and I figured it would fool trout on a pond rarely fished by other anglers, but when the rises stopped, I switched to one tied with a CDC feather. When that also failed to raise a trout, I changed to a Gold-ribbed Hare's Ear and then finally to one of my great-uncle's soft-hackled wet flies, but nothing seemed to pique the interest of the fish.

"Gonna try something different," I said. Digging through my fly boxes, I found a leech pattern.

The New Yorker scrunched up her pretty face when I told her that leeches slither around in the mud of most ponds in our region. Pointing over the canoe's gunwale, I added, "And if they're active, you might have a chance at a big fish."

After Diana lowered the weighted streamer to the bottom, I

instructed her on how to twist and tug the line to imitate the action of a leech, but after an hour we were unable to take a single fish.

I said, "It sometimes happens like this," and added with a dumb grin, "that's why they call it fishing and not catching."

As the sun receded, a chill crept into the air. I pulled out a sweater from my pack and offered it to the secretary. From across the pond there came a short, high-pitched howl, followed by another and then a few moments later, a series of yips interspersed with an occasional bark.

My sport looked in my direction. The crow's feet around her eyes wrinkled with concern. "Wolves?" she asked.

"Just a couple of coydogs caught themselves a hare for supper." I tried to put her at ease.

The light had faded by the time I pulled the canoe back on shore.

I pointed toward the northwest quadrant of the sky. "That's Jupiter." The planet's light remained steady rather than blinking like the stars that had appeared as we turned down the road.

There are no traffic lights on logging roads or street lamps on two-tracks, and the darkness seemed to unnerve my sport. We were walking side by side when we heard the coydogs again. The woman from New York drew noticeably closer while she looked over her shoulder.

"No worries," I reassured her. Giving her arm a squeeze, I said, "Really, they're harmless." After a moment, I added, "If you think about it, there's more to fear during your daily commute than there is out here." Overhead, the Milky Way had spread across the darkened sky.

On the way back to town, I managed to locate a moose—a female—probably born the previous year, but it was too dark for a photograph.

Diana Russo returned my sweater while settling up outside her motel room. When she promised to call me the following year, I suggested she reserve time in the spring when the rivers would provide fine fishing.

It was after ten by the time I walked into Sparky's. I'd developed a cramp in my leg from sitting in the canoe all afternoon and my head ached. I nodded to Thelma Louise, who was passing a Long Trail to a guy standing between two of the vultures. The tavern was crowded with a mix of locals and vacationers. I found Gilroy seated at our usual table. He was staring up at the television, where the Red Sox had just blown a three-run lead.

"I oughta knock that hat off his fuckin' head." Gilroy turned from the game and was now staring across the room at Wally Hancock.

Hancock wore the bill of his cap high on his head. He leaned against the jukebox while talking to a girl with wild red hair. She was wearing designer jeans. Her black heels made her appear as tall as the guide.

"You see the way he motored that boat into our water the other day?" Gilroy was working himself into another frenzy.

"Our water? Since when do we own the rights to the Magalloway River?"

"You know what I mean," Gilroy snarled.

When he rose to his feet, I said, "Tell ya what. I'm buying, but only if you promise to calm down."

"Good tip?"

I shrugged my shoulders. In fact, the lady had been exceedingly generous.

The State of Maine requires those wishing to receive payment for taking someone out into field or stream to be licensed and to receive that license they must pass a test. Gilroy, who knows the water as well as I do, would make a first-rate guide, but he refuses to take the test. More importantly, ever since that afternoon at Landing Pool, he couldn't bring himself to share the water with outsiders. Of course, that doesn't stop him from allowing me to pick up the tab with the money I earn doing what he won't do himself.

· *Chapter Eighteen* ·

A FEW DAYS AFTER THE NEW YEAR, MATILDA FERGUSON RETURNED from Sunday service complaining of pain in her stomach. It was a frigid but bright afternoon. I remember because it was the day before my twelfth birthday. When the pain would not subside, my great-aunt visited the local clinic. Upon the advice of Doc Woodward, she made the trip to Farmington, where tests revealed the pancreatic cancer that would take her life before summer's end.

The darkness that plagued my mother returned when she learned the news. As I remember it, my grandparents helped out as best as they could, dividing their time between my great-uncle's house and ours, while my father continued to commute back and forth to work each day.

During the six months that the cancer cells ravished his wife's insides, Angus rarely left their house. He and my grand did not do much fishing that year, and although I continued to get out on the water with Gilroy, my heart wasn't in it.

The house where I'd spent so much time as a kid had changed. With the curtains drawn, sunlight no longer poured through the windows. A musty smell had replaced the scent of freshly baked cookies. There was silence where once there had been laughter. With Matilda too weak to leave her bed, Angus devoted himself to her care. Thelma Louise came by my house often, but to be honest, the two of us walked up the block only a handful of times. I told myself that this was not how I wished to remember my great-aunt.

The truth is it scared me. It was Gilroy's mother we'd heard cry out that afternoon while messing around with Tom Rider's vehicles. It was his father who had fallen from the roof of one of the cabins. In the days that followed, we learned that Frank Gilroy had broken his back. Unable to rise from his bed, the man, who once had time to play with us kids, slowly withered away.

Gilroy's mother had been working at the motel when Donnie and I returned home from school one day to find his father lying in a pissed-stained bed with his mouth wide open. His skin was drawn and as pale as a dead chub lying along the bank of a stream. I wasn't any help to the Gilroy's, and I figured I wasn't going to do much better with my great-aunt and uncle.

When it comes right down to it, I should have been there for Angus and Matilda. I know that. Hell, they were always there for me, but what's done is done.

Although I wasn't present when my great-aunt died, I overheard Angus tell Harold about that evening. Lying in her bed, Matilda hadn't opened her eyes in days. The air passing through her parched lips made a raspy sound each time she breathed in. Although the sun was setting on that second day of July, the temperature outside the Ferguson's little cottage approached ninety degrees. Earlier, Angus had lifted his wife from their bed, placing her frail frame gently on the sofa while he changed the sheets. Angus told his brother that Matilda's body felt as if it weighed no more than a handful of the tiny flies he continued tying to take his mind off her illness.

After placing his wife back in bed, the old man called his brother and told him the end was near. Seated by Matilda's side, Angus placed a cool towel across his wife's brow. While he tucked in the crisp, white sheet around her waist, there came a rattle from her throat. After that, the rasping sound stopped. The room remained silent, except for the clicking of the clock that hung in the hall outside the bedroom. I imagined tears welling up in the old man's eyes as he removed the damp towel from his wife's forehead, kissing her on the cheek before collapsing in the chair beside their bed. His hand was still in hers when Harold entered the room.

My mother hadn't left her bedroom in days, but that afternoon I remember her seated at the kitchen table, a red-and-white checkered dishtowel gripped tightly in her hand as she held the phone to her ear. Anticipating the call, my father walked out from the den where he had been hunched over his files. My mother leaned into his side.

Outside the kitchen's open window, the melodic notes of a wood thrush hung in the air. A storm had been building throughout the previous evening. Thunderheads had threatened the last rays of sunlight. Sometime after dark the first clap of thunder followed a shard of lightning. The rain began with a few fat drops, but soon it intensified, filling the night with a rush of moisture that swept away the oppressive heat of that day.

We spent the next afternoon at my great-uncle's house. People from town came in and out carrying cakes and casseroles. Around noon, I asked my father to be excused and walked over to Thelma Louise's house where we played video games for the remainder of the day. Sometime after five, Gilroy showed up with a bundle of firecrackers he'd found in the back of Fogerty's station.

Pooling our money, the three of us walked down to the Pine Tree Frosty, where we bought lobster rolls. Seated alongside the pond behind the food stand, we lit firecrackers and tossed them over the water. When a woman yelled that she was going to call the cops, we scampered down the street.

Although the humidity had been swept away with the storm, the temperature that day rose into the eighties. After Gilroy threw out the last firecracker, we hitchhiked the short distance out of town to the Rangeley River. Smoking cigarettes Thelma Louise had taken from her mother's purse, Gilroy and I spent the evening wading the river in our cut-off shorts and sneakers. We took turns casting his dinged-up fly rod to a school of white perch that eagerly sucked down the ragged flies we offered them. Thelma preferred to lie back on a bed of moss while blowing smoke rings toward the cumulus clouds that ambled across the darkening blue sky.

The wake held on the following day wasn't our first, having attended the one for Gilroy's father. Even so, I was struck by the manner in which many of the adults conducted themselves. The women, weepy at first, broke into knots of twos and threes, swapping recipes and gossip. A group of men, who were friends of Harold and Angus, gathered in an adjacent room. They talked loudly while smoking cigarettes and passing around a pint bottle.

Early on, Petey's parents had walked inside. When I asked about their son, they told me it was best that he remained home. Sometime later, Donnie showed up with his mother and older brother. He was wearing a wrinkled jacket over a white shirt with a frayed collar. The jacket was two sizes too big for him, and I assumed he'd borrowed it from his brother. Not long after that, Thelma Louise arrived, accompanied by her mother and two stepbrothers. After she paid her respects, the two of us looked for Gilroy. We found him seated on the back steps of the funeral home.

Donnie and I were unaccustomed to wearing jackets and ties. The only other time I saw Thelma in a dress was at the funeral for Gilroy's father. The three of us stared at the hearse and two black limousines parked outside the door. Thelma Louise pointed to a pileated woodpecker. The bird's flaming red crest bounced up and down as it pounded on the trunk of a thick spruce tree.

Thelma pulled out a cigarette. Gilroy lit it. After taking a drag, she passed the cigarette to Donnie, who passed it on to me.

"Looks like Mr. Duggan got himself a new truck," Gilroy muttered after he exhaled.

"Dylan says Fords are shit," Thelma volunteered.

"Rather have a Ford than a Chevy," I said just to be contrary.

By the time our conversation turned to a newly released movie about a post-apocalyptic world, Gilroy and I had shed our jackets and loosened our ties. Thelma had removed her leather shoes and was wiggling her toes in the grass below the last step of the stoop. Little did we know that we'd be back, not once, but three more times before it was all over.

· Chapter Nineteen ·

THE FRAGRANT SCENT OF LEMON GRASS AND LIME LEAVES DRIFTED UP through the floorboards of my apartment. Emptying another long-neck, I lit a cigarette and turned up the sound on my iPod to listen to my best friend's favorite song, Willie Nelson's pot-smoking anthem, "Roll Me Up and Smoke Me When I Die." Looking over at the clock beside my bed, I could see it was a few minutes past two in the morning. I thought of texting Gilroy, but was too tired and a bit loopy from the beer to type out a message. The aroma of fried shrimp was added to the exotic smells that were wafting up from the restaurant below. When I relaxed the grip on the Thompson vise a little black ant fell into my palm.

It had been two weeks since I'd taken the Rangeley boat up Aziscohos Lake to the Camp Ten Bridge. Since the near miss of the hurricane, the rivers had returned to their low levels, with the fish backing down into the lakes. Unlike Diana Russo, most of my sports had stayed close to their homes. With only three-and-half weeks remaining in September, I spent my nights scanning the weather websites in search of rain, hoping we'd receive a prolonged downpour before the end of the month. Without rain, the spawning run would not begin in earnest until October when all but a few places would be closed to fishing.

Money was always a concern, and with the fishing slowing down, my main source of income came from flies I sold to the local stores. I knew the owner of the town's fly-fishing shop. He paid me for those hours behind the counter when he was out guiding. The storeowner also paid for well-tied patterns such as the three-dozen flying ants that swarmed around the bottles of Long Trails I'd emptied during the night. Putting out the cigarette in a dish containing a forest of butts, I turned off the light and stumbled over to my bed.

Besides working at the town's fly-fishing store, I had a handshake deal to sell my flies at a few of the sporting lodges, as well as at L.L. Cote, a sporting goods store that takes up a city block forty-five minutes west of Rangeley in Errol, New Hampshire. I thought about dropping in on Rusty and Jeanne Miller, the owners of a smaller store located only a few miles down Route 16 at the entrance of the tiny hamlet of Easie. They also stocked my flies.

Afterward, I could continue down the road to Black Brook Cove, where Jeff Lafleur might be interested in stocking some of my streamers that work well on Aziscohos Lake. Jeff and his wife, Barbara, run the general store and campgrounds at the bottom of the lake. While there, I'd motor the Rangeley up to Beaver Den Camps to see if Tom Rider had any work for me. But all that would have to wait because I'd agreed to spend the day with Petey Boy. I'd promised it would be just him and me. An afternoon of drinking pop and eating snacks while trolling for salmon from my Rangeley Boat.

My head ached when I bent down to unlace my boots. Still clothed, I laid back and stared at a crack that ran from one side of the ceiling to the other. The crack branched off into two tributaries that continued down the wall and around the window overlooking the main street of town. I closed my eyes while wondering what pattern of fly might take the trout that lingered there.

Startled by the shrillness of the alarm, I stretched an arm toward the bed stand and silenced the source of my discomfort. I stumbled into the shower, where cold water washed away the fog of the previous evening. I was due to meet Petey at Fogerty's by ten. Dressing quickly, I looked back at the bed stand. It was already ten-twenty.

I grabbed a shirt from a peg beside the door and rushed down the stairs. Squinting into the sunlit street, I stopped to light a cigarette. A few doors down, I looked up at the marquee of the town's movie theater and made a note to ask Thelma Louise if she wanted to see the latest Spiderman flick. I say "latest", but invariably films will play for months in the theaters downstate before making their way to our town.

After stopping at the diner to fill my cooler with lunch, I walked past the post office and dropped in at the sports store to firm up the deal for the three-dozen flies. Trotting down the steps of the shop, I said hello to Doc Woodward. When he was not on a stream or out on a lake, the retired physician spent much of his day walking up and down Main Street, stopping to chat with one or another of his former patients—just about anyone living in town over the last sixty years.

I found Petey seated on the curb between Fogerty's office and the single bay where the old mechanic spent much of his life resuscitating aging trucks and cars for those of us unable to purchase a new vehicle.

"He's pissed," whispered Daniel Fogerty, who had walked outside when he saw me stride past the pumps.

"Hey Pete, you ready to go?" I called.

"You're late." Petey's eyes were fixed on the pavement.

"He kept asking me the time." The old mechanic wiped his hands with a greasy rag he pulled from the back pocket of his greasy overalls. "I told him you'd be coming, but you know how he gets."

I knew.

I walked over to Petey. "It's a beautiful day to be out on the lake."

"You're late," he again grumbled, his eyes still on the macadam.

"Look, the Rangeley's on the trailer and the trailer's hooked to my truck." I pointed to the rig parked on the street beside the station.

Petey's arms were crossed against his chest. He refused to look up. I flipped my cigarette to the ground, using the tip of a work boot to crush it out. I sat down next to him on the curb.

"I've got a couple of cans of vanilla coke in the cooler." I poked a finger into Petey's side. "Whatdya say?"

He said nothing.

"And a Three Musketeers Bar." I poked him again.

Although he tried hard not to show interest, a smile crept across his face.

"Can I hold the rod when we're in the boat?" he asked.

"Sure," I said.

"And can we stop for ice cream when we're done?"

"Don't see why not."

Petey took my hand when I rose. Pulling him to his feet, we walked out of the station's lot and onto the street where I'd parked my rig the previous night.

Ten minutes later, I turned off the blacktop and onto the Morton Cutoff Road. We had the windows down and could hear the familiar sound of the aluminum trailer clanking behind us. The morning air was crisp, although the sun promised to warm things up. Turning onto Lincoln Pond Road, we bumped along for a mile or so before crossing over the wooden bridge that spans the Cupsuptic River. I turned again, this time onto the Green Top logging road, where a few moments later, we stopped for a ruffed grouse. The hen clucked as she stutter-stepped across the road.

"Grousey!" cheered Petey from the open window.

Around the next bend, we stopped for a logging crew that blocked our progress. On one side of the road a guy wearing a sap-stained T-shirt with a crimson maple leaf splashed across the chest sat inside the compartment of a knuckleboom—a machine that consists of a long mechanical arm with a metal claw at the end of it. The man worked the claw so as to grab a tree and feed it through a cylinder that removed any remaining branches. Afterward, the long boom swung the limbless tree toward a huge circular saw called a slasher.

A second fellow sat inside another machine. Its claw grasped a number of the logs previously cut to size by the slasher. The long arm of the second knuckleboom extended across the road where it deposited a fistful of timber onto the bed of an eighteen-wheeler.

When they saw us pull up, the two loggers swung their booms to either side of the road. Petey waved as the men suspended their operation. The guy with the maple leaf tee waved back. His wide smile revealed two missing teeth.

Not long after that, we turned onto the Camp Ten Bridge Road. As I drove over the four planks of wood that span Twin Brook, Petey turned to ask if we were there yet. I told him almost, while pulling out the ashtray from the dash and crushing my cigarette inside. A few minutes later, I backed the trailer down a dirt-and-gravel boat ramp located on the east side of The Magalloway River above Aziscohos Lake.

I've fished most of the ponds throughout the Rangeley Lakes Region, many shown to me by my grand and his brother. Gilroy and I prefer paddling a canoe on such smaller water, but on bigger lakes we depend upon my Rangeley Boat.

Although thirteen miles long, Aziscohos Lake is never so wide as to be unable to see the far shoreline. Even so, when the wind picks up, as it can do with little notice, a sturdy craft like the Rangeley is needed to fight through the waves and avoid being swamped.

The hardwood trees along the river had turned scarlet, gold, and orange. By the time I backed my rig into the water, the temperature had climbed into the seventies. A few soft clouds floated through a powder blue sky. Although beautiful, I would have been happy with a dank, dark morning preceded by three days of steady rain—the kind of morning preferred by turkeys, ducks, fish, and fishermen.

Petey cried, "Geronimo!" when the Rangeley slid off the trailer. While I transferred our gear from the bed of the truck, he picked up a stone and attempted to skip it across the water's surface. After stringing two rods for trolling, I turned to find him weaving along the shoreline in pursuit of a swallowtail.

When he returned, Petey pointed to a brace of cedar waxwings perched in the top branches of a popple.

"Waxy wings!" he called, that cheerful smile splashed across his face.

I helped him into the bow of the Rangeley, after adjusting a life preserver around his shoulders. Wading up to my calves, I pushed the boat out a few feet before hopping into the stern. The outboard started on the second pull, and I steered the wooden boat past the demarcation line that marked the upper river where only fly fishing is permitted. A few moments later we motored into the lake where we could troll.

Although a bit hazy on the history, I seem to remember Harold saying that Aziscohos Lake was formed sometime in the early nineteen hundreds when the dam above what is now Route 16 was constructed of concrete. This caused the river to flood the valley all the way up to the Camp Ten Bridge. Although the cold water releases from under the dam allow me to guide my sports over the tailwater fishery that developed in the lower portion of the river, I'd come to feel most at home above the gates located a number of miles north of the Camp Ten Bridge, where the Big and Little Magalloway Rivers continue to flow pretty much as they have since before John Danforth sought to make a living hunting and trapping.

Before handing the rod to Petey, I guided a thirty-foot-long monofilament leader into the water, followed by an additional sixty feet of sinking fly line. I did the same with the second trolling rod. After sliding the butt end of my rod into a metal holder secured against the boat's gunwale, I steered the Rangeley down the western side of the lake.

While most anglers use radar devices to locate fish and down riggers to bring their elaborate rigs to the exact depth where fish can be found, I've never varied from the simple techniques Harold and Angus taught me. They used sinking lines rather than downriggers to obtain the proper depth, while preferring hand tied streamers to metal lures and boats like my wooden Rangeley and its small outboard instead of fiberglass craft, with their larger engines able to streak up and down the length of the lake. Trolling requires knowledge of the lakes and the habits of the fish that live in them. In spring, big salmon and brook trout gravitate toward the surface where schools of smelt congregate after ice-out.

A floating fly line with the right streamer is all that I need to take fish until the water warms. As summer progresses, smelt seek colder water, swimming deeper and deeper. In the fall, as the water temperature grows cooler, they once again rise toward the surface. It's simple enough. Find the smelt and you'll find the salmon.

I steered into a cove and around an island opposite Beaver Den Camps. Tom Rider knelt at the end of his dock. He was helping a young woman into a kayak.

As I scanned the tin roofs of the small cabins set on either side of the main lodge, an overwhelming sense of melancholy swept over me. For a moment, I once again stood between Gilroy and Thelma Louise, while we listened to the shouts of men rise above the helpless sobs of Gilroy's mother.

"You gotta sit down!" I called out angrily when Petey stood up, his arm extended, a finger pointing to a line of spruce along the opposite shoreline.

After doing as I asked, he stared down at his sneakers. "Just wanted you to see the herrings," he whispered.

The bad memory had soured my mood, but I shouldn't have taken it out on Petey.

"Herons," I gently corrected him. Looking toward the tree line, I saw a number of great blue herons. The large, gray birds sat precariously on the very tops of the spruce trees.

I took a zigzag course down the lake in the hope it would provide action to the streamers trailing along either side of the boat.

Looking down at my watch, I realized that we had been on the water for a little over an hour. I told Petey to reel in his line while I did the same with mine. Deciding to switch to a darker pattern called a Black-nosed Dace, I snipped off the Gray Ghost streamers that had failed to produce a strike and once again let our lines drop to the bottom of the lake before proceeding forward. During the next two hours, my mood improved. I broke out a bag of potato chips and popped open cans of vanilla coke.

We took three shorts—salmon, no more than fourteen inches long—but that didn't lessen Petey's excitement. Each time one of our rods bent forward he screamed Geronimo! Once, while bending over the boat's gunwale to watch me detach the hook from the jaw of a fish, he nearly fell overboard, saved from a dunking when I grabbed his shirttail.

We saw only three other boats while working our way down the lake. Two were fire engine red kayaks similar to the one Tom Rider's sport had paddled away from his dock, the third an aluminum boat about the same size as the Rangeley. I never took to kayaks. Over the last few years they had become as plentiful on our lakes as black flies. Unlike a canoe, it takes little skill to paddle a kayak across still water. Gilroy hated the idea that anyone with enough money to purchase one could have access to wild waters he thought of as his own.

Steering into a quiet cove, I cut the engine while drawing Petey's attention to a moose that was standing up to her belly in the shadows cast by the tightly packed conifer forest that grew down to the shoreline. The big cow's head remained submerged under the water. Long strands of green vegetation hung from the sides of her bulbous mouth when the female looked in our direction. As we floated closer, the enormous animal lumbered toward the trees, rising out of the water and slipping noisily into the wood.

A half an hour later, I beached the Rangeley on a sandy shore. Grabbing the cooler from the bow of the boat, I handed Petey a peanut butter and jelly sandwich. After unwrapping an Italian sub, I twisted off the caps on two more vanilla cokes.

Petey had pulled off his sneakers and socks. After lunch, I helped turn up the bottom of his overalls so that he could walk along the edge of the water and then unwrapped a Snickers Bar, handing it to him before he tramped down the waterline in search of treasure.

Seated on the sandy shore, I closed my eyes as the sunshine washed over me. In some ways, the region hadn't changed since I was a kid—in others it had. Once known only by anglers interested in catching a trophy brook trout and hunters hoping to bag their limit of ruffed grouse, a moose, or black bear, Beaver Den Camps had become family-friendly. It was now an "eco-destination" resort, adding hikers, birders, and kayakers to Tom Rider's clientele. Hell, it wasn't that long ago that Tom would turn out the lights at ten each night to save on gas. That was before the camp owner installed a propane generator with a satellite dish that provided 24/7 access to the Internet and the use of the lodge's flat screen TV. Is that progress? And if so, is it a good thing? I've asked myself that question more than once. I'm still not sure of the answer.

A few of the guides I know are pretty old. Like Fogerty, they speak of a time "before the changes," and of people "from away." I sometimes catch myself using the same terms. I may no longer get along with my great-uncle, but I respect his appreciation for the traditions handed down through the generations, like preserving my Rangeley Boat. I sometimes think that I've more in common with the town's older farts—guys like Angus, Doc Woodward, and old man Fogerty, than I do with guys my own age.

Fogerty never tires of talking about the good old days, which for him were the thirties and forties. He's always complaining about the paper companies' greed. According to him, the forest had been primarily softwood—a mixture of pine, spruce, and balsam that protected the lakes and many of the streams from pollution and overfishing.

The aging mechanic argues that with the rapid change of ownership, the paper companies have less and less connection with the state, which has resulted in more and more intensive cutting. Salmon—and especially brook trout—depend upon clean, cold water for their survival. The forest provides shade along the rivers and insulates the lakes and ponds from siltation. With the politicians in their pockets, the paper companies have their crews logging closer and closer to shorelines, which has created less shade and more erosion, in some cases resulting in the destruction of natural hatcheries required for the continued propagation of the region's game fish.

Fogerty points to a little stream that acted as a natural hatchery for the large brook trout once commonly found in Rangeley Lake. Although attempts were made to restore a portion of the brook to its previous condition, siltation caused by logging along the shoreline filled in the once deep pools. As a result, a hatchery that produced large brook trout is no longer doing so.

Not so long ago, I was surprised to learn of damage to the headwaters of the Cupsuptic River, another natural brook trout hatchery. An older guide working out of Easie sounded the alarm. I forget his name, but he was the guy Gilroy and I saw that afternoon at Tom Rider's lodge, the guy working on the outboard with Rusty Miller—the I-talian. I sometimes see him in town walking with a ragged old dog, one with a scar down the side of his head. Anyway, he was the guy who first spread the word that someone was dredging the river for gold. A local cop was implicated in the illegal activity that took a number of years to clean up.

Doc Woodward likes to remind anyone who'll listen that in the eighteen hundreds it took large crews to accomplish what four or five men can now take out of the forest. Back then, loggers used oxen rather than skidders to drag trees to be processed. There were no eighteen-wheel trucks and few roads leading into the dense woodland. Sports had to use their legs to access many of the lakes, rivers, and streams. He'll tell you about the time, only a few winters back, when big logging rigs motored over the ice to take timber from a large island not far above Tom Rider's camps, leaving only a single line of spruce along the shoreline.

Many remember a time when gates, similar to those that continue to protect the Parmachenee Tract, blocked the logging road along the western shore of Aziscohos Lake as well as other stretches of prime water. These have long since been open, allowing the public easier access. Just last year, the paper company forged a new logging road along the eastern side of Aziscohos Lake. Those owning camps halfway up the thirteen-mile impoundment can now reach the upper river in half the time it once took.

But it's not just big business that's to blame. The warden who dragged

Gilroy and I up to my great-uncle's cabin grumbles about lax fishing regulations that, in his opinion, have resulted in a depletion of the region's fishery. But I don't need a warden to tell me what I can see for myself. Smelt replaced the blueback trout as the principal food of the region's brook trout. Without a healthy smelt population, the trout and salmon can no longer flourish, yet our local tradition of scooping bucketfuls of smelt from feeder streams continues without abatement.

Many of the guys my age won't admit it, but technology hasn't helped. Online forums explode whenever a run of fish come up the river or a new hatch of insects presents itself. Back in Fogerty's day, anglers didn't have the benefit of cell phones to spread the word or GPS to find those honey holes. Then there are the magazine articles published from time to time like the one Diana Russo read. One guy, I think he has a camp on Aziscohos Lake, even writes novels about the region.

It's funny though, most of us who complain are more than willing to take the money sports pay at the gas pump, in the stores around town, or to those of us who guide them. I mean, the better a guide does his job, the more fish are caught; and the more fish that are caught, the more sports come to the region.

But not Gilroy. Donnie lives by his own code. If it were up to him, only us locals would be allowed to fish the waters around town. That's one of the reasons he pulls down the signs along the logging roads. When we were kids, you had to learn your way around the dirt-and-gravel roads on your own. Over the last ten years, signs identifying the names of each logging road have appeared while mile markers now help anglers locate those waters once difficult to find. I understand that the signs and markers shorten the time it takes for wardens and emergency personnel to respond to emergencies, but they also make it easier for those not familiar with the region to navigate what once had been a mysterious web spun by loggers to harvest their product. Signage along Route 16 even designates where to pull off to fish or put in a boat. At first, I helped Gilroy pull them down, but with just about everyone having GPS in their vehicles, it seemed like a losing battle. Instead, I just try not to think about it.

More than any other angler I know, my great-uncle keeps to the old ways. Angus still fishes with flies first tied in Scotland. He consults that book passed down to him from his mother's father to tie his flies and casts a cane rod that is nearly as old as he is. Yet, he never complains about the changes like so many of the other guys. Even so, I have to agree with Fogerty, who if he had his druthers, would wish away *Google Maps* and every last GPS gadget, smartphone, and online forum.

"Harry, look." Petey was pointing toward a boat that had dropped anchor in a cove across the lake. Its chrome fittings sparkled in the sunlight.

Digging out binoculars from my pack, I glassed the opposite shoreline. When the Bayliner came into focus, I watched a woman about my age dive into the lake. A few moments later she climbed up a ladder fixed to the boat's stern. A guy holding a beer reached down to give her a hand, while another fiddled at the boat's controls. I swept the glasses over a second woman lying on her back across a set of red-and-white cushions. Her tanned skin glistened under the sun.

Sliding the glasses back into my pack, I wondered why it was that every motorboat of its type had at least one bikini-clad girl lying in the bow? I imagined the advertisement:

For Sale. Eighteen-foot Bayliner, one-hundred-and-twenty-horsepower engine with Bimini top. Slightly used twenty-something included at no additional charge. Comes with blonde hair and perfect proportions. Your choice of black or white bikini.

· *Chapter Twenty* ·

"I'LL GO." RALPH PETERSON SAT UP. IT TOOK A MOMENT TO REMEMBER that he was not in his own bed. He had felt a bit claustrophobic since their arrival at the tiny cabin a few days earlier. That sense of unease had returned as Ralph searched the darkness for the flannel robe his father-in-law had lent him for the weekend. A dog began barking. He realized it was the same sound that had awakened him from an uneasy sleep. His wife rolled onto her back. She murmured something Ralph didn't understand. Clawing sleep from his eyes, Ralph's bare feet touched down upon the cold floorboards.

The barking had stopped. He stood in the dark, hoping to slip back under the heavy wool blanket that had kept him warm throughout the cold night. Listening until the dog started up again, Ralph stooped down and slid on a pair of expensive leather slippers, the ones Shelly had presented to him last winter. It had been Christmas morning, the first in their new home, the children flying in to spend the holiday with them.

It took a few moments to locate the red-and-black-checkered garment hanging from a spruce notch beside the bureau—the only other furniture in the small bedroom. Although muffled, the barking persisted as he wrapped the frayed belt of the plaid robe around his waist. Hard to believe it could be so cold this early in October. Wisps of sleep slipped past as Ralph stared down at the battery-operated clock he had remembered to pack.

"Jesus," the former insurance executive muttered. It was ten minutes to six. Ralph hadn't been up that early since before he'd retired.

Staggering out into the main room of the cabin, he parted the bathrobe and slid a hand down his pajama bottom. Slipping his fingers under a pair of white boxers, he scratched his testicles.

The barking grew more intense as Ralph fumbled with the latch. His father-in-law's Brittany spaniel sprang into the cabin when he swung open the door.

"Damn mutt," Ralph growled.

The Brittany's stubby tail wagged back and forth as the young dog looked up at the man through amber eyes bright with intelligence that Ralph did not appreciate. The man stood, staring warily down at the animal. The Brittany's orange-and-white coat glistened with dew. Burrs were imbedded in its fur. Ralph assumed it wanted something, but had no idea what that could be.

Ralph's mother would not permit pets in the house, explaining to her children that dogs were filthy animals containing lice and fleas. Although Shelly grew up with dogs and cats, she had bent to her husband's will, raising their children in a suburban home without any animals.

Ralph padded over to a table that had been painted forest-green and pulled out a chair. The cabin consisted of a single ten-by-twenty-foot rect-angular room flanked by two bedrooms, each no bigger than the walk-in closet Shelly had insisted upon when they built their retirement home. The dog remained seated beside the door while Ralph stared across the room. At the far end, a large cooking stove stood beside a kitchen count-er. Cabinets flanked a porcelain sink and an ancient Servel refrigerator leaned against the opposite wall. He remembered his father-in-law ex-plaining that the stove and fridge were powered by propane. Only a few hundred feet from the front door of the cabin, the lake provided water.

Against the wall, across from the shiny green table where he sat, a bureau contained linens and towels while an old sofa with ornate wood-en arms and tired green cushions dominated another wall. Ralph still found it hard to believe that after all these years his wife's father had failed to install indoor plumbing.

The young dog had been his father-in-law's constant companion since Shelly's mother died a few years back. The Brittany now walked toward the table, stared up at Ralph, and then circled back to the door while looking over her shoulder. Ignoring the animal, Ralph walked toward the cast-iron stove that squatted in the near corner of the room. He thought about rekindling the fire that died out during the night, but wasn't sure how. The dog began to whine.

Maybe she's got to take a shit, Ralph thought.

Sighing, he shuffled back through the kitchen and opened the door.

While Ralph urinated off the side of the porch, the dog raced down the steps. While she waited in the grass, her docked tail continued to wag. The man strained to see the lake, but a dense fog made that impossible. Ralph shivered. At home, he never paid much attention to the temperature. Too cold and he turned up the heat; too hot, the air conditioner. His Lexus was always warm, parked overnight in the attached garage. Why Shelly had insisted on dragging him up to the old man's cabin was beyond him.

The dog began to once more bark, each time running a few feet up the grassy drive beside the cabin and then back toward Ralph. Suddenly, a feeling of dread drained away the last remnants of sleep. It wasn't the claustrophobic feeling Ralph had experienced since arriving at the cabin, but the realization of what the dog was trying to tell him.

He remembered slipping under the covers the previous evening, lying under the wool blanket while Shelly sat in the kitchen with her father. He'd left the two of them sipping coffee from mismatched mugs. While lying in bed, Ralph had overheard the old man tell his daughter that he'd be up early, asking if she thought he, Ralph, would be interested in hunting for partridge. Ralph recalled Shelly's laugh. How, afterward, she'd tried to talk her elderly father out of going alone.

"Sally'll be with me," he had said with that annoying chuckle of his. At that point, Ralph had grown bored with the conversation. Turning to the wall in the darkened bedroom, his thoughts, like a kaleidoscope tumbling one after the other, settled on the twosome scheduled for that Monday morning with Roy Wilkinson.

Ignoring the dog's continued barking, Ralph turned and walked back inside the cabin. He wondered how hard it would be to sell the run-down shack and what they might get for it.

Now, I don't know if any of that is true. To be honest, I kinda pieced it together, at least in my imagination. I first learned of Sid Phelps' death the following spring, when my great-uncle asked if I would accompany him to the old man's cabin. You see, Angus had done work for Sid, the two becoming friends over many years. I was fourteen and didn't hesitate when my great-uncle asked me to go with him. Back then I'd follow the guy anywhere. It always seemed to end in one interesting adventure or another. This time was no exception.

I can remember sitting at the wheel of the pickup Angus borrowed from Daniel Fogerty.

"It's four cabins up the Heights road," the old man had said as I turned off the Lincoln Pond logging road and onto the ALCA Heights road. ALCA was short for Aziscohos Lake Campers Association. The paper company had a road crew out grading the Morton Cutoff Road, which forced us to take Route 16 until Angus turned right at the sign for the Black Brook Cove Campgrounds. Once on the Lincoln Pond logging road, he suddenly braked and asked if I wanted to drive.

"Really?" I'd never taken the wheel before.

"Aye, bit no tellin' yer maw or da," he warned.

After losing his wife, Angus had become more withdrawn. He sold the house in town and spent most of his time at the cabin beside Parmachenee Lake. I hadn't seen him in a while and he looked older if that was even possible.

The empty aluminum trailer he towed behind the borrowed vehicle clanged as we crossed over the wooden planks that spanned the narrow width of Lincoln Brook. I asked why we needed a trailer, but with a twinkle in his eye, the old man simply replied, "Patience, laddie."

As we crossed the little rivulet, I looked down at the current that ran high with snowmelt. Although the leaves on maples and oaks had begun to bud out, the branches of the aspens remained bare. The sun was strong as it slipped past the ridgeline of Big Buck Mountain. The temperature had fallen into the forties overnight, but was slowly rising as the morning progressed. The big fish had followed the smelt up the river more or less on time that year, and I was hoping Angus might suggest that we take an hour or so to cast a line before heading back to town.

It was the third week in May—that first day of spring when the sun is warm enough to roll up your sleeves. The kind of day when young men drive their cars with the windows open and radios turned up loud; a day when young women pull out their short skirts. But for sportsmen it was the beginning of the new fishing season.

The gears of the old truck grinded when I attempted to downshift. The vehicle struggled up a hill, the right front tire dipping into a pothole filled with water. A few moments later, I turned down the drive that led to Sid Phelps' camp.

"Sorry for yer loss," Angus muttered to Shelly Peterson. I nodded while averting my eyes.

"He lived to ninety-three." The inflection in her voice seemed to imply that ninety-three years had been more than enough time to get the job done. I had the feeling that Angus wasn't so sure, but he said nothing.

Shelly told my great-uncle that when her husband relayed what he suspected, she quickly dressed and called the warden's service on her cell phone, which she could only do after driving her Range Rover up the logging road until she was able to get enough bars. Two hours later, a young warden found her father face down near a stand of spruce, the old man's 20 Gauge side-by-side lying on the ground next to him.

As she concluded the story, Sid's Brittany spaniel trotted up from the lake. The dog's tail appeared to wag her entire back end. When I bent forward to scratch the orange patch on the top of the young Brittany's head, she raised her paws to my shoulders, pushing me onto the damp grass.

"Sally!"

We all turned toward the cabin when Ralph Peterson screeched out the dog's name.

"Sorry about that," Shelly's husband had walked down the steps and over to where Angus stood beside his wife. "Damn dog is always underfoot," he said while extending a hand in my great-uncle's direction.

Getting to my feet, I ran down the trail that led to the nearby lake, with the spaniel following at my heels.

After listing the cabin for sale with a local realtor, Shelly had called Angus, who she knew did odd jobs for her father. The two men had hunted and fished together for over thirty years. She had contracted him to haul away what Ralph Peterson referred to as "junk." Over the winter, Angus had driven up the lake on his snow machine to look the place over, agreeing to return in the spring.

The Brittany remained close while I helped my great-uncle haul the old sofa and then the forest-green table onto the bed of the pickup. After removing two mattresses and their frames, we loaded the bedroom bureaus, which were surprisingly heavy, onto the truck. Angus could see that they were well-crafted pieces of furniture and was surprised that the Peterson's had no interest in keeping them. Ralph wanted us to take the cast-iron stove, but Angus convinced him that it would add to the price of the camp that required the stove for heat even in the summertime.

From the shed behind the cabin, we carried away piping, a number of two-by-fours, and a stack of pine boards left over from the cabin floor.

"Ye sure yi'll want me tae tak' th' boot?" Angus asked Shelly, who had walked outside with a pitcher of lemonade. A Rangeley Boat lay upside down on blocks beside the shed. The faded gray paint was peeling. Moss grew in spots along the upturned hull. In places, the seams had expanded enough so you could see the ground underneath. Angus pulled a small knife from the pocket of his green work pants. Unfolding it, he poked the wood that was spongy in spots. He explained to Sid's daughter that the Rangeley, although in pretty bad shape, could still fetch a nice price. Shelly said that neither she nor her husband had the time for such a project and would be glad if he would haul it away.

After we secured the weather-weary craft to the trailer, I asked Angus what would happen to Sally. He said he didn't know. When I asked if we could take her with us, he frowned.

"Yer da wouldn't lik' it," he said while the dog sat in the grass between us as if listening to her fate.

While Ralph Peterson settled up with my great-uncle, I heard Angus ask about the dog.

"Sally?" The other man snorted.

After talking it over with his wife, Peterson told my uncle that Sally was his.

I spent more time with Angus during the next twelve months than I had since his wife died. All throughout that fishing season, we worked on the Rangeley. Angus replaced the planks that had dry rot. After corking and sanding the cedar hull of the sixteen-foot boat, we gave it two coats of paint. During that time, Sally remained by my great-uncle's side, eager to play whenever I arrived at the cabin by the lake. During the fall, the three of us hunted grouse, the Brittany proving to be a fine bird dog.

On a warm afternoon in June of the following year, Angus walked around the restored craft as sunlight glistened off its newly painted hull. Although my grand had been laid up with a bad hip from a fall taken while wading the river, he lent his brother the Jeep. With Sally and I in the back seat, my great-uncle double-checked the straps securing the wooden boat to the trailer he'd once again borrowed from Fogerty.

Forty minutes later we turned onto the dirt road that passes by Mill Brook and ends at a cement boat ramp in a sheltered cove on Richardson Lake. Sally jumped to the ground when Angus opened the door of the Jeep. She raced along the shoreline with her nose to the ground while I directed my great-uncle as he backed the trailer down the ramp. A few mosquitoes flew out of the nearby forest on a reconnaissance mission, but gave up the chase when we rowed out into the lake.

Wearing a T-shirt and shorts, I sat in the stern of the Rangeley with my legs stretched out. The wooden hull felt good against my bare feet.

Angus had the sleeves of his khaki shirt rolled above his elbows. He gripped the corncob pipe between his teeth while taking the oars. Sally stood in the bow, staring straight ahead.

As the Rangeley cut smoothly through the sun-speckled wavelets, I asked Angus to tell me about the boat's history. I never tired of hearing the story, which he had repeated half-a-dozen times while we repaired and repainted the sturdy craft. Now, between strokes of the oars, Angus explained how the Rangeleys were originally called Indian Rock boats after a landmark located on the Kennebago River near the Oquossoc Angling Association's lodge.

"Th' foremost boots had lap-streaked hulls. They wur langer than ours, measuring more than sixteen feet 'n' pointed at baith ends. Unlike th' featherlight craft bult in th' Adirondacks, th' Rangeleys wur heavy in order tae withstand th' big water 'n' rough waither that ye know kin build quickly oot 'ere." Angus stopped rowing and swept his hand out over the wide expanse of the lake.

After a half an hour or so, I asked if I could have a turn at the oars. The two of us traded places on the rounded milk-stool seats that my great-uncle installed to match the type once used on older models of the boat.

When a branch floated past, the Brittany raced across our laps, hanging off the stern in an effort to grab it. My great-uncle pulled a biscuit from his pocket, calling to Sally, who sat at his command. While the dog munched on the treat, Angus dragged a Styrofoam cooler between his legs. Twisting off the caps on two bottles of pop, he handed one to me. After taking a long pull, he continued the story.

"Sometime in th' nineteen twenties, th' Barrett brothers opened a shop in toun 'n' th' name quickly became synonymous wi' th' Rangeley. Th' square stern oan thair boot wis a development tae accommodate th' outboard that became popular in th' nineteen thirties."

Although knowing the answer, I nevertheless asked why so few of the boats remained on the water.

"It takes a lot o' wirk tae maintain a Rangeley. Efter World War

II, aluminum 'n' fiberglass made boots virtually maintenance-free. Thay soon replaced th' wooden craft. By then, Herb Ellis wis building Rangeleys, usin' th' Barrett design. This 'ere is one of Ellis' boots." He clanked his empty pop bottle against the gunwale.

I was caught by surprise, when later that afternoon, Angus offered to sell me the boat for three hundred dollars, which was less than the old man spent in restoring it and not nearly what it was worth. That summer I supplemented my income bussing tables at the Red Onion by working at Fogerty's. Throughout the fall, winter, and the following spring, I continued working at the garage each day after school to earn enough money to call the boat my own.

It would be another few years before I could afford to purchase a six-horse-power Johnson, the outboard that continues to power the Rangeley to this day. I bought the engine used from Fogerty, who threw in a trailer at no extra charge.

The following winter Sally passed on. Although still young, she had been growing thin, eventually refusing to eat. When Angus brought the dog into Easie, the veterinarian there said she had cancer. For the second time, the disease stole away someone the old man had dearly loved.

· *Chapter Twenty-One* ·

"CAN WE GET ICE CREAM NOW?" PETEY ASKED. WE WERE DRIVING along the east side of the lake. The tires rumbled over the dirt road's washboard surface. Dust billowed up behind us. With the windows open, we could hear the trailer carrying the Rangeley Boat clanging behind my truck.

"Sure," I answered.

Instead of turning left and following the Camp Ten Bridge Road toward Green Top Mountain, I took the new road that would bring us to the bottom of the lake, where we could buy an ice cream cone at the Black Brook Cove Campground's General Store. On the radio, Guy Clark sang about cold dog soup and rainbow pie. Outside, the cloud of dust rose higher as I pressed down on the accelerator. My speed bumped thirty miles an hour, which is about as fast as one can go while towing a trailer carrying a wooden boat on a logging road.

I slowed as we approached Black Brook Cove Campground. A number of vehicles were stopped along my side of the dirt road. A Ford Expedition with Massachusetts plates hunkered down on the other side. Two Yamaha Wave Runners sat on a trailer attached to the back of the shiny black Ford. A truck and another SUV were parked nearby. Both had the logo of the Maine Department of Inland Fisheries and Wildlife painted on the doors.

A warden stood beside the trailer containing the two jet skis. Two men, who looked to be about my age leaned against the Ford. They wore expensive wraparound sunglasses, T-shirts, and flip-flops. Baggy bathing suits hung down past their knees.

I recognized the warden standing beside the trailer. He had been the backup quarterback for the football team the year I began high school. I watched him take pictures of the personal watercraft that glittered under the dappled sunlight.

A second game warden motioned for me to stop behind the other vehicles parked along the side of the road. Following his instructions, I pulled in back of a four-door Jeep Cherokee, where a third warden was asking the driver to exit his vehicle. Farther down the road a fourth warden stood with his legs parted, arms folded across his chest. He wore mirrored sunglasses that masked his eyes.

All but one of the four men wore Kevlar vests over olive shirts. A sergeant's bars were stitched on the sleeve of the guy who was speaking with the driver of the Cherokee. The warden taking photographs was the exception. He wore a green T-shirt with the words GAME WARDEN stenciled in gold across the back. All four sported olive baseball caps with the Fish-and-Game insignia on the front. None were smiling.

The sergeant took a while interrogating the Jeep's driver. He eventually allowed him back into his vehicle. After waving the Cherokee forward, he walked in our direction. Placing his hand on the roof of my truck, the warden scanned the inside of the cab. I didn't recognize him.

"Nice afternoon to be out on the lake." His eyes moved around the truck's interior.

He was older than his subordinate across the road. His face and hands were tan from the sun and leathery from spending time out of doors. Creases like furrows on a newly plowed field ran across his forehead.

"Harry let me fish." Petey smiled broadly.

I turned off the radio.

"That right?" The sergeant shifted his eyes toward Petey, but quickly moved them back in my direction when I leaned over to open the glove compartment. He stepped back. His hand slid toward the weapon holstered on his side. He appeared nervous.

"Just getting my license." I quickly pulled out my identification.

The warden moved back to the window. "How did ya do out there?" he asked.

"Released a few shorts." Trying to sound casual, I felt guilty even though we hadn't done anything wrong.

The sergeant glanced back toward the bed of the pickup and then the rig.

"A restored Rangeley. You don't see many of those these days."

"Suppose not." I could feel my anger build. If the dumb ass had a problem with me why didn't he just come out and say so.

"You carrying any firearms?"

"Firearms? No. No firearms, just two old trolling rods." I pointed to the fly rods held by Velcro ties under the Rangeley's gunwales.

"Mind if I check for myself?" The warden walked around the back of the truck. He eyeballed the inside of the Rangeley as he crossed behind the trailer and walked up the other side. He stopped beside the open window, where Petey grinned down at him.

"Would you mind stepping outside?" the sergeant asked as the warden wearing the T-shirt crossed the road.

"What's this all about, Ronnie?" I asked the younger of the two men. We'd shared beers at Sparky's, even fished together on a few occasions. Once, over a year ago, I'd dropped off a baker's dozen of flies at his trailer that was located in a grove of birch trees alongside Route 16. Word was, he was dating a girl who spent more time in New York City than she did in Maine.

Ronnie Adams pointed toward the two men, who milled around the SUV on the other side of the road. One walked around in circles. He had his arm raised and was unsuccessfully attempting to obtain enough bars to call out on his phone.

"Someone took issue with those gentlemen exercising their constitutional right to the pursuit of happiness."

I frowned, not certain what he meant.

"Put a few bullet holes in their toys," the older warden growled.

I did my best to suppress a smile. If there was anything I hated more than kayaks and Bayliners, it was jet skis.

Like most of us living above beyond, I knew the younger warden had no love for the shallow-draft watercraft that could speed through places other boats like mine could not reach. I'd never seen one on Aziscohos Lake, but had witnessed them on the larger lakes. I'd seen their riders scare loons from their nests. They'd harass the birds by circling around them as the craft sprayed water ten feet into the air. I'd read that Jet skis spew twice as much pollutant as my six-horse-power outboard and knew from experience that their annoying roar is also much louder. You can hear the sound reverberating up and down the water for minutes after one speeds by. Petitions have been signed and legislation proposed to keep them off the semi-wild lakes of the region, but each time the boat lobby triumphs.

"Too bad for them," I mumbled.

"One of those guys almost drowned, another was sent to the hospital, may have broken his shoulder when he hit the water." The sergeant did not hide his annoyance with my attitude.

Screw you, I thought, but grunted, "Like I said, tough luck."

"You wouldn't know anything about it?" The older warden wasn't letting up.

I turned toward the warden who I knew. "C'mon Ronnie, I may not like the assholes who ride those things, but I'm not about to shoot one of them. Besides, I don't pack heat when I'm out fishing." I chuckled trying to lighten the mood.

"It's not a laughing matter," Adams' superior snapped. "We have a guy in the hospital. Lucky he didn't end up in the morgue," he continued.

"Can we get ice cream now?" Petey looked over at me.

"What's with him?" the older warden asked.

"He's okay, Sarge." Ronnie replied before I could answer.

The third warden walked up the road as they were talking.

"Mind if we check the inside of your truck?" the sergeant asked.

"Knock yourselves out," I replied, feeling my anger swell.

While Petey and I stood outside, the sergeant searched the cab. The other wardens checked the inside of the boat. One of them opened the cooler to look inside.

"You seen Gilroy today?" Ronnie Adams asked when they had finished.

I knew Gilroy had been on law enforcement's radar since high school. "No," I lied.

"Well if you do, tell 'im we'd like to talk. Better he comes to us rather than the other way 'round." Opening the door of my truck, Ronnie motioned for me to get back inside.

"You don't really think—?" Before I could complete my sentence, another truck barreled down the road, the wardens moving away and the sergeant putting out a hand.

A few minutes later I was turning left onto the blacktop. After slowing at the stop sign beside the wooden bear outside the town of Easie, I continued into Rangeley and didn't stop until we pulled in front of the Pine Tree Frosty. After buying Petey a strawberry cone with sprinkles, I drove back up the street and into Fogerty's Garage.

"You hear 'bout Gilroy?" The station's owner had walked out of the repair bay when I swung the truck beside the pumps.

One thing about living in a small town—news travels fast.

"Harry bought me ice cream." Petey walked over to where he had left Rolling Thunder leaning against the outside wall of Fogerty's little office. A river of ice cream flowed down the outside of the cone, and when Petey changed hands a large dollop splattered on the ground.

"Cops want to talk to him," Fogerty continued. "Seems someone took a few potshots at a couple of kids. They was racing around on those infernal jet skis." He plucked a cigarette from the corner of his mouth and flipped it toward the sidewalk.

I stepped out of the truck. "Why do they think it was Gilroy?"

He removed the cap from the Ford's gas tank and slid the nozzle inside. "Don't know what they think. Just know they weren't messin' 'round when they came by here earlier this afternoon."

After adding ten dollars' worth of gas, Fogerty screwed the cap back onto the tank and replaced the nozzle on the side of the pump.

"When was this?" I asked.

The old man stuffed the ten I gave him into the pocket of his overalls.

"'Bout an hour ago," he said.

"So, what did you tell them?"

"Well, Donnie had been in here about twenty minutes before the cops." Fogerty waited as if he expected me to reply, but when I didn't, he continued.

"He was gassing up that snot-colored Subaru of his when he kinda chuckled. You know that way he's got about laughing to himself as if he knows about something funny, but he ain't gonna let you in on the joke?"

The guy could take forever to get out a simple thought. "Yeah?" I prolonged the word, making it more of a question than an affirmation; my patience wearing as thin as the cirrus clouds that hung high in the sky above us.

"Well, he was talking crazy-like. Tells me about seeing these guys on their wave runners and how you could hear the engines from a mile away and how the only way to get something done is to do it yourself."

"This was when?" I cut him off.

"About two hours ago."

"And you told the cops this?" I pulled off my cap and swept back my hair.

"Of course not. Told 'em I hadn't seen him in days."

Petey had hopped on Rolling Thunder. Holding the remains of the ice cream cone in one hand while grabbing the bicycle's handlebar with the other, he rode toward the gas pumps. I set my cap back down and adjusted its brim before climbing back into the cab of the truck.

"You'll watch Petey Boy?" I asked while turning the key in the ignition.

"Sure. He can hang here until he gets bored and then I'll send him home for dinner. I always call his mother to be sure she's on the lookout for him." Fogerty looked over at Petey, who was riding between the pumps and the office. "Blasted jet skis," he mumbled to himself.

Pulling out of the station, I looked back through the truck's rear view mirror to see Petey on his bike. A thin line of strawberry ice cream trailed behind him in the shape of the number eight.

· *Chapter Twenty-Two* ·

B Y THE TIME I REACHED FIFTEEN, I'D LEARNED TO DRIVE A TRUCK AND had restored a Rangeley Boat. That was also the year I obtained my Junior Maine Guide patch.

I'd managed only a C average by the end of my first year of high school, preferring the books on my great-uncle's shelves to those at school. By then, I'd learned more about fly fishing from Angus and his brother than most men come to know in a lifetime. By my sophomore year, I'd advanced through the technical classics—books like Ray Bergman's *Trout* and Gary LaFontaine's *Caddisflies*.

When not exploring "how to" texts, I scoured our local library for anything written about the region. After reading Graydon Hillyard's book about Carrie Stevens, I found *Chasing Danforth*, a book written by Robert Cook about the guy who may have spent time in the little cave Gilroy and I discovered when we were younger. After that, I checked out Stephen Cole's *The Rangeley and Its Region*, sometimes walking down Lake Street after school, reading until dark on a bench that overlooks Rangeley Lake.

Books written in another century by writers from a different country also captured my imagination, although they sometimes left me confused. I found it hard to believe that into the early part of the nineteen hundreds two Englishmen waged an intellectual battle over whether fishing with nymphs should be an accepted practice. But then, I remembered what my great-uncle had said about fishing being no different than politics, religion, or any other human endeavor. Donnie said the controversy reminded him of the blunt versus bong debate.

I was surprised to learn that sometime during the nineteen fifties, Frank Sawyer, an Englishman who wrote a book entitled *Nymphs and The Trout*, created a pattern called the pheasant-tail nymph that Gilroy and I cast when dredging the deeper pools of the Magalloway River.

On one of my birthdays—it was during my teens, but I can't remember which one—Angus presented me with his copy of *Where the Bright Waters Meet*, a memoir written by Harry Plunket Greene. My great-uncle was of the opinion that the book says all there is to say about the fragility of our rivers, lakes, and ponds.

If not fishing, or when not reading, I'd often deconstruct one of Angus's flies, carefully stripping away the grouse collars, rabbit or mole fur, and the different color silk to better understand how each imitation was put together. On one particular afternoon, I sat at the table with the short legs as a steady rain beat against the tin roof of the old man's cabin. Harold hadn't been feeling well and had been spending less time at his brother's camp. My great-uncle was lazing around, waiting for the weather to break so we could take the Rangeley out on the lake. I was pulling apart two Gold-ribbed Hare's Ears, one tied by Angus and the other purchased through a fishing catalogue. I separated the ingredients of each wet fly into two piles of fur, feathers, tinsel and silk. After finishing, I asked my great-uncle why his fly had been fashioned differently than the store-bought one.

In response, he limped into his bedroom. Angus came back with Edmonds & Lee's *Brook & River Trouting*. Handing it to me, he said, "Oor grand wis tae poor tae purchase this book whin 'twas first published, bit he wrote doon near every word from th' copy he found in th' Lord's library, while adding his observations abit flies, fish, and th' water he wis hired tae maintain." Angus pointed to the leather-bound book he often consulted when tying his flies. "That wis back whin I wis a wee laddie."

He liked to say that the soft-hackled patterns fashioned by his grand and passed down to him looked "fishy." Growing older, I found myself gravitating toward modern patterns that more closely imitated the aquatic insects, which form part of the trout's diet in the streams of western Maine. I eventually abandoned the impressionistic flies preferred by the tiny man with the sharp nose. Even so, I had to admit that my great-uncle continued to outfish everyone else on the water.

For a good portion of this time, my mother was lost, periodically finding a trail back through the darkness, only to once again lose her way. My father spent more time at the bank, if that was possible, as if unwilling to acknowledge his wife's slow descent into depression. When at home, he remained shut in his study as my mother slid farther and farther down the rabbit hole.

My grand had been fond of saying that my mother's eyes were the color of emeralds. Harold and Emily's daughter had been a beauty. As an adult, her raven-black hair fell out of the sides of a straw hat that she liked to wear when working the gardens that brought her so much joy. The hat's wide brim sheltered her alabastrine features from the sun.

Clementine Ferguson was a happy child who enjoyed the forest. She often accompanied her father and his brother on their frequent visits to the surrounding lakes and streams. There were times, however, when for no apparent reason, she would withdraw into herself, sometimes for days at a time. Her mother would say that there was nothing to do when the sadness came upon her daughter.

My grand would tell me that as a child, my mother always had a pencil in her hand. When she started school, her skill as an artist became evident. She carried a notebook wherever she went and often sketched her father and uncle while they fished, rowed, or hiked. Clementine was especially talented at capturing the wild nature of the flora and fauna she encountered while traveling with the two men.

My grandmother once explained that her daughter had planned to attend art school. Instead, she married Edward Duncan shortly after graduating from high school. The two had been dating through their senior year. Clementine initially declined Edward's proposal of marriage. It was a decision that upset her mother, but with which my grand agreed.

That spring, my mother had been accepted to the Rhode Island School of Design, but afterward went into an unexpected funk that she could not shake. Clementine was unwilling to leave her room. After missing school for nearly two weeks, Emily and Harold asked Edward to speak with their daughter. When he proposed a second time, Clementine accepted. The two were married shortly after their graduation from high school. Edward took a position at the local bank, where he had worked as a teller the previous summer. Putting aside her acceptance to the prestigious college, Clementine maintained their apartment and later, the home they purchased with the money loaned to them by Edward's mother.

The year after their wedding, my parents announced my impending entrance into the world. Knowing the demands that an infant can make upon a first-time mother, Harold and Emily worried that their daughter's melancholy might return. At first, it seemed their fears were unfounded, but halfway through her eighth month, Clementine refused to leave her bed. Fearing for both mother and baby, the family called the doctor.

After taking the pills prescribed by Doc Woodward, the malaise passed. All was well after my birth. For the next few years, my father devoted his energies to climbing up the bank's corporate ladder, while my mother cared for me. I remember playing in the warm grass while my mother painted pictures of song birds that flew to the feeders she hung from the branches of trees and the birdhouses she nailed to cedar posts around the edges of her newly-planted gardens.

I recall one Monday morning that should have been no different than any other. My mother failed to rise from her bed no matter how I pleaded. As was my father's habit, he had left for the office before the bus arrived to take me to school. No more than six at the time, I can remember being afraid to move, unable to walk toward the front door, where sitting at the wheel of the bus, Greta Hanson waited to transport me to my first-grade class. For a long time, I sat at the kitchen table and listened to the patter of the birds outside the window. Eventually, I summoned the courage to leave the house. Running up the block and around the corner, I knocked on my grandparents' door.

My mother remained in her room for three days, returning to our world after she resumed the medication she had previously flushed down the toilet.

Once, when they didn't know I was listening, my mother described her bouts of depression to my grandmother. She said they began like thunderheads, building slowly until she was engulfed by the blackness. I listened to her explain how she had stopped taking the drugs prescribed by Doc Woodward because they fogged her brain and made her fat, something my mother could not abide.

The most recent storm, the one that swept over her after my great-aunt's death, was more like a hurricane. It ripped at whatever under-pinnings might have remained over the years of intermittent darkness. Only with the help of the pills that she loathed to take was Clementine Ferguson able to return to us, if only for a while.

· *Chapter Twenty-Three* ·

THELMA LOUISE LOOKED UP TO SEE A MAN IN UNIFORM. HE WAS silhouetted in the shock of sunlight that flooded the tavern when the door momentarily opened. She had been stacking longnecks under the bar when the young cop entered and walked directly toward her. The sudden burst of light was extinguished when the door closed. Thelma made out the words Rangeley P.D. printed in big block letters across the front of the officer's baseball cap. The cap's bill failed to hide the scars that rippled down the right side of the man's face.

"Whit," she said as he drew closer.

"T.L.," he replied.

The police officer grunted as he climbed onto an empty stool. It was three in the afternoon, and with the exception of the few vultures stooped over their glasses, the place was empty.

"You seen Donnie?" he asked.

"Not for a few days." Thelma Louise would have given the same answer even if it weren't true.

The wide-screen television was tuned to ESPN. While waiting to learn the latest trouble her friend had gotten himself into, Thelma looked up to find an attractive woman discussing the previous evening's basketball game. *I could do that*, she thought.

"Everyone's out looking for him." The cop stared across at Thelma Louise, who resumed stacking the beers.

"Everyone? For Gilroy?" She set aside the last bottle and swiped a cloth across the top of the bar.

"Well, we are, for one and then there's the Franklin and Oxford

County Departments, the boys from the state, and the warden service. Even the border patrol has been put on alert."

As he sat there waiting for Thelma Louise to take in what he was saying, she was wondering what on earth her friend could have done.

"Can I get you anything?" she asked.

The young officer shook his head from side to side while studying Thelma's face for a clue as to whether she knew where to find Gilroy.

"Yesterday afternoon, just around two o'clock, someone took a couple of shots at some fellas up from Boston."

Thelma scrunched up her face unsure as to what this might have to do with her friend.

The cop continued, "They were riding WaveRunners on Aziscohos Lake. A guy almost drowned and another was hospitalized. They could have been killed."

"And you think Donnie did it?" The thought was by no means inconceivable. After all, the chip on Donnie Gilroy's shoulder was larger than the hump on Quasimodo's back. Thelma knew how her friend felt about jet skis.

"One of the guys was swimming to shore when he saw a pea-green Subaru with Maine plates drive off. You know anyone else around here with a vehicle that matches that description?"

Thelma Louise shrugged. That didn't seem to be enough to point the finger at Gilroy. As if anticipating her reticence, Whitney added, "The wardens on the scene took statements from Wally Hancock and two of his sports. They were out in that bowrider of his. They heard the shots and Hancock says he saw Donnie running toward his car a few moments later."

Thelma didn't like the sound of that.

"Look, T., I know he's your friend, but it would be better for Gilroy if I found him before anyone else does."

Thelma couldn't decide whether the young cop's eyes were sad or just tired. She didn't know much about Whitney Parker. She remembered him hiring on as a cop soon after graduating from the regional high school. Everyone in town knew the story about how he enlisted in the marines a day or two after 9/11. How the IED that exploded under his Humvee killed most of the men in his unit and left him with permanent burns that disfigured his face. The rumor around town was that he'd been unable to speak for a time after his return from Afghanistan as the result of an injury to his brain.

After more than a year of rehabilitation, Whitney Parker reclaimed his position on the town's police force. He married a girl a few years older than Thelma Louise. Thelma thought the girl's name was Sophia MacDougall. One of the smart kids in school, she remembered that Sophia had graduated at the top of her class. Her parents ran a small sheep farm outside of town. Thelma supposed she knew enough about Whitney to trust him. Even so…

The vulture hovering to the left of the young cop suddenly came to life. He pushed his shot glass toward Thelma Louise, who turned to pull a bottle of rye from the back shelf. After pouring the amber contents into the glass, she accepted the card the police officer handed to her.

"Call me if you hear anything," Whitney said as he slid off the stool. Before turning toward the door, he added, "It really would be better if he came in with me rather than…" Although failing to finish the sentence, it didn't take much imagination to envision the bad ending that could easily occur.

When Gilroy didn't answer his phone, Thelma called to tell me what Whitney said. "No way. Not even Gilroy's that stupid." I held the phone to my ear while waiting in my truck for two girls to cross between the post office and the Town and Lake Motel. In their early teens, they wore skinny jeans and different colored belly shirts. The girl with short blond hair and a little jewel fastened to her nose waved to me. The other, the one with longer brown hair, pulled her friend's arm down. The two were still giggling as they reached the sidewalk.

Gilroy's mother walked out of one of the motel rooms carrying an armload of sheets and towels that she dumped into a plastic container.

Susan Gilroy waved in my direction when I caught her eye.

It was only a few years back that Donnie, Thelma, and I used to get high on weed, pretending to be characters in the latest version of Grand Theft Auto. The three of us would shoot at bottles in the sand pit up along the western side of the Kennebago River with the rifle Gilroy inherited from his father. I knew it didn't take much for his emotions to get the better of him. I also knew that in addition to his father's rifle, Donnie sometimes carried an unlicensed revolver he'd bought at a gun show.

I waved at Gilroy's mother and then winked at the two young girls while accelerating up the block. Looking in the rearview mirror, I watched them burst into laughter. Passing by the Building and Supply, I climbed the long hill that leads out of town.

By the time I'd passed the wooden bear that stands outside the town of Easie, it occurred to me that Gilroy might be hunkered down in his mother's basement. Turning the truck around, I sped back down the hill. A few minutes later I slowed, once again passing by the Town and Lake Motel. Two white SUV's were now parked outside. Each had the border patrol insignia painted on the door. Four men dressed in olive shirts, their fatigues tucked into leather boots, stood outside the building speaking with Gilroy's mother.

Good luck with that, I thought. Susan Gilroy was a tough nut. Never remarrying after her husband's death, she raised Donnie and his older brother, until Eddie Gilroy left town in 2013 for West Texas. Word was that when the oil boom collapsed, Eddie moved to Pennsylvania and then New York State, taking fracking jobs wherever he could find them. Susan Gilroy had done the very best she could, cleaning rooms at the motel on weekdays and waiting tables at the Red Onion on weekends.

I turned left onto Allen Street and pulled into a driveway a few houses up from the little Cape Cod with the swayback roof.

Checking things out through the rearview mirror, I counted two Ford Explorers and a nondescript Chevy clogging the short drive beside the Gilroy house. The SUVs had the Rangeley Police logo painted across the doors. I figured the nondescript Impala belonged to the State Police. I remembered how, when we were kids, Donnie referred to such cars as Sneaky Petes. One bit of good news—I didn't see Gilroy's Subaru. Knowing he wouldn't make it easy for the cops to take him, I wondered if he'd had time to collect his stash of drugs.

After a few minutes, I drove back down the block, turned right onto Main Street, and once again headed out of town. Glancing over at the ruffled surface of Dodge Pond, I debated what to do next. When a shadow slipped across the water, I looked up to find a large cumulus cloud in the shape of a big fat Buddha. When I looked closer, the Buddha appeared to be smiling down at me. Right or wrong, good or bad, Gilroy was my friend, and I needed to get to him before anyone else did. I thought back to when his father died, where he had gone, returning only after he'd run out of food.

A few minutes later, I passed the farmhouse that is a familiar sight between the towns of Rangeley and Easie. A tractor pulled a brush hog through a field leaving the tall summer grass to stand in the shape of the letters U S A.

It would take a few minutes to reach the Morton Cutoff Road and another twenty to get to the gate. A few miles along the road that bends around the east side of Parmachenee Lake, there is a culvert through which a little brook sometimes flows if enough rain has fallen. From there it's a long, tough slog up the side of a hill, which is where I was pretty sure I'd find my friend.

· *Chapter Twenty-Four* ·

I PASSED THE TEST FOR MY GUIDE'S LICENSE AT ABOUT THE TIME WE entered our third year of high school, but didn't do much with it on account of most sports were unwilling to entrust their few hours on the water to a kid. Meanwhile, Gilroy's pockets were always full of cash. He had made friends with a guy, who knew a guy, who could get anything you wanted for the right price. At first, it was bootleg CDs and videos. Then it was parts for cars and trucks for less than half the price at the NAPA store and even less than old man Fogerty charged.

Although there was no shortage of boys willing to sleep with Thelma Louise, she found herself alone at the end of each summer. Even so, she continued to dream of moving to Boston or New York City, sometimes to L.A. Depending on the season, Thelma's mood, and menstrual cycle, she hoped to become a newscaster, model, actress or weather woman. The spring before Gilroy and I graduated, Thelma Louise decided her best chance to escape our little town was to become the beautician to the stars.

Gilroy's mother lent us her car, and a few days after ice-out we picked up Thelma Louise and headed south. After driving two hours, we entered Lewiston. Making a left on Cedar Street, we crossed over the Androscoggin River. The water was running high with snowmelt, and Gilroy and I debated whether it contained trout this far south. It certainly didn't look like the same river we fished. Gone were the spruce and pine. In their place stood traffic lights and stop signs. Tires, shopping carts, and other man-made debris replaced the bald eagles and loons we'd seen along the northern stretch of river. A few moments after turning onto Lisbon Street, Thelma Louise pointed to the sign for Mr. Lee's

School of Hair Fashion.

Gilroy and I sat in a small waiting room while a woman with big breasts and bigger hair escorted Thelma Louise through a door. Forty-five minutes or so later, we heard Thelma's voice coming from down a hall. We later learned that the woman with the big hair had concluded her interview by asking if Thelma Louise had ever been convicted of a crime. Thelma had worried about the twelve-thousand-dollar tuition, but hoped to qualify for a scholarship. What she never suspected was that her encounter with the judge's son would adversely affect her right to join the ranks of Mr. Lee's hairstylists. So, when the woman with the big hair informed her that a conviction for assault, although a juvenile offense, was below the high standards set by Mr. Lee, Thelma Louise Shannon lost it.

"You mean to tell me your Mr. Lee won't accept me into his school because I punched some kid in the nose when I was twelve?" Thelma was reaching some pretty high notes by the time a girl in a nearby room stuck her head out of a door.

Racing down the hall, Gilroy and I found the lady with the big hair reading from Mr. Lee's School of Hair Fashion's Code of Ethics. "It's posted on our website," she screeched defensively.

By then, Thelma had climbed over a desk to reach for the woman, who had backed against the wall with the Code of Ethics clutched in her meaty fingers.

"Do you believe this bitch?" Thelma screamed as we pulled her down from the desk. "I mean, look at that rat's nest she calls a hairdo," she continued to rant as Gilroy and I led her out of the room. Donnie wanted to drive to a 7-Eleven and buy a carton of eggs, but I talked him out of it. Instead, as we pulled away from the school, he mooned the women staring out of the windows while Thelma and I raised our middle fingers out either side of the car.

Thelma Louise tried hard to hide her disappointment.

"You don't need no school to teach you the beautification process,"

Gilroy said, trying to raise her spirits.

She had shaved the sides of her head while letting the center grow out. Her latest dye-job was not quite blue, closer to dun colored, with a white streak down the middle. She reminded me of a great blue heron. I said, "Who knows more about hair than you, T. L.?"

Using our fake IDs, we spent the afternoon at a local bar. Later, while weaving north on Route 4, Thelma Louise proclaimed her intention to become a country-western singer. By the time we drove down Rangeley's main street, she and I were singing Lovesick Blues, with Gilroy giving his best Hank Williams yodel at the end of each stanza.

Two years behind Thelma Louise, Petey Boy was struggling through his Special Ed classes. Thelma Louise had convinced me that after graduating from high school, I should put my plan to become a fishing guide on hold while signing up for community college. By the time Gilroy and I managed to graduate high school, he had begun dealing dope. Marijuana was still illegal in Maine. Donnie found selling the stuff more lucrative than stolen electronics and hot car parts, which is how he was able to afford two bamboo rods and still have enough money to purchase a used Subaru. Back then, it was Gilroy who bought the beers.

A week or so after graduation, I started the college courses. While I commuted to Farmington three days a week, Thelma Louise began working weeknights at Sparky's. By then, she had fully committed to pursuing her plan to become the next Shania Twain.

Hoping to make it big as a country-western singer, Thelma spent all her free time preparing for her debut performance at the Wooden Nickel, a roadhouse located down the street in the town of Easie that featured an open-mic every Thursday.

Gilroy and I were there on the big night with Petey Boy standing between the two of us in the back of the room. While we hooted and hollered Petey stared, his mouth open, as Thelma took the stage. She was no Taylor Swift, not even a Brittany Spears, but our girl gave it her best shot. I thought she looked slick in her short denim skirt and red satin blouse, stomping across the stage in a new pair of cowgirl boots.

"At least she remembered the words," Gilroy bent over to whisper in my ear as Thelma Louise worked hard on a song made popular by the Dixie Chicks.

There was a scattering of applause from the ten or twelve other customers when Thelma finished. A local guy whistled while she looked uncertainly toward one end of the stage before making her retreat. The main act wouldn't begin until sometime after eleven, which is when the place would fill up.

Thelma Louise was working on her second beer when Gilroy drained his longneck, saying he had business that couldn't wait. Not long afterward, I remembered my obligation to return Petey Boy to his parents. After we climbed into my pickup, I backed out of the lot in front of the roadhouse. Thelma lit a cigarette and passed it to me as I drove toward the stone bridge that marks the entrance to the town. She started pointing to a figure standing in the shadows on the deck of Ollie Stubbs' general store when Petey cried out, "Look!"

Turning our attention away from the general store, Thelma and I stared up at a crescent moon that had slipped over the roof of Lakeview Sports.

It wasn't until the following afternoon that we learned what had happened. The way Gilroy told it, he had pulled beside the deck of the general store a few minutes before eleven. Not long after he arrived, the lights in the apartment above the store went out.

Except for the Wooden Nickel, there's not much happening in Easie after dark. Down the block, vehicles were beginning to fill the lot outside the roadhouse. He could hear music whenever someone opened the door, but otherwise the street was quiet. It was so quiet he could hear a hum coming from a black box fixed to the top of a pole that had all sorts of wires running in and out of it.

Gilroy had watched the crescent moon ascend over the Millers' sporting goods store. He'd seen us pass and a few minutes later watched a BMW drive over the stone bridge. Following the vehicle's progress as it passed the store and pulled in front of the roadhouse, Gilroy inhaled on a cigarette. He was still standing on the general store's deck when the fancy sedan pulled out of the gravel lot and drove slowly back up the street. Flipping the cigarette into the pea stone below the deck, Gilroy watched the expensive sports car brake under the light above the box with the hum and then turn in beside his recently purchased Subaru.

Noticing the Connecticut plates, Gilroy could see, but not hear, the guy behind the wheel say something to a younger woman seated beside him. He stared down from the deck when the car doors opened. Gilroy figured the driver to be in his mid-to-late twenties. He wore designer jeans and a polo shirt. They were clearly not locals, most likely on vacation from Hartford, or maybe Bridgewater or Danbury. The woman's short skirt rode up her thighs as she swung her legs from the passenger seat.

Roger Cook, one of Gilroy's regular customers, had vouched for the guy. Said his parents owned a million-dollar camp on Mooselookmeguntic Lake and that he was up for the Labor Day Weekend and looking for some product.

"Hey." The guy grinned at Gilroy as he ambled up the steps and onto the deck.

Gilroy had caught a flash of panty when the woman turned to slide her lean frame from the car. *Red*, he thought, but couldn't be sure.

He smiled to himself as she held a phone in the air. Ignoring the guy who had drawn closer, Gilroy watched the young woman extend her arms. The woman turned in a circle and pointed the phone above her head, but then slipped it back into her purse when she was unable to obtain sufficient bars.

The woman wore a dark blue leather skirt, with a dark bra under a light blue, see-through sleeveless blouse. Her blond hair was cut short. Her bangs fell down to her eyes.

She has money, he thought.

Donnie was still checking out her legs when the man extended his hand. Gilroy declined the offer. Instead, he said, "Do I know you?"

"Roger says you're the man to see around here." The man lowered his arm.

Something about the guy's manner annoyed him. Maybe it was his smile. Gilroy wanted to ask what was so funny, but instead, said, "What can I do you for?" He was staring at the woman, who had pulled a nail file from her purse. She stared back at him. The faintest smile slipped across her lips.

"My parents are gone for the weekend and I'm throwin' a party." He pronounced the last word "partay." While working the file over her nails, the woman leaned back against the sedan. Her legs were now crossed at the ankles.

"And?" Gilroy turned back to the guy. He decided there was something hinky about him. Donnie told me later that he would have left, had he not looked back down at the woman, who momentarily caught his eye.

"Come on dude, I need something to keep the natives from getting restless."

Still not trusting the guy, Gilroy pulled a cigarette from the pack in his jeans.

"Jay, why not ask your friend to come along?" The woman called, her eyes on Gilroy.

"Hey, why not?" the guy said. He leaned in close and whispered, "Pam's a bit wild. To tell ya the truth, she's a handful. I'd just as soon you take her off my hands."

Gilroy took a drag on his cigarette. He definitely didn't like the guy. Too much attitude. He was thinking of walking away when Pam pulled a pack of smokes from her purse. Walking closer to the deck, she called to him for a light.

He leaned down and lit the tip of her cigarette.

She let out a plume of smoke while saying to her friend, "Forget it, Jay. I know a guy in Errol. He can hook us up."

"How 'bout some Kush?" Gilroy wasn't sure why he made the offer.

He was surprised to hear the words coming from his mouth.

"How much you got?" the guy asked.

"How much you want?" Gilroy noticed that Pam had red nails. He wondered again if that was the color he had caught a glimpse of when she'd stepped out of the car.

"Two, three ounces."

"That's an awful lot for one party," Gilroy said, once again growing suspicious.

"We're talkin' three days here. Don't want to run out."

The woman was staring up at him, a thin curl of smoke rising from the tip of her cigarette.

Gilroy thought for a moment. "How does two hundred and fifty an ounce sound? Call it seven hundred for three."

The guy pulled out his wallet and peeled out ten one-hun-dred-dollar bills.

It was Gilroy's turn to smile.

Trotting down the steps, he passed under the light cast by the lamp above the deck. The woman dropped the cigarette to the ground. Crushing it with the tip of one navy-blue stiletto, she turned to follow Gilroy, who had walked into the shadows. Opening the back door of the pea-green Subaru, he yanked the back seat upward. Ten one-ounce bags of marijuana were hidden underneath.

Removing three bags, Gilroy turned to find the woman facing him. A State Police badge dangled from a chain around her neck. The under-cover cop was pointing the barrel of a handgun at him. A few steps away, her partner had his gun pointed in the same direction.

I remember Donnie's dopey smile, when many months later he de-scribed how the cop in the short skirt stood with her legs apart. She kept her gun pointed at his head while he lay on the ground with his hands cuffed behind him. According to Gilroy, he took a great deal of satisfac-tion upon looking up and seeing that her nails had indeed matched the color of her panties.

· *Chapter Twenty-Five* ·

ALTHOUGH I HADN'T RETURNED TO CAMP DANFORTH SINCE WE WERE kids, I knew that Gilroy treated the place as his personal hole-in-the-wall hideaway. He'd spent a week in the cave after his father's funeral. Another time, he had held up there when the wardens were looking for him in connection with a sudden spate of missing signs along the Lincoln Pond logging road.

After the narcs confiscated the dope Donnie had packed into the Subaru, they tore apart his mother's house, but only found a small stash he'd hidden behind the basement paneling. Unaware of Gilroy's home-away-from-home, the cops failed to uncover the two additional ounces he'd hidden on the hill behind the gates of the Parmachenee Tract.

Gilroy was sentenced to nine months at Mountain View Youth Development Center, which was extended to a year and three months when he broke the cheekbone of another kid who'd made the mistake of picking a fight with him. Although Mountain View might sound like a vacation camp, it is, in fact, the juvenile detention facility for the northern part of the state. Had Donnie been busted a month later, he would have been sentenced as an adult.

Instead of spending his first day of freedom fishing the upper stretches of the Magalloway, upon his return from the detention center, Gilroy drove over to Rumford where he sold one of the hidden ounces to a logger in exchange for a key to the western gate below Parmachenee Lake. He sold half of the other ounce to a guy willing to duplicate the key even though it was illegal to do so. After that, we no longer had to rely upon my great-uncle for access to the river above the gates.

Driving along the shoreline of Aziscohos Lake, I hadn't noticed the clouds drifting in from the south. A few drops sprinkled down as I locked the western gate behind me. It hadn't rained in weeks. The rivers remained low as the season drew to a close. Only an hour ago, I'd been standing outside my apartment staring up at a sunlit sky, and although I hadn't been expecting any precipitation, the weather in this part of the country can turn on a dime.

I switched on the truck's windshield wipers while driving over the top of Parmachenee Lake. Continuing down its eastern shoreline, I passed the two-track that led down to Angus's cabin. Not long afterward, I crossed over the culvert through which a brooklet ran and parked my truck down another two-track that dead-ended in an open field once used to stack timber during a long-ago logging operation. Summer grass had grown up the middle of the seldom-used road. Saplings closed in from either side.

After strapping a pack to my back, I slipped a camo poncho over my head. Not wanting to take any chances, I used a camp axe to hack off a number of spruce branches and placed them over the truck before tramping toward the main logging road.

It was a ten-minute walk to the culvert. The little stream had begun to rise from the rain that had intensified. I stepped into the forest and followed the brook up the side of the hill while weaving around the tightly packed trees. The climb was steeper than I'd remembered, and it took me longer than expected to reach my destination. I tried not to leave too much sign, working between oak and maple, stooping under the sodden branches of balsam and spruce, doubling back a few times, while losing my way at least once. I hadn't hiked the hill since we were kids and had difficulty finding the shelter we had discovered all those years ago. After slip-sliding around in the rain for nearly an hour, I came upon a familiar boulder. Twenty minutes later I stumbled upon a wooden shack built into the side of the hill. Gilroy had added spruce and pine branches to the sides of the logs making it nearly impossible to spot from even a few yards away. As I approached, Donnie broke out of the wood to my left, his father's rifle slung over a shoulder.

"You walked by the place twice." He fell in beside me, that dopey grin plastered across his face.

"Brought food," I grunted as Gilroy removed a large spruce limb that covered a door constructed of wood planks.

"Welcome to Camp Danforth." His smile grew broader.

I was surprised at what Gilroy had done to the cave we had discovered as kids. Sometime over the years, he'd hauled logs up the side of the hill to build wood walls around the original opening. Donnie added a tarpaper roof to keep the weather out and a floor layered with balsam boughs. The wooden sign we had carved all those years ago hung above the door.

Inside the log enclosure, Gilroy had placed a small propane heater we'd salvaged from the Rangeley Walmart. He'd constructed shelves along the inside of one wall and stocked them with canned goods and other provisions. There was just enough room in the cave for one bedroll, and he had rigged a rudimentary wooden frame with rope on which he had placed a sleeping bag.

Donnie Gilroy slipped out of his rain gear and sat cross-legged on the makeshift bed. After bending down to enter the opening of the wooden structure, I too, removed my poncho.

"What do ya think?" he asked.

"All the comforts of home," I muttered.

Slinging the pack off my shoulders, I sat on the floor, with my back against the log wall. The old propane stove heated the small enclosure without any smoke. I removed a few cans of soup, a can of beans, and another of tuna fish. As Gilroy arranged them on the shelves beside his other supplies, I handed him a box of cereal and a container of non-perishable milk called Parmalat.

"You got cops from two counties looking for you, not to mention state troopers. They been out to your place. The border patrol guys talked to your maw. Whitney Parker's been over to see T.L. Says it'll be better if you turn yourself in to him."

"Like that's gonna happen."

"What were you thinking?" I asked, unloading a six-pack from the bottom of my pack.

"Not here," Gilroy whispered. "Let's eat first." He picked up one of the Italians I'd bought in Errol while driving back and forth over Route 16 to be sure no one was following me. Passing him a beer, I began to work on my sandwich.

After we ate the foot-longs, I donned my poncho and followed Gilroy back outside. He climbed up to the top of the hill and worked his way down the other side. At one point Gilroy turned to me and said, "Didn't want to talk back there." He pointed up the hill. "Between the FBI, CIA, and NSA, you can't be too careful."

"Whatever. Just tell me you didn't do it," I said as he continued down the hill.

"What can I say, Harry. A man's gotta do what a man's gotta do."

"Jesus, Donnie. This ain't the wild west."

"I can't go back, Harry. Juvie was bad enough. This time it'll be the real thing."

"I don't know as you have much of a choice." I stared down at my boots. The rain dripped off the brim of my cap.

"I have a plan." Gilroy had worked his way to another rill. He stopped when he came to a boulder that leaned against a tree. After pushing it aside, Donnie reached in and pulled up a small canvas pack from a hole he'd dug under the large rock. Inside the pack were three plastic bags containing marijuana.

"There's three pounds here. Everything I have. Over seven thousand dollars' worth of product. All I have to do is make one quick score and then hop over the border until things cool down. I know a guy who'll be happy to take the stuff off my hands. It'll be enough for me to get a new start in Montreal. But I need you to set up the meet."

There was noise about grass becoming legal in our state, but until it happened, the cops took dealing seriously.

"Why not just text him?" I asked. "Why do you need me?"

"I told you. They could be listening in. Tracing my calls, my texts. Besides, can't get no bars out here. You know that." Gilroy unzipped a baggie and after removing his phone, raised his arm over his head. "See," he said, moving the phone in one direction and then in another.

I didn't like it. I'd never sold dope and didn't want to start, but Gilroy needed my help. After placing the phone back in the plastic bag, he gave me the guy's name and contact information. We agreed that I'd bring him up to the Camp Ten Bridge at midnight, the night after next. I was to turn the lights off and on twice if everything was cool. Once would mean it was a no go, in which case we'd meet back at the shack the following morning.

The rain had slowed and gradually stopped. After a while it grew quiet. We listened to the water dripping off the leaves and the current that rushed alongside the hill. From somewhere off to our right a raven called. Another answered from farther back in the forest.

"You hear that?" Gilroy pointed toward a stand of spruce. I hadn't heard anything except the two birds and told him so. I figured his paranoia was working overtime. We waited for a few minutes longer, but neither of us heard another sound except for the current passing by our boots.

Moisture spiraled up from the forest floor. A red squirrel chattered from a spruce limb. We stayed in the moment for as long as we could, neither wanting to return to what had become of our lives. Peeking down into the little mountain brook, I hoped to catch a glimpse of a fin against the dun-and-rust colored streambed.

"Wish we had our fly rods." Gilroy had turned back up the hill.

A step behind him, I pulled down the hood of my poncho and replied, "The trout should be looking toward the surface now that the water is coming up."

· *Chapter Twenty-Six* ·

A FEW WEEKS AFTER GILROY RETURNED FROM MOUNTAIN VIEW, I QUIT college to become a full-time guide. By then, Thelma had gone from country-western singer to web designer, helping me create a website to advertise my services as well as the flies that I was now selling to most of the stores in the region.

I handed out my cards to just about everyone in town. I left a stack in each of the local stores. The owner of the town's fly-fishing shop agreed to display them on his counter while over in Easie, Rusty Miller agreed to do the same at Lakeview Sports. Thelma Louise knew the daughter of the owners of L.L. Cote, the New Hampshire sporting goods store, who also agreed to talk me up to their customers.

I received the news of my grand's death while standing on the porch of Thelma's house. I was smiling down at the card my mother had designed, the words: BIGGEST BROOK TROUT SOUTH OF LABRADOR were printed in bold letters under a black-and-white fish breaking water to grab a mayfly. I had felt a sense of pride at seeing the words 'Registered Maine Guide' after my name.

Thelma Louise came out from inside the kitchen where she had been fixing lunch. She handed me the portable phone with a stricken expression on her face. At first I thought something had happened to my mother, but felt no better when my father told me my grand had been rushed to the hospital. I later learned that he never regained consciousness; the heart attack was as massive as it was sudden.

To my relief, my mother did not fall into a depression. She attended her father's funeral. Seated by her mother's side, Clementine Duncan held the older woman's hand as tears stained their cheeks. My father and I stood beside my mother. We greeted the mourners as they formed a line down one side of the room. Each had taken a turn kneeling in front of the coffin that had a banner draped across the side with the Duncan family crest stitched upon it.

Many of the men who attended my grand's funeral were ancient. Quite a few hobbled into the room on legs they could no longer trust. Many leaned on canes, while a few were confined to wheelchairs. I knew many of them, but not all, later learning that men Harold knew while living in Massachusetts had made the long drive to pay their respects. Fogerty was there, nodding gravely as he walked over. The mechanic bent forward to take my mother's hand and then the hand of my grand-mother. He'd slicked back his white hair. Although he shaved, his razor had missed a number of whiskers that were sprinkled across his chin and over his neck. These stragglers reminded me of those few trees left by loggers after they clear-cut a section of forest. I could see the old man's shoulders sag as he folded his arms around my great-uncle. The two men were visibly sobbing as they hugged one another.

I knew my grand and great-uncle were old, but until then, had never given much thought of losing either of them. To be honest, I assumed they would be around forever, but on that afternoon Angus Ferguson looked like all the other frail old men.

The room was packed. Some of the men were my father's age or younger. Most of them looked uncomfortable in ill-fitting jackets and ties. Each took a moment to look down at the coffin before walking over to my family and whispering a condolence. Just about every guide in the region showed up, as did the wardens, who wore their dress uniforms. I watched the tall warden who had nabbed Gilroy and me enter the room. He stood for a moment in his red-and-and-black tunic. The warden held a wide-brimmed hat in a gnarly hand. His leather boots were spit-shined. After stopping at the coffin, he leaned down to whisper something to my great-uncle before exchanging words with the rest of our family.

As with the other funerals I'd attended, some of the men eventually retired to a second room, which is where I retreated when the minister walked in to pray over my grand's lifeless body. Harold's friends sat on a long sofa centered against a wall, a few in chairs with upholstery that matched that of the sofa. A number of them unfolded metal chairs that the funeral director carried into the room. As a result of a new law, a sign on the wall prohibited smoking.

Above the sofa, a small flock of canvasbacks swept through a dark sky with low-hanging clouds. I wasn't sure if the gilt-edged painting was meant to depict dusk or dawn, but the gray marsh below the ducks fit my mood. Lamps set on tables placed on either end of the sofa cast a soft light over those gathered in the room. Brochures titled "Coping with Death" were neatly stacked on each table. A few jackets hung from hooks on a brass rack standing in the near corner of the room.

The men huddled around the table grew silent when I entered. Like the murmur of a distant stream, voices from the other room rose in response to the minister's prayers. Fogerty clapped me on the back. When a man offered him a flask, he passed it to me. Those around us resumed their chatter that quickly drowned out the invocation of the faithful.

During the evening session, I walked outside, followed by Gilroy and Thelma Louise. The three of us passed around a joint while staring up at the stars that stared back at us in cold silence. I wondered out loud if the God evoked by the mourners paid any more attention to their sorrow than the stars did to the earth. Gilroy figured it was all nonsense and that we were on our own in the Big Suck. Leaning her head on my shoulder, Thelma whispered that all we had was each other.

The three of us walked back inside when we heard the sound of bagpipes. Three men dressed in kilts lined up along the back wall. The men from the other room had fallen in on either side of the pipers. My father slipped his arm around my mother's waist as they stood with their backs to the crowd. The little man with the sharp nose stood beside my grandmother. Her hand was in his. The old men looked straight ahead. The few in wheelchairs struggled to rise when the pipers began to play "Scotland the Brave." By the time the last note struck, I was sure that even the stars were wiping away their tears.

A few weeks after the funeral, my mother set up an easel beside her bedroom window. We watched for the blackness, but as the month progressed, she appeared to go into overdrive, trying hard to capture the autumn color that had already begun to change. When not painting, she spent much of her time with her mother. My father, who had taken a few days off to help the two women, resumed his long days at the bank.

With the September spawning run in full swing, I wanted to spend time with my great-uncle, but he had retreated to his cabin. Thelma Louise dropped by our house more often. I'd catch her talking with my mother and grandmother. About what, I had no idea. Although my father's concern grew as cable news warned of a major collapse on Wall Street, I found it hard to believe that anything happening in New York City could have an effect on our lives.

What I remember most about that month was the silence that followed a long piercing cry. It was sometime after five in the afternoon. My father had not yet returned from the bank. I had been in my room listening to a Bob Marley CD. Taking the steps two at a time, I entered the kitchen to find the phone dangling from its cord. My mother had collapsed on the floor. With her arms around her raised knees, she rocked back and forth as silent as a crying star.

· *Chapter Twenty-Seven* ·

"WHY NOW?" I ASKED.
"Why not now?" Thelma Louise answered.

We were lying on my bed, a sheet covering our bodies. The rain that let up the previous afternoon had resumed sometime overnight. It continued to come down hard throughout the morning, but slowed while I picked up Thelma Louise, with the sun slipping out from behind the clouds by the time I parked my truck.

Nearing the end of September, it was unseasonably warm. After the rain abated, the air outside grew as still as the air inside my apartment. We lay on our backs. It would be another hour or so before Thelma Louise began her shift at Sparky's. I had my hands clasped behind my head. One of Thelma's legs stretched out from under the sheet. Her knee touched my thigh. I was thinking of Gilroy back in his hidey-hole, like some wise old brown trout, waiting out the daylight hours tight against the riverbank, peeking out from amongst the roots of a pin oak, hidden under the shadow cast by the tree's overhanging limbs.

"Come with me," Thelma Louise whispered. The sheet fell completely away when she shifted her body to place a hand on my chest. A pink nipple stood at attention on her pale breast.

"But what about Gilroy?"

Thelma bent forward and kissed me slow and deep. Raising her leg, she straddled my pelvis. Her fingers were entwined in mine. Falling into a familiar rhythm, I unclasped my hands and slid them toward her waist as she began to slowly rock back and forth.

Beads of sweat bathed our flesh when we were again lying on our backs. I reached for the pack of cigarettes on the table beside my bed. A moment later smoke curled above our heads. Slowly drifting toward the open window, the gray cloud momentarily masked the pervasive smell of peanut sauce coming from the restaurant below the apartment.

"I can't let Gilroy down," I muttered, drawing on the cigarette.

"Whit says it's best if he turns himself in. That he's gonna get himself killed if he doesn't."

"Parker? He's a cop. What do you expect him to say?"

"Whitney's okay. You know that."

"Donnie says one last deal and he can skip over the border." I believed his chances of success less than Thelma did.

"You're no drug dealer." Thelma Louise reached over to take the cigarette from between my fingers. "And neither is Gilroy." When I rolled my eyes, she said, "Not really."

She took a drag and blew the smoke toward the ceiling. "Christ, Harry, three pounds? He's in way over his head." Thelma returned the cigarette.

I knew she was right.

Shifting her weight onto her hip, she raised up on an elbow.

"So, are you coming with me or not?"

"I can't T., Gilroy's counting on me."

"He's gonna get himself killed and maybe you with him. Can't you see that?" Her voice sounded as shrill as a kingfisher disturbed by a streamside angler.

"But T., you're the one who's always saying we have to stick together. All that crap about all for one."

She scowled at me, saying something about what an ass I could be.

"Besides, all I know is the river." My smile only angered her more. Thelma swung her legs over the side of the bed. Reaching down toward the floor, she grabbed her bra from where it had fallen.

"I get it. You're a fishing guide. But there are other rivers." Thelma adjusted the black cups over her breasts. She hated to lose an argument.

"In New Jersey?" I slipped the cigarette butt into an empty longneck on the bed stand.

Earlier, she had told me about her latest plan to move away.

Unlike Thelma Louise's mother, Thelma's two aunts had moved out of town while they were still young. One now lived in Florida, the other in New Jersey. A few winters ago, Thelma Louise and her mother had taken a Greyhound down to Orlando, where they spent the holidays. While there, Thelma checked out a club where her cousin worked. Upon her return, she announced that the owner had offered her a job. "A strip club?" Gilroy had asked.

"A gentlemen's club," Thelma Louise had replied.

"Stripping?" I said.

"Waitressing!" she screamed back at me.

But like her past plans, this one faded as winter turned to spring.

Earlier this afternoon, she announced that the aunt in New Jersey had offered to take her in. Thelma Louise said that her aunt worked for a community college, which entitled anyone in her family to free tuition. The aunt also promised Thelma a part-time job as a secretary at the college.

Although I protested that she knew nothing about being a secretary, Thelma Louise countered that she had taken a typing course and knew enough about computers to get by.

"New Jersey's not so bad," she now said while pulling on a pink tank top. "My uncle says they got plenty of trout streams, and you can still be a fishing guide if that's what you want to do."

"Trout streams in New Jersey? You gotta be kiddin." What I knew about the state came from Bruce Springsteen CDs and TV shows like *The Sopranos* and *The Jersey Shore*.

"Well, I'm going whether you come or not." She sucked in her stomach while pulling on a pair of skinny jeans.

"Can't you wait until this business with Gilroy is over?" I figured by then Thelma would be on to her next get-out-of-town scheme.

"I've made up my mind. The lease is up on the Wrangler and I've decided not to renew it. I already bought my ticket. Bought it before I knew what Donnie had done. It's up to you Mister Man. Fogerty's agreed to drive me down to Augusta tomorrow morning. The bus is scheduled to leave at eight."

She padded into the bathroom. Grabbing my briefs from the floor, I walked toward the open door. Thelma Louise was flushing the toilet as I walked inside.

"I thought we had plans," I pleaded as she buttoned her jeans.

Thelma Louise turned toward the sink. She ran the tap while squeezing out a blob of toothpaste into her mouth.

"C'mon T." I slid my hands around her waist.

"Don't T. me!" Thelma snarled through a mouth of white foam.

She spit the toothpaste into the sink. "What am I supposed to do in this town while you spend your days on that damn river?" She glared back at me through the mirror.

"But I thought…"

"You thought. You're gonna get yourself killed!" she screamed.

Before I could reply, she turned toward me. "You know, Harry, you're always bitchin' about how your father spent his entire life hiding away in that bank of his, but what about you? You and that river of yours! You tell me, what's the difference between you and your father?"

Thelma Louise pushed past me. "I'll be at Fogerty's by seven." She slipped on her red sneakers. "Meet me there if you change your mind. If not, well…" She hesitated then said, "It's been real." There were tears in her eyes when she rose on her toes to kiss me on the cheek.

After Thelma Louise left, I called the number Gilroy had scratched out on a scrap of paper. The guy on the other end of the line was cautious, but when I explained the problem and Gilroy's asking price for the weed, he agreed to meet me at Sparky's later that evening.

I was nervous about the drug deal and upset about what Thelma Louise had laid on me, especially the part about me being like my old man. I didn't want to believe it and told myself that I was nothing like him. Hell, I never forgave the fucker for what he did to my mother and I never would. I knew that Thelma tended to go off half-cocked when she was on the losing end of an argument. That she'd say anything to make her point. But as much as I hated to admit it, after the next twenty-four hours nothing would be the same. Thelma would be on her way to New Jersey and Gilroy to Canada. God only knows what would happen to Petey Boy. I felt trapped, but couldn't see any way out. I suppose I always knew it wouldn't last.

Walking down the steps of my apartment, I told myself that there was always the river. Opening the door, I half expected the earth to have stopped rotating. Instead, it was pretty much the way I'd left it, except for a fine mist that had begun to fall. It seemed that I was not the only one unable to make up my mind as to what to do.

Running back up the stairs, I grabbed a poncho from a peg beside the door. Once more outside, I pulled the hood up around my head. Moisture glistened on the white-and-red petals along a line of Geraniums planted in a flowerbox under the window of the Thai restaurant. Lighting a cigarette, I stared across at the Rangeley Historical Society Building. The parking spaces outside the stores on either side of Main Street were taken. Up the block, a car parked outside of the Alpine Shop displayed a Florida license plate; the one beside it had a plate from Connecticut.

As I had come to learn, like the out-of-state vehicles and the line of geraniums, like the rain now falling from the overcast sky and the planet spinning evenly on its axis, the leaf peepers hustling past the window of the Thai restaurant took no interest in my life or the lives of my three friends.

With time to kill before meeting Gilroy's connection, I decided to leave my troubles beside the apartment door and spend the remainder of the afternoon wading through the cool water upstream from Little Kennebago Lake. Forty-five minutes later, I pulled off a two-track and into the same gravel pit where as kids we'd taken turns shooting at pop bottles.

· *Chapter Twenty-Eight* ·

FOR THE MOMENT, THE EVENTS OF THE LAST FEW WEEKS HAD SLIPPED toward the back of my mind. Sitting at the kitchen table, I watched a gang of hummingbirds compete for nectar around a flying-saucer-like feeder hanging outside our kitchen window. Earlier that morning, I'd filled the red plastic bowl with more than enough sweet liquid for each bird to sit side by side around the six openings. Instead, unwilling to share, they drove each other away, their feathers iridescent in the sunlight that broke through the shifting clouds.

Had it been nearly a month since my mother sat at the same table? She had been wearing a sleeveless blouse and shorts down to her knees. I was wearing a T-shirt and jeans. The two of us had watched chickadees and titmice flitting around a tube feeder. It was later that same afternoon, before the phone rang, that my mother had boiled the red liquid favored by the rowdy little hummers and placed it in the fridge to cool.

On this morning, while staring out the kitchen window, I wore a flannel shirt, the sleeves rolled up to my elbows. Overnight an early frost had coated the lawn, but now, at ten in the morning, the grass was damp. The maple tree down by the pond was turning color, its leaves tinged with scarlet, while a few feet away the leaves of an old oak remained green. My mother's vegetable garden, the one that bordered the forest along the back of our property, had been left untended. Lupines, daisies, and black-eyed Susans withered away in a flower garden planted closer to the house. A few Queen Anne's lace rose gracefully above an invading mass of dock, plantain, and fleabane. I thought about pulling weeds, but could feel my ambition wane before it had a chance to move me.

"You okay?" My father entered the kitchen where I had remained seated. The hummingbirds outside the window continued their competition for the sweet nectar.

I glared at him, but said nothing.

"You want me to make some breakfast?" He walked toward the refrigerator.

"Fuck you," I cried.

When she learned of her mother's death, Clementine Ferguson was unable to find her way back from the melancholy that descended upon her like a blizzard roaring down the Boundary Mountains. It was a neighbor, Ingrid Dexter, who had witnessed the accident. It was she who telephoned our home that afternoon. The police arrived at our house an hour or so later. Whitney Parker, who had graduated from high school the previous spring, stood outside the front door in his new uniform. He shifted from one black shoe to the other while the cop beside him explained that the guy driving the car was only nineteen. He had struck my grandmother after spending the day at Sparky's. The cop said the kid had backed out of the lot in front of the tavern. He never saw the old woman crossing behind him.

I had carried my mother up the stairs after she'd collapsed. My father had returned from the bank by the time the police arrived at the door. I stood a step behind him. Staring up at the stairs, I was more concerned about my mother than what the cops had to say about my grandmother, who wasn't coming back no matter how she left.

This time, the depression that gripped Clementine Duncan was as unrelenting as any cancer. Unable to attend another funeral, my mother remained confined to her bed. She remained lost in some dark hinterland. The pills prescribed by Doctor Woodward had little effect. I remained by her bedside, speaking to her of the birds that were beginning their migrations, of the last of the flowers blooming in her gardens, and of the river and how the big fish were about to make their spawning run.

My grandmother died on a Saturday and was buried on a Monday, with only a one-day wake. After the funeral, my father worked from home. When not in his study or on the phone with his office, he looked in on my mother. We took turns trying to coax her back to the land of the living, but she remained lost in her despair.

It was the beginning of my last year of high school. At first, my father groused when I refused to go to class, but after the first few days he no longer complained. By then, the people in charge at my school had pretty much given up on me, and so they paid little heed to my absence.

I remember sitting in my usual place at the end of the old green couch in our living room. I was watching the Price Is Right while listening to Robert Earl Keene on my iPod when the phone rang late on a Monday afternoon. My father, who was in the kitchen fixing a sandwich, answered it. A minute or two later he walked into the room and sat in the easy chair beside the couch.

"That was the office," he said, placing his plate on an end table. His face had turned pale.

I pulled my headphones off and looked over at him.

"I said, that was the office. They need me. I have to go in."

He continued talking, something about Wall Street and Lehman Brothers, but by then I'd tuned him out.

"You gonna be okay?" he asked.

Rather than reply to his question, I said, "I'm gonna check on mom." Slipping the headphones back on, I stomped up the stairs.

I returned to the kitchen table after my father left for work. The hummingbirds were still whirling around the feeder when my great-uncle called from the front door. Angus had visited a few times since my grandmother's death, but he continued to spend most of his time at the cabin beside Parmachenee Lake. I didn't have the energy to rise and waited for him to walk through the house.

"Harry," he greeted me as he had done so many times in the past.

"Angus," I replied, pushing aside a bowl of cornflakes.

"Time tae git back tae school, dinnae ye think?" He pulled out a chair and sat across from me.

"But what about mom?" I stared toward the kitchen door.

A mop of unruly grass had grown up around the red canoe that lay on its side. Not far behind, a heron stood motionless, its cold yellow eye staring down into the shallows of the pond that shimmered in the late afternoon sunlight.

"That's yer da's responsibility. Yer's is tae finish school."

"He tell you to talk to me?" I rose from the table and slipped the bowl into a sink of dirty water.

"Dinnae be lik' that, Harry. Yer da's a good bloke."

I stared at the soggy cornflakes floating in the sink like flotsam after a shipwreck.

"Whatever." I felt defeated.

I looked out the window from the bird feeders to my mother's gardens, from there to the reeds along the edge of the pond. My eyes rested upon the canoe that lay a few feet from the shoreline. I wondered if my mother and I would ever again spend a summer afternoon paddling around the pond together.

"C'moan now, Bucko," Angus patted my shoulder.

The next morning a woman arrived a few minutes before my father left for the bank. Reluctant to walk downstairs, I stood by the open door of my bedroom listening to them talk. Later, after my father left for the office, I found the woman seated at the kitchen table drinking a mug of coffee. She shifted her massive frame as I walked past. Her hair was more gray than brown and piled on top of her head in a giant bun. The woman wore men's work boots under a shapeless dress that fell down to her ankles. She had more hair on her upper lip than Gilroy could grow on his face in a month. A raspberry-colored growth hung off of one cheek.

"My name Malina," she said. "You go to school. I take care of mother."

I turned and walked out the front door.

For the next few weeks Malina arrived at about the same time each morning, leaving not long after I walked in from school. In the mornings, when I'd walk down the stairs from my bedroom, she'd be seated at the kitchen table drinking coffee. When I returned in the afternoon, she'd be in the same chair, with the same mug in her hand. I swore she hadn't moved the entire day.

One afternoon, I returned from school to find my father at the door. It was unlike him to be home so early. Inside, I found Angus seated on the couch next to Doc Woodward. I turned toward the stairs, but my father grabbed my arm.

"Sit," was all he said.

When I did, Doc Woodward explained that they had admitted my mother to Riverview Psychiatric Center. I thought, *First Gilroy, then my mother.* I could see the advertisement:

Welcome to Mountain View: Come for the view, stay for the broken jaw.

And the one for the psychiatric facility:

Enjoy the scenery while we strap you down and run four-hundred-and-fifty volts through your brain.

I remember thinking that our state has one hell of a sense of humor.

· *Chapter Twenty-Nine* ·

I HEARD THE VEHICLE. THE SOUND GREW LOUDER UNTIL THE JEEP MY great-uncle inherited from his brother rounded a curve and pulled into the gravel pit. The rain had once again abated, but the leaves on the trees and bushes remained laden with moisture. I pulled down the hood of my poncho after climbing out of my pickup.

I hadn't seen Angus since the morning he'd caught that humongous salmon below the Camp Ten Bridge. We'd barely spoken after what had happened to my mother. I couldn't remember the last time we had a real conversation. Over the last few years, our encounters were limited to a few chance meetings on the water that required the formality of a greeting, but nothing more.

As far as I knew, he spent most of his time on one part or another of the upper Magalloway. I was surprised to find him this far east of the Parmachenee Tract. He looked older than I remembered. His gait was slower. His limp appeared more pronounced as he exited the Jeep and walked over to my side.

"Harry." His one-word greeting hung in the air like the humidity on that damp afternoon.

I stood, the two sections of lightly flamed cane held in my hands. "Angus," was my one-word reply.

"Ye think it's a wee bit time we stoap this pish?" He extended an arm in my direction. His flesh rippled across the top of his hand like the surface of a lake on a breezy afternoon.

My hippers flopped over my bare legs. Rather than respond, I bent down to snap the buckles around the loops of my shorts.

He lowered his arm. "Fishing light today?" Angus decided to switch to a subject with which we were both comfortable.

I had left my fly vest in the truck's cab. The fly box that I'd shoved into my shirt pocket contained three or four Royal Wulff dry-fly patterns and an equal number of wet flies—all that would be needed to play tag with the little brook trout of the headwater stream.

"I suppose." If he had something to say, I wished he would just say it and leave me to deal with the mess that was my life.

Unwilling to give him anything, I joined the two sections of bamboo. While the man with the hawk-like nose shifted weight from his bad leg to the good, I waited to see why he had ventured so far from the cabin by the lake.

I was about to turn away when he asked, "Ye gonnae follow thro' wi' that plan yer pal concocted?"

"What plan?" He had caught me by surprise. It took a moment, but then I assumed Thelma Louise had enlisted his assistance in dissuading me from helping Gilroy.

Before I replied, he continued, "That wis me yer eejit friend heard efter ye 'greed tae meet up oan th' Camp Ten Bridge."

"What—what were you doin'...," I stammered.

"Ah first saw him whin he climbed up tae that cave th' two o' ye foun' as wee ones. Have bin watchin' him ever since, figured th' dumb neap micht need some hulp, 'n' then ye shawed up."

"I didn't think you cared about anyone except yourself." Although not certain, I thought my blade found flesh with that one.

"Ah heard everything," he said taking a step closer to me.

"What you gonna do? Turn me in?" I sneered.

"Harry, ye gotta be daft tae git involved in sellin' drugs."

"What do you know about it?"

"I ken enough tae tell ye every cop, game warden 'n' border patrol agent wi'in a hundred miles o' that bridge is oan th' lookout fur yer buddy 'n' likelie ye as well. Wouldn't be surprised if we aren't bein' surveilled richt noo."

I stared up at the hill overlooking the gravel pit.

"Just stay out of it, Angus, you're good at that." I saw my great-uncle's cheek twitch.

"Aye, laddie. I suppose ye got me thare."

I'd finished rigging the little six-foot rod and crossed over the two-track, walking toward the rain-drenched alders that grew hard along the bank of the stream.

The old man, who had taught me so much of what I knew about the river, grabbed my arm and swung me around to once again face him.

"Look laddie, mibbie you're richt aboot me. Mibbie ah did screw up whin it cam tae yer maw, bit ye git yer da all wrong."

I could feel my temple throb. I clenched the fist of my free hand.

"Yer da did th' best he cuid. Yer maw was sick, Harry. She hud bin since she wis a wee lassie."

I tried to pull my arm free, but the old Scott was stronger than he looked.

"Th' pills Doc Woodward gave her weren't helping anymair. Putting yer maw in that place wis th' only thing yer da cuid think tae do."

"Easy for you to say." Like a sudden storm sweeping over a lake, a burst of rage surged through my body.

"Whin ye wur young, yer da spent more time at home, bit as yer maw's dark spells grew mare frequent, he just didn't ken whit tae do, sae he retreated tae th' bank."

"You mean like you did with that cabin of yours?" I wanted to bloody the old man's face.

"I'm nae saying he wis right. Whit a'm saying is," he hesitated for a moment, but then continued. "Whit i'm saying is, 'twas th' best he cuid do. I know that 'twas th' best I cuid do."

We stood no more than a foot from each other. Resentment had re-placed rage.

"Harry, wur jist men. Ye, me, yer da, even that delinquent pal o' yers. There ur no bad guys. Weel, almost no bad guys. There certainly aren't any guid ones. Just folk trying ta git by."

A chipmunk chattered away from the protection of the alders. I looked down at my boots and thought of my mother. A certain sadness came upon me.

"Give him a break. Give yersel' a break." The old man grabbed my shoulder with his boney hand.

Unwilling to let my anger go, I once again turned toward the stream.

"Cannae ye see, Harry? Ye're juist like him!" he called after me.

In all the years I'd known him, this was the first time Angus had raised his voice. Now I was the one who hesitated, remembering what Thelma Louise had said.

"Some men may have done better, bit yer da did th' best he cuid, 'n' that's all ye kin ask o' any man."

I stood in the dirt road as Angus hobbled to my side. Patting me on the shoulder, he said, "Look laddie, I've lived abit as lang as a man shuid. Caught all th' fish a man haes a right tae catch. Ye wur right tae turn yer back oan me. I cuid have done more fur yer maw. Ah ken that noo, bit at th' time it seemed lik' th' best thing tae do. Doc Woodward, yer da, they're educated men, 'n' I figured thay knew whit was best fur dear Clem."

He stopped short, thought for a moment and then said, "Really, Harry, yer da did whit he thought wis best. Right or wrong, he wis trying tae do th' right thing fur ye 'n' yer maw. Mibbie his best wasn't guid enough, bit then again, oor best rarely is. It's th' tryin' that counts, Harry."

I can't say I understood everything he was telling me, but some of it seeped through.

After a moment, he said, "I've git a plan. One that'll wirk better than yer friend's, if you'll hear me out."

I was still thinking about what he had said about my father.

"There may be a wey oot here," Angus continued.

I suddenly felt very tired, my thighs as wobbly as jelly. I thought about squatting down in the wet grass by the side of the road. It would be nice to leave my problems behind. Just lean my back against a boulder, close my eyes, and sleep for a very long time.

"Tell ye whit, Harry. Gimme a moment tae string up mah rod 'n' we kin blether while we fish."

My great-uncle didn't wait for me to reply. Instead, he turned toward his vehicle. "Wait til ye see this fly ah fashioned oot o' a wee bit o' beaver 'n' tinsel. It's gonnae drive th' fish mad."

The little man limped back to the Jeep where he gathered his gear.

Afterward, we zipped up our rain jackets and bushwhacked through the moisture-laden alders. Mud sucked at our boots. Coffee-stained water rose to our thighs. By the time we reached solid ground, a shock of cold water had slid down the inside of my left hipper. Standing side by side, we cast our flies into a dark pool. As the old man predicted, the little trout of the backwoods stream favored his pattern over my Royal Wulff.

Although the biggest trout fit snugly in my palm, the fish were eager. The sun had once again peeked out from behind the shifting clouds. Steam swirled up from the gravel beneath our feet. Angus had carried a frying pan in his backpack, and while I made a twig fire, he cleaned the fish, leaving the guts on a boulder, an unexpected treat for some passing mink or otter. My great-uncle laid six trout in the black skillet. After boiling water in an aluminum pot, we removed our ponchos and used them to sit on a shoal. We leaned our backs against a fallen tree and ate the fish with our fingers. As we sipped tea from tin cups, Angus described his plan. At first it sounded outlandish, but then again, Gilroy's idea wasn't much better.

"You're sure about this?" I asked when he concluded.

"Aye, ah'm feelin' lik' ah owe ye this much," he said, staring out over the surface of the stream.

Without making any promises, I agreed to consider his proposal. Afterward, we sat with our legs outstretched, listening to the sound of the little brook sweep over the cobble streambed. Deciding to change the subject, I asked, "How's the Lady?"

"Saw her th' ither day," he said. Licking the taste of trout from the tips of his fingers, he continued, "Cam' doon tae eat some scraps I put oot."

"She must be getting old."

"Aye! But aren't we all," he chuckled.

When the old man's legs resisted his effort to straighten up, I lowered a hand that he refused.

"Not that old," he grunted.

As I grabbed the skillet, he limped down to the pool and filled the coffee pot. Embers hissed when he poured water onto the stick fire. After pouring out a second pot, we kicked grit and stone over the smoldering coals. Humping back to the vehicles, we stripped out of our rain gear and hippers. While Angus packed away the cooking utensils, I used an old towel to dry off. A red squirrel chattered from a branch in a nearby spruce as we broke down our fly rods.

I wanted to thank Angus, to tell him how much I missed spending time with him, but before I could, he said, "Ye know, Harry, th' water is a fine place tae spend time. Th' forest haes its lessons tae teach 'n' ye have learned thaim well. Bit it's th' fowk in oor lives who mak' it worthwhile. Yer pal kin be a bit dunderheided fur mah taste, bit he's yer friend 'n' that's whit counts."

"I wish things had turned out differently," I said.

"It's a sair fecht," was all he replied.

I looked up at the sky that had once again turned ashen and then over at the man who had taught me most of what I knew about fishing and perhaps about life.

"Well?" my great-uncle asked as he hobbled around to the driver's side of his vehicle.

"I'm still thinking." Climbing into my truck, I wasn't convinced that either plan had a chance in hell of working.

As he backed the Jeep out of the gravel pit, Angus called me over.

"While yer'e thinking, ye might wantae consider that lassie o' yers."

"T.L.?" I asked.

There was a twinkle in the geezer's eye when he said, "Seems tae me she's a keeper."

A few drops sprinkled down on my shoulders as Angus stepped down on the accelerator. I was still standing there when it began to pour.

· *Chapter Thirty* ·

I WALKED OUT OF THE DOOR THAT AFTERNOON AND DIDN'T RETURN until a few days later. My father was at the office. What else was new? I gathered some clothes, my Thompson vise, bags of material to tie my flies, a few of my other things and moved in with Gilroy while we finished out the last few weeks of high school. I moved a second time a few days after Donnie started his stint at Mountain View, borrowing enough money from one of Thelma Louise's brothers to put down a security deposit on the apartment above the Thai restaurant.

Not long afterward, I'd visited my mother. It was the first and only time I saw her in that place. I wasn't sure what to expect, but seeing her there was too much to bear. It was probably me, but it seemed that the staff couldn't give a shit. I nearly got into a fistfight with a guy dressed in a white shirt and pants. He had a dragon tattoo running down his right forearm. It looked to me like he was bullying a patient, and when I said something he got in my face. The two of us were about to go at it when some guy in a suit called him off. Anyway, after that four-hour round trip, I never did get back down to Augusta.

Seven months later I found myself back in my parents' house. I sat at my usual place in the living room. Untying and then retying the laces of my boots, I walked over to the mirror above the bureau wedged into the corner of the room. I ran a hand through my hair and then sat back down on the couch only to jump up a moment later when my father pulled into the drive. I watched him walk around his Volvo, open the door, and help my mother out of the car. The temperature hadn't climbed out of the thirties, although it was the third week of April. With the sun out, water dripped from the tips of icicles that hung like daggers off the gutters. There was a few inches of snow still on the ground. Earlier, I'd shoveled away another dusting of flakes that had fallen while my father drove to the psychiatric hospital where Clementine Duncan was compelled to reside. My mother looked up at me from beside the car, but did not smile. She clung to my father as they walked toward the front door of their home. I wanted to run down and hug her, but remained on the stoop. I stepped aside as my parents shuffled into the foyer where my father slipped off my mother's winter coat and hung it on a hook next to my green parka.

At first we sat in the living room, my mother on the couch, my father beside her, and me in the big easy chair with the cushion that sinks down nearly to the floor. They had stolen her beauty. She had lost weight, her face gaunt, black circles under her eyes. She looked so frail. I noticed wrinkles on the tops of her hands and across her forehead. Her once long black hair had been cut short.

My father explained that my mother had a weekend pass—Friday through Sunday. According to him, her time at home would increase as she showed signs of recovery.

My mother stared across the room. Her eyes fixed on the photographs that flanked either side of a clock on the mantel over the fireplace. One was of her parents taken in their middle years, the other of my great-aunt and uncle. She continued looking around the room, shifting her attention to a set of smaller photos atop the bureau, images caught during a happier time when I was younger.

"Can I get you anything?" I asked. The ticking of the clock was magnified by the silence that bathed the room.

My mother appeared to have trouble processing the question.

"A cup of tea, soda, a glass of water?" I sounded like a goddamned stewardess.

Doped up on whatever they gave her, she shook her head from side to side.

After that, none of us said very much. The clock continued to tick away our lives until my father suggested that my mother take a nap. Although she didn't reply, he helped her up the stairs.

"I suppose you'll be off to the office now?" I said, when he returned a few minutes later.

"Give it a rest, Harry." He walked into the kitchen and pulled out a beer from the refrigerator.

I'd never known him to drink and said so.

Raising the can to his lips, he replied, "There's a lot about me you don't know."

Reaching into my pocket, I took out a pack of Marlboros.

"Since when do you smoke?" he asked.

"Back atcha." I put a plate on the kitchen table to use as an ashtray. "Gilroy and T.L. wanted to stop by to say hello to mom if that's okay."

"Maybe we should give her some time. Your mother's still dealing with a lot." He walked over to the window and looked out across the snow.

"I'm gonna check in on her." I put the cigarette out on the plate.

My mother was standing at the window. The bedroom was dark, and a streak of sunlight created a kind of glow around her body. She didn't turn when I walked toward her, but said in a low voice that I had to strain to hear, "I was thinking about that summer we watched the ducklings down by the pond. You remember?"

I thought for a moment. "The mallards?"

"You couldn't have been more than four or five years old."

"Each morning we'd put out cracked corn for them."

She smiled, still staring out the window.

I stood beside her, looked out onto the pond that had lost its ice. It was the first body of water to do so each spring. It was the subject about which most everyone in town had an opinion. Some swore it was because of the pond's sheltered location while others theorized it was the shallow depths.

"We watched those ducklings grow up. The four babies, always in a line, following their mum." My mother turned. "By September there was only one," she said in a near whisper.

I didn't know what to say to that.

"Is that our canoe down there?" She pointed to a smudge of red sticking out of a pile of snow. Beyond, a slight breeze rippled across the surface of the sunlit pond.

"In another few weeks, we'll be able to go for a paddle like we used to," I said.

Rather than reply, she walked over to the mirror above her dresser.

"I must look a fright." She managed another weak smile.

"You look great. I only wish you could stay home."

She walked back to the window.

"I forgot how pretty the yard looks with snow on the ground."

"A flock of grosbeaks flew in no more than twenty minutes before you arrived. I filled the feeders. Maybe later we can sit at the kitchen window and watch the birds."

My mother exhaled. "That would be nice, Harry. Thank you."

"It's gonna be okay, mom. You'll see."

"Sure, Harry. Just like it was." My mother raised a trembling hand to the side of my face. "Guess I'll take that nap after all."

She slipped off her shoes and lay back in her slacks. I found a quilt in a trunk at the end of the bed. "I'll come back up after a while and check in on you."

She smiled weakly and then closed her eyes. After pulling the blanket around her shoulders, I walked into the hall.

That evening, my father made meatloaf for dinner, which wasn't half bad. My mother appeared more engaged, saying that they should go food shopping in the morning. She was delighted that I'd enrolled in community college, saying how much she looked forward to my graduation and asking about Thelma, Gilroy, and Petey.

The previous evening, my father had made a special trip to the IGA to purchase a quart of chocolate ice cream. It was my mother's favorite, and she had two large scoops. When my mother decided to retire for the night, she insisted on walking up the steps without our help. "I'm not an invalid, after all." Her chuckle sounded more like a croak.

That night I slept in my old room. Rising early, I walked toward my parents' bedroom, but the door was closed. I found my father in the kitchen. He was still dressed in his pajamas and open-back slippers. He had the belt around a flannel bathrobe tied around his waist.

"Doc Woodward says diet has a lot to do with it." He was squeezing oranges into a glass pitcher.

"She seemed to be doing pretty well last night," I said. "Maybe she should stay home for a few more days?"

"It's not up to me." My father handed me a fork. Pointing to the bacon that was spitting fat in a large skillet, he began breaking eggs into a bowl.

"Still don't understand how you could have put her in that place." I glared at him. "Seems to me that if you spent more time at home…"

"Jesus, Harry," he cut me off, but before we could continue my mother padded in.

"Something smells good," she sounded like her old self.

After we ate breakfast my mother insisted on washing the dishes. When I offered to dry, my father said he was going to spend some time in his study.

"Just like old times, hey dad?" I called as he walked into the hall.

"Don't be so hard on him." My mother squeezed a bottle, squirting blue detergent into the sink.

"I love you both, Harry," she said while scrubbing a dish. "Promise me you'll never forget that."

Later that morning Thelma Louise called. She wanted to come over and see my mother, but my father thought it might be too soon. Instead, after my parents drove down to the IGA, I walked over to Thelma's house. My father was in his study when I returned.

"Where's mom?" I asked.

He looked up from a stack of files. "Taking a nap."

My mother wasn't in her bedroom when I opened the door. Walking across the room, I looked out the window. My eyes were drawn to the red canoe that was floating toward the middle of the pond.

· *Chapter Thirty-One* ·

I STOPPED THE TRUCK ON THE EAST END OF THE CAMP TEN BRIDGE. Rain had been falling steadily since Angus left me standing in the gravel pit. I switched the lights off and then on. I did it again, but no Gilroy.

I'd driven slowly back to town after leaving the stream, trying to decide whether to accept my great-uncle's offer of help or meet with the drug dealer, who was waiting for me at Sparky's. Since Angus had no phone at his cabin, he instructed me to call Fogerty in the morning and let him know whether it was to be a go. Scheduled to meet the dealer at ten, I took until then to make up my mind.

Now, with rain splashing against the windshield of my truck, I pulled a sleeve away from my watch and saw that it was ten minutes after midnight. I worried that Donnie might have abandoned his plan to meet me. Then there was my great-uncle, who might take matters into his own hands. Listening to the rain ping against the roof of the cab, I waited for another few moments before adjusting the bill of my cap under the hood of my rain jacket. The man seated beside me had agreed to remain in the truck until I motioned for him to come forward. Nodding in his direction before stepping out into the rain, I hoped I'd made the right decision.

The truck door creaked when I opened it. I could hear the rain-engorged current sweeping under the wooden planks twenty feet below my boots. I looked back at the truck. I had shut its lights before climbing out of the cab. With the rain splashing against the windshield I couldn't see its other occupant. *Just as well*, I thought.

"Donnie?" I called into the dark. After another moment, I called again. Stopping halfway across the bridge, I looked up and down the river, but found only darkness. I unzipped my jacket. Reaching inside, I plucked a cigarette from the pack in my shirt pocket. Wind whipped down the river. The rain was falling harder. I cupped a hand over my lighter, inhaling deeply until the tip of the cigarette glowed orange. I took a long drag, and then once again called out Gilroy's name.

The night we fished Widow Maker seemed a lifetime ago. I smiled at the thought of the green glow of Koz's night-vision glasses and thought how they'd come in handy on a night like this one. With the high water would come the spawning run. Brook trout and salmon would soon be working their way up the river. As I was about to turn back to the truck, there came a rustling sound along the west side of the bridge.

"Donnie?" I called again, while staring into the dark void on that side of the river.

It could have been a porcupine or some other small animal, but it grew louder as it came down the trail. Maybe a moose, I told myself.

But then I saw him at the edge of the path, standing near one of the bridge's concrete columns.

"Harry," he called to me as if it were any old night.

"The hogs have arrived."

I could almost make out that dumbass grin through the blackness. Gilroy grabbed an alder branch, slipping and sliding while scrambling up the muddy path.

He swung a canvas pack from his shoulder and asked, "Did you bring him?"

"Look, we don't have much time, so just listen," I said as he lowered the satchel to the wooden bridge.

Gilroy looked toward the truck. The lights were off, the windshield swept with rain. He took a step back and said, "What's going on, Harry?"

"Change of plans, Donnie." I grabbed for the pack that lay on the planks between us, but Gilroy reached toward his belt and pulled out a gun.

"Donnie, you've got to listen to me. You're not going to jail for shooting those Massholes, and if you let me have what's in that bag you won't be going to jail at all." I stood between him and the truck, hoping that Whitney Parker couldn't see the revolver that was pointed at my gut.

"I spoke with Angus. He's got a plan." I was talking rapidly, hoping Whit would give me the chance that he promised.

"Angus? What does the old man have to do with this?"

"He saw us up at the cave. He knows about your plan to sell the dope and the two of us meeting tonight, but he says you'll never make it over the border. All the crossings are staked out, even the ones above the Cupsuptic and Kennebago."

"He wants me to just turn myself in?"I looked over my shoulder and then back at Gilroy, who hadn't lowered the gun.

"He's gonna tell 'em he did it. That he thought the jet skis were some kind of Loch Ness thing. Make it look like he's got the Alzheimer's."

"Why would he do that?"

"I don't know. I think it has something to do with my mother."

Gilroy looked puzzled. He may have lowered the gun a bit, but the muzzle was still only a few feet from my stomach.

"Angus said they'll never put someone his age in jail, especially a senile old man. Even smiled when he said it. He figures the worst that could happen, he gets probation or something."

"Angus smiled?" Gilroy lowered the handgun. "So, how's this gonna go down?" he asked.

"You'll give yourself up to Whitney and Angus will show up at the station first thing tomorrow morning. When he confesses, they'll have to let you go. But I need you to give me that gun and we've got to get rid of the dope and do it now."

Gilroy looked over my shoulder.

Before he could say anything, we heard a loud whoop, whoop, whoop sound coming from around the bend of the river south of the bridge. I guessed Whitney heard it as well because the lights of the truck suddenly lit up the bridge.

"Jesus, Harry," Gilroy cried.

A helicopter swung into view before either of us could move. Someone called out to us on a bullhorn, but the words were lost in the noise of the wind and rain and the sound of the copter's blades. Whitney had his two arms extended, the firearm in his hands pointed in our direction. He was calling for us to get down on our stomachs. On the other end of the bridge two wardens and a state trooper appeared from the rain-soaked brambles. The trooper also had a handgun pointed at us.

Gilroy bent down. As the helicopter hovered closer, he grabbed the straps of the pack. Looking back at me, he yelled, "Some plan!" before leaping over the side of the bridge. A moment later, I followed him.

I braced myself for the fall, expecting to break a leg, if not my neck, on one of the boulders that protruded from the water's surface, but the rising current swept me quickly downriver. Unable to gain my footing, I stared back over my shoulder to see a number of figures leaning over the side of the bridge. Their flashlights created small circles of dull light upon the river's surface.

The helicopter had backed off. Its spotlight splayed across the dark water, crisscrossing from one bank to the other.

The river was shockingly cold, but I managed to swim toward the east bank. After a few moments, I struggled to my feet in the shallow channel that ran between a thin spit of land and the far shoreline. Crawling among tall grass and a few partially submerged alders, I ducked below the copter's spotlight when it swept over the little island.

"Harry!" I heard a hushed voice call from the spruce trees between the riverbank and the logging road.

"Harry!" I heard the voice call my name a second time.

I looked out across the river and watched the searchlight working the opposite shore, where it would have been easier to climb out of the stream. I staggered across the shallows, stepped into a pool where the water rose over my head, and swam across to the bank. The wet dirt under my boots was as slick as ice, but I grabbed a sapling and rose out of the river. Grasping the branch of another tree, I worked my way up the muddy embankment. As I reached the top, Angus grabbed my out-stretched hand and pulled me over the edge. I gasped for breath as the helicopter turned its light back in our direction.

"Follow me," my great-uncle whispered as we darted across the dirt road. At the edge of the forest, I found Gilroy squatting under a large spruce tree.

"This way, laddies," Angus muttered.

"What are you doing here?" I asked him, my voice tinged with surprise.

"Figured ye two might gum up th' wirks, so I decided it best tae bade close."

We followed the old man when he turned into the forest. I assumed he would bushwhack toward his cabin, but when Angus hiked around his camp, I stopped to question him.

"They'll be looking fur ye at mah cabin. Hell, ye two made such a fine mess o' things, they'll be looking fur ye everywhere."

"So, where you taking us?" Gilroy asked through chattering teeth. It hadn't been an especially cold night, but after standing out on the bridge in the rain and then going for a swim in the Magalloway, we were chilled to the bone.

"I figure th' one place thay don't know abit is that auld shack o' yers."

Forty minutes later we crawled into Camp Danforth. After work-ing his way into the wooden structure surrounding the entrance to the cave, Gilroy reached up to a shelf bolted to the wall and clicked on a battery-operated lantern. Stooping down to the earthen floor, he lit the kerosene stove.

"Noo this is howfur it's gonnae wirk," Angus said, rubbing his hands in front of the little stove. In the meager light cast by the lantern, he really did look like an elf with his thin frame and aquiline nose.

"Here." Gilroy handed me a wool blanket that he pulled out of a beat-up trunk. I pulled off my boots and socks. Dumping his backpack in the corner of the room, Gilroy began to peel off his shirt. He hesitated when

Angus asked for his rifle and the handgun, but then handed them over.

Angus pointed to the canvas pack. "Harry, ye git rid o' that jobby so's it ne'er finds its wey back tae oor door. I'll climb doon aff this hill 'n' git a night's kip. To'morra, I'll drive intae town wi' th' rifle 'n' mah fingerprints all ower it, 'n' tell 'em 'twas me that shot at those jet skiers."

It took another twenty minutes for us to warm up. While we hunched over the kerosene heater, I thought once more of my mother and how hard it was to let her go. The night before her funeral, I'd asked Angus his opinion as to why she did it. He repeated what the police officer had told him, that the coroner had classified her death an accident. But I wasn't so sure. I'll never understand what made her dig that canoe out of the snow.

Afterward, Angus slid back into his rain gear. We watched the old man shimmy out into the rain.

As he faded into the shadows, I turned to Gilroy. "Now let me tell you the rest of the plan. Here's the key to my truck. You'll find the certificate of title along with one for the Rangeley in the glove compartment. I assume the police will release it after Angus gives them his confession."

Gilroy turned the key over and over as if it were some mysterious talisman.

"They're yours now. The truck, boat, and trailer," I said.

"Mine?"

I pulled a wad of wet bills from the pocket of my jeans. "There's a bit over six hundred dollars here, all I've managed to save."

"I can't take this," he said, still not understanding what I was telling him.

"Put it in the bank. You'll need it if the truck breaks down. It's also about time you get the hell out of your mother's basement, so I paid the Mookjais a year's rent in advance and told them you'd be moving in."

I'd rarely seen such a puzzled expression on Donnie Gilroy's face.

"And for God's sake, get your guide's license. I'll email you my client list and the bookings for next season."

"What's this all about?"

"I'm leaving, bud. Gonna try to make it work with T."

Gilroy grinned. Quoting Yoda again, he said, "Difficult to see. Always in motion is the future."

I extended my hand, but he grabbed me by the shoulders and squeezed me in a bear hug. It took me a moment to catch my breath after he loosened his grip.

"I dropped by Petey's house earlier tonight and explained how I would be gone for a while and that he's to mind you. Treat him right, Donnie. You're the only one he can depend upon now."

"I will, Harry. I promise."

"Oh, and one more thing."

He raised an eyebrow.

I gripped his shoulder with my hand. "No more dope."

"Next you'll be telling me I can't go to Sparky's," he laughed.

After walking out into the darkness, I pressed the little knob on the side of my watch. I was glad to see it was still working. The illuminated dial confirmed it was nearly two o'clock. I had a long way to go and not much time to get there.

· *Chapter Thirty-Two* ·

THE BUS STATION CONSISTED OF ONE LARGE ROOM. TO SAY IT WASN'T crowded would be an understatement. Three marines dressed in desert fatigues sat along one wall with their duffel bags scattered around them. One guy thumbed the keys of his phone. Like bookends, his two buddies sat on either side of him with their eyes closed, legs extended and boots crossed at the ankles. Across the room, an old man and woman stared at me from where they sat.

A middle-aged man in a rumpled suit had listened intently as I recounted the story of how it came to be that I found myself seated beside him, beginning with the night Gilroy and I waded through Widow Maker and ending with the two of us jumping off the Camp Ten Bridge. Besides the woman working behind the counter, the only other person in the station was a custodian dressed in green pants and shirt. He was at least as old as old man Fogerty. The custodian was tall, slightly bent forward, and as thin as a reed. His skin was chalky black. The crevasse dug into his left cheek reminded me of a jagged washout I'd passed earlier that morning while crossing the logging road leading out of the Parmachenee wilderness. Daryl—that was the name stitched above the custodian's shirt pocket—shuffled more than walked while hunched over a mop that he swished across the floor. The old guy occasionally stopped to slide the mop into a bucket of murky water, running the dirty fibers through a ringer before continuing on his way.

The man in the suit had been seated when I first arrived. I'm not sure why I told him my story, but the guy proved to be a good listener and the words seemed to pour out of my mouth like the current of the

Magalloway that carried me away from the Camp Ten Bridge earlier that morning.

By the time I finished my tale, the clock on the wall over the ticket booth had ticked toward eight-forty. The rain had stopped sometime after six. The sun was now streaming through the windows along one wall of the room.

I'd walked into the Concord Coach Line Terminal a few minutes after the eight o'clock bus to Boston pulled out of the station. The woman at the ticket booth explained that upon arriving in Boston, its passengers could take a bus to anywhere on the east coast, including New Jersey. Now, staring up at the clock on the wall, I saw that the next bus would be departing in another twenty minutes.

"You sure you saw her?" I asked the man. "Short red hair, pointed in different directions—kinda like the feathers of a parrot caught out in the rain? She had a bit of purple up front." Thelma Louise's latest fashion statement was hard to miss.

"Sounds like her, all right." The man pulled a bus ticket from his shirt pocket, stared at it for a moment and then placed the ticket back in his pocket. "She was wearing tight black jeans and those red sneakers you mentioned."

The custodian had worked his way back across the room. I walked over to a water cooler and filled up a paper cup. After drinking the contents, I tramped back to my seat.

"And you say she got on the bus?" I asked the middle-aged man.

"I'm not really sure. I mean there weren't many people around, no more than now. She was seated over there." He pointed to a row of plastic chairs set along the glass wall adjacent to the ticket booth where the sun warmed the elderly couple.

"She walked in with an old man with white hair. He sat down beside her. I watched the two of them, the older guy doing most of the talking. Seemed like an odd couple, you know?" The man continued, "I was at the ticket booth chatting up blondie over there when they walked inside."

Somewhere north of forty, the woman behind the ticket booth appeared in need of a good night's sleep rather than what the man in the rumpled suit had in mind. Her heavy makeup barely hid the crow's feet extending out from the corner of each eye and failed to mask the fold of flesh that drooped down below her chin. Streaks of gray invaded the not-so-blond hair pinned up on her head.

"So, did she get on the bus or what?"

"Your girlfriend?" He chuckled and then said, "Well to tell ya the truth, I was kinda checking her out."

I stared at the man.

"Come on. You said yourself she has a killer body."

I wanted to punch the guy in the face.

"Well, you said it, not me. Anyway, I'm pretty sure she and the old man with the white hair walked outside when the bus pulled in."

"Pretty sure?"

"I had to take a leak. When I came back from the men's room they were gone. A few minutes later I saw the bus pull out." He pointed to the gravel drive outside the windows.

The man stretched out his arms. "Gonna get a coffee from the vending machine. You want one?"

I waved him off. Earlier, I'd borrowed the guy's cell phone to call Thelma Louise, but she didn't pick up.

As the man rose to his feet I asked to borrow his phone again.

"Knock yourself out. I've got unlimited minutes," he said, tossing it to me.

I tried Thelma a second time, but again no answer. I wondered if she'd changed her mind. Maybe Fogerty drove her back to town. Maybe. There were too many maybes. Like trying to figure what rising trout are taking when overlapping hatches of caddis and mayflies are fluttering over the surface of the river. I tapped in Gilroy's number. He answered on the fourth or fifth ring.

"Donnie? You okay?"

"Dude. Spent the morning up at the shack. Came off the hill after the rain stopped. Hung out in one of those wilderness campsites beside Twin Brook. Mooched some food off one of the campers. Gonna wait until after ten to call Whitney. Figure by then Angus will have turned himself in. And Harry, you wouldn't believe the fishing."

"The fishing?"

For the first time in a long time the last thing on my mind was the fishing.

"It took a while but eventually Five-O got into their vehicles." Gilroy was shouting above the sound of the Magalloway's current. "At first, I thought it was some kind of trap, but when they drove off I figured what the hell. With the water up and all, I headed back to the river, and sure enough the fish were there. I took six. Was releasing the seventh when you called. It was a real bruiser."

Almost as an afterthought, he put on his best Tony Soprano accent when he asked, "How 'bout you guys? On your way to New Joisey?"

The guy in the suit returned to his seat. He was holding a Styrofoam cup in one hand and a Danish that looked like a pile of dog crap preserved in a plastic wrapper.

I gave him a thumbs-up and then walked over to the large windows overlooking the pavement in front of the building. I nodded to the old couple. The woman looked away while the man stared down at his shoes. I couldn't blame them. After my short swim and long night in the rain my clothes remained damp, while my boots were caked with mud from tramping down the river and through the wood. The bottoms of my jeans were not much better.

"Hardly," I muttered into the phone.

The sunlight streaming through the windows felt good against my face. I lost the connection after Gilroy asked how I managed to get past the cops. Calling him back, I described how the wardens were waiting at the gate closest to Parmachenee Lake, forcing me to bushwhack through the spruce and balsam until I came out below the southwest gate.

Staying away from the logging roads, I kept to the east of Aziscohos Lake. The wardens had blocked off the Lincoln Pond logging road at about the same location where they stopped me and Petey Boy on the afternoon of the shooting.

I told him how the parking lot outside the Black Brook Cove General Store was lit up like daytime, with vehicles parked every which way.

"How did you get across Route 16?" he asked.

"I managed to reach it before sunrise," I said. "From the edge of the wood, I watched that damn helicopter swing over the paved road. Its spotlight illuminated the blacktop as it turned east toward Rangeley. It came back a few minutes later and headed in the opposite direction. Soon after that, a border patrol truck came tearing up the road. I figured the cops would be crawling all over Rangeley, so there was no way I was taking Route 4 down to Augusta. I decided to take Route 16 through New Hampshire and cut across Route 2."

I explained how it took another twenty minutes to work my way back toward the Magalloway.

"I managed to make my way down to the long pool below that set of waterfalls."

"Where I took that twenty-inch salmon year before last?" Gilroy broke in.

"It took another hour, maybe more, to come into sight of the little bridge above Wilsons Mills. By then, the sun had risen and the first cars were driving by. I could see that the state troopers had the bridge blocked. After that, I climbed through the briars behind the Magalloway River Farm and scuttled in and out of backyards until coming to the little diner a quarter-mile or so up the road."

"The one that closed?"

"Yeah. I lost my phone in the river and there was no way I was going to make it to the bus station on my own."

"Gotta keep it in a baggie. That's what I do. Never know when you're gonna take a dunking," Gilroy interrupted.

"Well, I broke a window and climbed inside to use the phone. Lucky for me it was still working. I wasn't sure who to call. Figured old man Fogerty left his station to drive Thelma Louise down here. I eventually decided on T.L.'s brother."

"Dylan?"

"Dylan didn't answer, but I got Jake."

The connection went dead again and I had to call Gilroy back a second time. I described how Jake picked me up on the other side of the roadblock, and how I hunkered down in the back seat all the way through Errol and even afterward as we took the long way around to Augusta.

Before wishing Gilroy good luck, I explained that I wasn't sure if Thelma Louise had even left Rangeley.

By the time I returned his phone, the man in the rumpled suit had eaten the sugar-frosted pile of dung and was washing down the last bite with a gulp of the sludge he'd purchased from the vending machine.

Just then, the nine o'clock bus to Boston pulled in beside the station.

"Time to go." The man set down his cup of coffee.

"You coming?" he asked.

I hesitated as the three soldiers strode past. The old couple followed them out the door. As the elderly husband helped his wife board the bus, the middle-aged man turned toward me and said, "Guess I'm gonna miss the ending of your story."

I shrugged my shoulders.

"Sure you're not coming?" he called as he reached the door.

I walked toward the lady behind the ticket booth. She couldn't confirm whether Thelma Louise had boarded the earlier bus nor would she tell me if Thelma had cashed in her ticket. I asked if I could cash in mine, but before she answered, Daniel Fogerty tromped though the door.

"Why, Harry Duncan, right on time as usual," Thelma Louise Shannon had followed Fogerty into the station. "I was all set to get on that bus, but Daniel here reminded me how you operate on a different time schedule. That's when I took him up on his generous offer to buy me breakfast down at the local Dunkin."

After saying our goodbyes to Fogerty, Thelma and I found seats near the back of the bus. With her head on my shoulder, Thelma Louise quickly fell asleep and did not wake until we entered the city limits of Portland.

Staring up at me, she asked through half-closed eyes, "What are you smiling about?"

"Difficult to see. Always in motion is the future," I replied.